Wallflowers to Wives

Out of the shadows, into the marriage bed!

In Regency England, young women
were defined by their prospects in the
marriage market. But what of the girls who were
presented to society...and *not* snapped up?

Bronwyn Scott invites you to

The Left Behind Girls' Club

Three years after their debut
and still without rings on their fingers,
Claire Welton, Evie Milham, May Worth and
Beatrice Penrose are ready to leave the shadows
and step into the light. Now London will have to
prepare itself...because these overlooked girls
are about to take the *ton* by storm!

Read Claire's story in

Unbuttoning the Innocent Miss

Read Evie's story in

Awakening the Shy Miss

Both available now!

And watch for more **Wallflowers to Wives** stories—
coming soon!

Author Note

A couple of years ago I read a nonfiction book that espoused the idea that if you do what you love, the rest will follow. This is a theme that many people struggle to balance with "reality" through their lifetimes. Do we pursue our dreams even when we can't see how those dreams will pay the bills or keep our families secure, or do we "do the right thing" and follow the traditional paths laid out by society?

I wanted to explore this theme with Evie and Dimitri's story. They are both trapped by social expectations and have spent their lives living up, or in Evie's case, living down, to those standards at great personal cost to themselves. Their relationship allows both of them to explore who they truly want to be. Of course, it's easy to say "follow your dreams." The truth is, the reality of doing that is a lot harder. What I like best about this story is that Dimitri and Evie don't simply say, "To hell with society, we'll strike out for ourselves." That's not how it works for them or for us. What makes this story special is how they find a way through all that without compromising and without jeopardizing others—ultimately, this is a story about love's great balancing act.

I hope you enjoy Evie and the Prince of Kuban in their story. Here's a teaser for you—look for May's and Beatrice's stories next, and beyond that, look for a chance to meet four other princes of Kuban in a new Bronwyn Scott series.

Stay in touch at bronwynswriting.blogspot.com or at my webpage, bronwynnscott.com.

Bronwyn Scott

———

Awakening
the Shy Miss

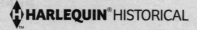

Recycling programs for this product may not exist in your area.

ISBN-13: 978-0-373-29900-3

Awakening the Shy Miss

Copyright © 2016 by Nikki Poppen

Printed in U.S.A.

www.Harlequin.com

Bronwyn Scott is a communications instructor at Pierce College in the United States, and is the proud mother of three wonderful children—one boy and two girls. When she's not teaching or writing, she enjoys playing the piano, traveling—especially to Florence, Italy—and studying history and foreign languages. Readers can stay in touch on Bronwyn's website, bronwynscott.com, or at her blog, bronwynswriting.blogspot.com. She loves to hear from readers.

Books by Bronwyn Scott

**Harlequin Historical
and Harlequin Historical *Undone!* ebooks**

Wallflowers to Wives

Unbuttoning the Innocent Miss
Awakening the Shy Miss

Rakes on Tour

Rake Most Likely to Rebel
Rake Most Likely to Thrill
Rake Most Likely to Seduce
Rake Most Likely to Sin

Rakes of the Caribbean

Playing the Rake's Game
Breaking the Rake's Rules
Craving the Rake's Touch (Undone!)

Rakes Who Make Husbands Jealous

Secrets of a Gentleman Escort
London's Most Wanted Rake
An Officer But No Gentleman (Undone!)
A Most Indecent Gentleman (Undone!)

Visit the Author Profile page
at Harlequin.com for more titles.

For Tonia, who spent six great months with us.

Chapter One

Evie Milham desperately wanted to get into *his* trousers. Judging from the extraordinary amount of females crammed into Little Westbury's assembly-room-cum-lecture hall this warm August night, she wasn't the only one. Although, Evie doubted the rest of the female population wanted into them for the same reason.

Regardless of female motive, there was no disputing this was the most well-attended archaeological lecture in the history of West Sussex, perhaps in the history of England. Not even the Elgin Marbles had engendered such an enthusiastic response in retrieving the past. Then again, the Elgin Marbles didn't look like *him*, Dimitri Petrovich, Prince of Kuban. Evie was certain he could talk about pickled herring and still draw a crowd. He was tall, with sleek dark hair that flowed over his shoulders, his face chiselled with strong lines that hinted at exotic antecedents. Women would travel miles to stare at those cheekbones with their high slant. And his clothes, oh, those clothes! He wore them like a god's own mantle. Evie's fingers started to twitch in anticipation. How she wanted to get her hands on those trousers! If she could just study them up close for a few moments! Whoever his tailor was, the man was a genius.

Evie craned her neck, trying for a better glimpse. If she'd known he'd be so exquisitely dressed, she would have sat closer to the front. She'd not chosen this particular seat near the back for him, but for another him. Andrew Adair sat just two convenient rows ahead of her, his golden head a beacon for her eyes except, apparently, when those eyes were looking at Prince Dimitri Petrovich, which was more frequently than she had anticipated. It was hard not to. When one wasn't looking at his trousers, one could easily stare at his hands. He didn't gesture like an Englishman. There was a loose fluidity to his gestures that made him appear all the more foreign.

She might as well look, Evie reasoned. It wasn't as if Andrew minded or was even aware of her visual perfidy, more was the pity. She often thought she could dance naked on a stage and Andrew wouldn't notice. Not that she would. Evie Milham might entertain such wild notions, but she *never* acted on them.

Tonight was supposed to change that. Tonight was her chance to claim Andrew's notice after six years of anonymity. Admittedly, for two of those years, she hadn't been 'out', hardly eligible for his attentions even if they had been neighbours for two decades. The other three years, he'd been in Europe on his Grand Tour while she debuted in London. This year it would be different. Their trajectories were finally in alignment. She was 'out' and he was home. Better yet, he'd made it clear during the recently ended Season he was looking to marry. Evie drew a deep breath. She would make him notice her.

Her eyes strayed from the back of Andrew's golden head once more. Up on stage, the Prince of Pleats—it must be the pleats that caused his trousers to lie so exquisitely across those lean hips—made one of his exotic gestures to footmen carrying trays of champagne. She forced her eyes back to Andrew. Now was not the time to be distracted by a set of pleats. If she'd learned anything this last Season it was that nothing changed until *you* did. She couldn't merely *wait* for Andrew's notice. Hadn't her friend Claire's whirlwind marriage to the dashing diplomat, Jonathon Lashley, a few weeks ago, proven the motto true? Claire had *made* Jonathon notice her. She simply had to do the same with Andrew and her own happy-ever-after wouldn't be far behind. After all, Andrew couldn't be blamed for not noticing her if she had done nothing to help that notice along.

'Champagne, miss? Compliments of the Prince for the toast.' A footman offered her a tray of cold, sweating flutes. Not just champagne, but *chilled* champagne. Iced champagne in the country in August was a luxury indeed. Evie took a glass and the footman moved on. At the front of the room, the Prince raised his glass, signalling the audience to rise. It was a noisy, rustling affair as the crowd took to its feet, careful not to spill a collective drop. Inspiration struck Evie. What if she moved up a couple of rows? No one would notice if she edged forward and took a place at Andrew's elbow. It was the perfect plan. He would turn and see her. He'd have to clink glasses with her, he would look into her eyes…

Move, you ninny! she chastised herself. The toast would be over and she would still be standing here dreaming about the moment while the moment passed. Evie gathered her courage and made the journey forward two rows, all of ten feet. Her heartbeat sped up. Never had she dared to place herself so directly in Andrew's path. The Prince was speaking but her thoughts were too preoccupied to pick up more than snatches of his speech. 'I am pleased to announce I have taken up residence here in Little Westbury for the purpose of excavating… I am proud to be joined in this venture by fellow enthusiasts for history such as…' She didn't hear the names until he reached the end of his recitations. 'And most of all, I am joined generously by my friend and fellow traveller, Mr Andrew Adair, without whom this venture would not be possible.'

That got her attention. Andrew was bosom bows with the Prince? Andrew was interested in historical preservation? All these years of living next door to him and she'd had no idea on either account. She'd just reached Andrew's side on the aisle when the toast went up, people clinking everywhere. The room sounded like a series of chiming crystal bells. Andrew clinked to his right, then with the people in front of him and behind him. Finally, he turned to his left. His fair brows knit in startled surprise, taking a moment to process her presence. 'Oh, Evie, it's you. What are you doing here?' He touched his glass to hers. She searched her mind for something to say.

'I wanted to hear the Prince speak.' Partially true. 'Congratulations, by the way, on the evening.'

'Oh, yes.' His response was vague. 'This is big, very big.' His eyes were already drifting back to the stage, his attention on the Prince when it was supposed to have lingered on her.

Evie struggled to hold his interest. 'I had no idea you were so interested in—' she began, but he cut her off with a raised index finger signalling for a pause.

'If you'll excuse me for a moment, Evie?' Andrew brushed past her into the centre of the aisle. If she didn't know better, the interruption bordered on rude. She might have been insulted by his abrupt behaviour. But she understood the reason for it. As a close friend of the Prince, Andrew would be expected to offer a reciprocal toast. She should have anticipated that. Andrew wasn't being rude. He was just doing his duty.

Andrew lifted his own glass as the noise ebbed, the motion causing all eyes to swivel his direction. And hers. Evie recognised too late she was caught in the view of the audience's collective gaze. She wanted to step back, but the crowd was too thick around her. She'd only wanted Andrew's notice, not the entire room's. When she'd approached Andrew, she'd made another serious miscalculation. She'd not bargained on this much attention.

Andrew raised his voice, commanding and confident, to address the crowd. She envied and admired his confidence. 'To the Prince!' Within moments he was swept towards the stage to join the Prince and she was left behind. Again. And that was that. Her bid for Andrew's attention had come to an abrupt end.

No. Go after him! That was Claire's voice in her head. Claire would never stand here like a wooden doll. Evie pushed forward and let herself be caught in the crowd surging towards the stage, everyone eager to meet the Prince. It was surprisingly easy to let the jostling move her closer to Andrew. When the jostling stopped she stood beside Andrew, watching in genuine astonishment as the Prince of Kuban swept him into a brotherly embrace, definitely not the kind of embrace English gentleman gave one another. This one was far too full bodied. 'My friend! It is good to see you. Did you like the talk?'

Andrew returned the embrace, but his movements were awkward, as if he were not quite comfortable with such intimate male contact. 'Very much, the points you made about the importance of history were eloquently put,' Andrew effused with a charming smile. 'West Sussex agrees with you, old chap. You are looking quite fit.'

The Prince grinned. 'Indeed it does!' He threw his arms out wide to encompass the room and beyond. 'What a beautiful piece of earth you call home. You are a lucky man.' He meant it too, Evie thought. There was an air of sincerity about the Prince that made him appear more human, less royal, than one might expect, although she doubted any of the folks tonight would let him forget the royal part. But then the very human prince turned his dark eyes in her direction and Evie froze, no longer a comfortable observer in the conversation, but a participant. The Prince's eyes were on her, two decadent brown pools of chocolate silk. His gaze was as full bodied as his embrace, those eyes taking in all of her as if he really saw her—Evie the needleworker, Evie the seamstress, Evie who helped her father with his historical research—and he didn't find those truths lacking or socially backwards. It was a bold gaze, another way in which the mere physical presence of him announced to the world he wasn't English. 'Andrew, we've been remiss. Who might this charming young woman be?'

There was a scold beneath his words for Andrew. It was the second time that night Andrew had been borderline rude in her presence. A lady should never have to introduce herself. She sensed Andrew's fraction-of-a-second hesitation as he found himself yet again surprised to see her beside him. She wished her attendance would stop being such a revelation to him.

Andrew smiled his recovery. 'This is Evie Milham, my neighbour.' Evie fought the urge to cringe. He'd called her 'Evie' in front of the Prince! Surely meeting a prince, even if it was amid the milieu of Little Westbury's assembly hall, required more formality than that. The Prince seemed to think so too. One of his slim dark eyebrows went up in a querying arch.

Evie lifted her chin in defiance of the slight. Unintended as it might have been, it was a slight none the less. She faced the Prince and dipped a curtsy, taking the introduction into her own hands. 'I'm Miss Milham.' This might be the country and Andrew and the Prince might be bosom friends, but she knew what a prince was due, Sussex assembly room or not. She knew what she was due too and it was high time she gathered the courage to claim it, demand it if need be. If she didn't value herself, no one else would either. Beatrice and Claire had taught her that. She was missing Claire very much just now, Claire who spoke five languages. Claire would know what to say and how to say it. Claire could speak Russian with him, or whatever it was they spoke in Kuban.

Evie summoned her courage, trying not to feel plain and shy in the presence of such a man. She offered the Prince her hand, hoping he would never guess just how much courage the simple gesture had taken. It would have been far easier to slink back into the crowd. The effort was worth it, though. He bent over her hand, lips brushing knuckles, chocolate eyes holding hers. Heat spread warm and slow through her. He made her feel like the only woman in the room when he looked at her that way. Perhaps that was the difference between a prince and other men.

'Evie?' His accent feathered the ends of his words, making his speech exotic. 'Is that short for something?' He was giving her a chance to recover from Andrew's slight, and elegantly so.

'Evaine.'

His warm eyes lit in recognition. The pool of warmth in her stomach deepened. 'Ah, the aunt of Sir Lancelot in your Camelot legends.'

The Prince smiled appreciably. Melting was complete. No wonder good English mothers warned their daughters about the influence of foreign men. This was a man who could sweep a woman off her feet without lifting his arms, a reminder that he had her melting and he didn't even mean to. She knew the hand kissing, the direct gaze, were all just politeness. Heaven help a woman when he applied himself. Evie had to fight back images of what that application might look like, what form it might take.

'You know your literature.' Evie nodded her approval. She seldom met a gentleman who was well schooled enough to know the origins of her name. In these parts, if it wasn't about a hound or a horse, gentlemen were surprisingly lacking in their education no matter how many years they had spent at Eton. Evie shot a covert glance in Andrew's direction. She was still digesting the revelation that Andrew had an interest in archaeology and history. She'd definitely classified him as the hound-and-horse sort. He certainly wasn't the repentant sort. Even with the Prince's implicit scold over his lack of manners, Andrew had done nothing to make amends.

'I'm a great follower of the Arthur legends,' the Prince offered by way of explanation. He was patient as if he didn't have an entire room of far more attractive women waiting to meet him. But Andrew wasn't nearly as relaxed. He was edgy and anxious beside her, eager to get on with the socialising.

'You should visit the Milhams some time, then.' Andrew's tone was brisk. 'Evie's father is our local historian.' He said 'local' with a hint of distaste as if that explained why her father hadn't been included in the initial investors in the site, all men from London with further-reaching historical interests.

The Prince looked at her with encouragement, as if he'd like to hear more. Evie took the opening to elaborate. 'Yes, we have a tapestry that is somewhat noteworthy.'

Andrew was smiling now too, but his was a gesture meant to silence, not to encourage. 'Later, Evie. If you tell him about it now, there won't be anything to reveal when he sees it.' Andrew's hand went to the Prince's arm, his face wearing another smile, this one meant to cajole. 'Besides, we have people to meet, Dimitri.' The message could not have been clearer. While people stood by, suitably enthralled by the royal presence among them, Andrew called the Prince by his first name. Andrew had risen above the country commonness of Little Westbury; risen above her. Evie suddenly felt very small, very burdensome, as if she was a child who'd forced her unwanted self into the company of adults. Perhaps melting wasn't a bad idea after all.

The Prince stood his ground long enough to politely take his leave. 'I shall look forward to the tapestry, Miss Milham.' She thought she saw an apology in his eyes for the abruptness of their meeting. But surely he understood Andrew's need to move on as well. Once again she'd miscalculated. She should have anticipated the evening's demands on Andrew's time.

'I look forward to it.' Evie dipped another curtsy and watched them move away, the pair immediately engulfed by the other guests craving their attention. She was alone again after a brief moment in the sun of Andrew's attention. In some ways it felt worse now that she'd had a taste of that attention, what it felt like to stand beside him.

She had to stop the self-pity! She was being ridiculous. What had she expected? That somehow Andrew would take her up with them? Include her in his rounds tonight? Why shouldn't the Prince and Andrew be popular and sought after? They made a handsome pair of males, the Prince with his dark hair and warm eyes; Andrew with his golden, English good looks.

Evie smiled softly to herself, her mind already justifying Andrew's behaviour. This was a big night for him. He had a lot on his mind, there were people for the Prince to meet. It was no wonder Andrew didn't want to stand around talking about tapestries or exchanging pleasantries with someone who wasn't important to his cause this evening. She was selfish to want to keep him all to herself. She had made her first overture, she had to be content with that. And she was. Claire and Beatrice and May would be proud of her. She'd not accepted the first opportunity to be defeated. She'd gone to the stage instead and put herself forward. That in itself was a big step—one of many she'd have to take in this quest to capture Andrew's affections.

Even if Andrew's behaviour had bordered on rude, she understood the reasons for it *and* he had noticed her in the end. She had to take baby steps. She had to get Andrew's attentions first, then his affections would follow. As her father was fond of saying, Rome wasn't built in a day. Evie drifted to the perimeter of the assembly hall now that the evening's goals had been met. She needed to celebrate her victories, not wallow in her defeats.

Chapter Two

The night had been a success! Dimitri Petrovich, Prince of Kuban, allowed himself the rare private luxury of slouching into one of Andrew's comfortably shabby overstuffed chairs. People had been interested in his project and in him. He didn't fool himself. Interest in the latter was usually a strong recommendation for interest in the former. Being a prince had its merits even if it came with inordinate amounts of fawning. But the cause was worth it.

He pulled at his cravat and let out a sigh. 'Ah, that feels better.' Interest was a good sign. It meant the funds would come. Right now, the funds to start the project were all his, but eventually he would want to turn this project over to the people of Little Westbury and they would need to support it. For now, his mind could confidently race ahead to getting the project underway and all the next steps that would entail. There were arrangements to make, men to hire. But all that would keep for tomorrow. Tonight had been a start.

Not a finish. Dimitri pushed the thought away immediately and without tolerance. He wouldn't allow himself to dwell on what else this evening was; the beginning of the end. This was the last project, his final foray abroad before he had to return to Kuban and take his place at court as all loyal, royal Kubanian males did when they turned thirty. He'd known this day would come. He'd been raised for it, but knowing its imminence didn't make it any easier to accept. To give up this world and all its riches now, when there was so much more to learn, seemed a great tragedy. But not yet. There were still a few months. There was still time and he would be damned if he'd let the future pollute the present.

He turned his attention to Andrew at the sideboard preparing brandies. 'You, my friend, were rude this evening.' It would be far better to occupy his thoughts with more immediate issues. Andrew usually behaved with good manners. Not so tonight.

'Rude?' Andrew laughed and handed him a brandy before taking the seat opposite and settling in. A cool evening breeze drifted in from the open French doors of the study, a perfect late summer night. 'To whom? I was charming to everyone who matters.'

Dimitri cocked an eyebrow and engaged in good-humoured debate. 'The pretty girl doesn't matter? That's not like you, Andrew. I thought pretty girls were your specialty.' Pretty, *rich* girls. But Dimitri was too much of a friend to say that out loud.

'There were lots of pretty girls tonight.' Andrew grinned and sipped his brandy. 'Which one?'

'The first one. Evaine,' Dimitri prompted.

'Evaine? Oh, Evie.' Andrew shrugged dismissively. 'She's always around. Good sort, I suppose. Rather shy. You think she's pretty? We grew up together. I suppose I never thought of her as pretty or otherwise.'

'Well, she's clearly thought of you,' Dimitri probed. The girl had been eager for Andrew's attention, all smiles and doting eyes whenever he looked at her, which was seldom. Andrew had been oblivious. His friend might not have noticed Evaine Milham, but *he* had. It was a habit of his, to excavate people the way he excavated sites. He liked looking beyond their surfaces to find their true natures. It made him a better judge of character. He'd seen a far different woman than the girl Andrew so readily dismissed.

Behind the plain upsweep of her hair and the quiet way she presented herself, Evaine Milham had fine features and a wide, generous mouth that lit up her face when she smiled—which was not in public company. She'd been uncomfortable tonight. Her hair might have been simply styled, but its colour was lustrous, a deep chestnut that reminded him of autumn afternoons. Her gown, also simple in fashion, had been intricately embroidered around the hem, where no one would notice. Another sign that she was not a woman who craved attention. Yet there was a certain quiet steel to her. When she'd been pushed to it, she had stood up for herself, demanding the respect she was due.

Taken together, these were no minor clues that Evie Milham was more than she appeared. It was too bad people didn't look close enough to see those things. He would wager there were secret depths to Miss Milham. 'I think she might be pretty if she were to do something with her hair.' Dimitri decided to nudge the point. 'Perhaps you should give her a second look. It's no small thing to have a woman's affection.' A man could lay claim to no greater prize in this world than a woman's loyalty. His parents' marriage had taught him that. It had also taught him that such a gift should be protected, not shunned with the casual disregard Andrew showed Miss Milham.

Andrew gave another shrug as if to suggest it was nothing new, that he was used to having the women of West Sussex fall at his feet with adoring eyes. It was probably true. Andrew had never been short on female attention when they'd travelled together. His new friend had a knack for finding the loveliest, wealthiest woman in a room and latching on to her.

'Evie's not my type.' Andrew's tone was dismissive without hesitation. Miss Evie Milham would be disappointed to hear she'd been summarily discarded. She'd seemed quite interested, as if Andrew was *her* type. Andrew took a healthy swallow from his glass. 'Never has been, never will be. She's not rich enough by far. I suppose it's a good thing I haven't noticed her looks. It would hardly matter how beautiful she was if there's no money to go with her, and in her case there isn't. At least, not enough for me. Her father's a baronet, not exactly a gold mine.'

Dimitri nodded noncommittally on both accounts, keeping his thoughts to himself. Andrew was not usually so harsh when it came to women. Tonight, he was downright callous. It was also the closest Andrew had ever come to admitting he was in the market for a certain type of bride. Dimitri had noticed, of course—the desire to be with the richest women, the state of the furnishings in Andrew's home, which were comfortably worn out of necessity as opposed to a fashion choice. Still, Andrew was no pauper. Andrew lived well. He drank the finest brandies. In Paris, he'd spent money on opera seats and the expensive opera singers that went with them. Andrew simply didn't like making economies. Apparently, Evaine Milham was an economy.

Dimitri gave his brandy a contemplative swirl. He had to be careful here. Who was he to judge? He was a prince with no apparent financial limitations. He had wealth untold as long as he returned to Kuban on time. He would never have to worry about economies. And yet, Andrew had the one thing that eluded him. Freedom. The freedom to go anywhere, to do anything, to be anything. There were nights when Dimitri thought he'd trade all the wealth of Kuban for that freedom and a pair of shabby chairs. He leaned back and sighed contentedly. 'It was a good idea to come here, Andrew. Thank you for this opportunity.'

There were nights when Andrew knew without question he'd trade everything he had, everything he was, to be Dimitri Petrovich, Prince of Kuban: rich, handsome, charismatic, with the world at his feet. This was one of those nights. He'd seen the people approach Dimitri with something close to awe, the men impressed with his title and knowledge, the women impressed with just him. Andrew longed to command a room like that. He had his own charisma, it was true, but he knew it didn't rival Dimitri's magnetism. Of course, money probably had something to do with it. Money always had something to do with everything.

It was also one of those nights when he found Dimitri irritatingly high-minded. Of course, it was easy to be without sin when one was wealthy enough not to have to care. Andrew rose and poured another glass of brandy—the good stuff. If he had to listen to Dimitri go on and on about his plans for the villa excavation, he might as well enjoy himself. 'This will be good for Little Westbury. The excavation will provide jobs.' Andrew tuned it out. He had heard it all before, how retrieving history created a sense of local pride in small communities, how it helped the economy, not just labourers at the site, but the businesses that supported a large labour force: farmers, bakers, butchers who supplied the food required for such an endeavour; tourism and news stories that would bring people here, people who might require more services than a single inn or tavern could provide. The town might need two such places. The Prince had vision and he had the talent to give others vision too, Andrew would give him that.

After all, hadn't the Prince given him vision? The vision of how dusty, broken artefacts could be translated into shiny gold. Once Andrew had seen the possibilities, history had become a lot more interesting. This villa excavation was going to be his own personal gold mine. He'd finally have the funds he needed, the prestige he needed, to live at the standard he wanted. There would be no more tatty chairs and worn curtains, no more carefully going over the account ledgers of his grandfather's shrinking estate to make sure the books balanced. Andrew was not interested in what the excavation would do for Little Westbury, but what it could do for him. He would finally be free.

Chapter Three

'So, how did it go last night?' The question hit Evie the moment two of her best friends stepped down from the open carriage. It was mid-morning and the sun was riding high towards its noon heat. Soon it would be hot, but for now it was pleasantly warm and Evie let Beatrice and May link their arms through hers, flanking her on either side as they set off for shopping in the village.

Anyone watching them advance down the street would see three young, chattering women, all smiles and laughter, even carefree. In part, that might be true. Evie knew the primary purpose for this shopping expedition was to hear about the excitement of her evening. No one saw the other agenda that brought them together. No one could be allowed to. It was their secret. Time was running out. They might not be together much longer. Already, their fourth, Claire, was on her honeymoon far away in Vienna, where she'd live with her new husband. Beatrice would be the next to go, probably in a few weeks.

Evie shot a covert glance at Beatrice's middle,

softly rounding beneath the loose cotton muslin of her summer gown, proof that *it* was going to happen. Beatrice was pregnant. And unwed. She would be leaving for Scotland soon, where she could have her baby at a distant relative's home and her family could forget about her shame. Beatrice's stay in Little Westbury was merely a two week stop-over in preparation for that journey.

'Well?' May prompted with a mischievous glint in her eyes. 'Did anything happen last night? I heard the assembly hall was a crush.'

Evie smiled at each of her friends in turn as she related her story; how she'd sat behind Andrew and found a way to move up next to him for the toast; how she hadn't given up and followed Andrew to the stage. She left out other details like Andrew's disregard.

'Well done!' May commended her, gesturing to the shop window on her right. 'Let's stop in here at the Emporium. I need to get some drawing paper and pens.'

Masterson's Emporium was the social hub of Little Westbury, a shop that carried a variety of goods ranging from planting seeds to ready-made gloves straight from London. Customers milled about, looking over the goods in the dim coolness of the shop. A few children ogled the row of sweets displayed in glass jars.

'How did Andrew take your presence?' Beatrice sifted through a bin of soaps, lifting them at random to sniff as they waited for May.

'He was surprised,' Evie answered honestly. 'He didn't expect to see me and it flustered him.' She didn't want to admit Andrew had forgotten to introduce her. Beatrice didn't like Andrew as it was. Bea thought he wasn't worthy of her. This would just give Bea fuel for that fire. 'I met the Prince,' Evie offered brightly, hoping to distract Bea.

'How was he? Arrogant? Haughty?' Bea sniffed a citrus-scented soap and wrinkled her nose before putting it back down.

'No, he was neither.' Evie gave Bea a quizzical glance. 'Why would you think that?'

'He's a prince. Men like him have a certain tendency towards pretension.'

Evie laughed. 'Be nice, Bea. He was very cordial last night.' More than cordial. She couldn't recall the last time a man had been that 'cordial' to *her*. She couldn't forget those eyes, her body couldn't forget the feel of his lips brushing her knuckles. Her mind had rebelliously kept her awake last night with a hungry curiosity. What would it be like to be a woman who truly caught his attentions? She would never be that woman. But it was harmless to wonder from afar.

Bea gave a soft smile. 'You're too kind, Evie, always looking for the best in all of us.'

May hurried up to them, a brown wrapped package under her arm. 'I'm ready to go. Where to next?'

'The draper's, I need to get some fabric. I've a new dress in mind for autumn.' It was a beautiful russet silk she'd ordered from a warehouse in London when she'd been in town. She could hardly wait to get started on it. Evie smiled as they set off down the street. 'You've heard all my news, now I want to hear yours.' The threesome had not seen each other since Claire's farewell ball in London. Evie and her family had set out for home immediately afterwards, arriving a week ago. May and Bea had only reached

Little Westbury the day before after a sudden delay in departure plans.

'I don't think there's much to tell,' Beatrice began slowly. Too slowly. Evie sensed there was something afoot, but there was no time to enquire.

May squeezed her arm, whispering in frantic excitement, 'Who is *that*? He's crossing the street and coming towards us!'

Evie looked down the street where a tall man in high boots and summer buckskin *sans* pleats strode towards them swinging a walking stick at his side. She recognised him immediately, pleats or not. 'That's the Prince of Kuban, Dimitri Petrovich, himself.' All six feet and two inches of himself. Her sartorial eye noted the excellence of his wardrobe. He was dressed for an English summer day in a single-breasted tailcoat of camel with a waistcoat in bone linen, set off with a deep green cravat the colour of the forest. But no matter how English his clothing, no one would mistake him for an Englishman, not with that long hair pulled into a sleek tail behind him, making his high cheekbones all the more prominent, his eyes all that more exotic.

'He is certainly *all* man,' May murmured appreciatively. 'Just look at that swagger.' Against her better judgement, Evie's eyes drifted down to his open-hipped stroll, which bordered on decadent. Even his walk was exotic. Good heavens, she really had to find a new word. He *was* handsome. Perhaps if she wasn't focused on Andrew, she might find him attractive in a more personal way. For now, though, the attraction was limited to his mannerisms, his fashion. She truly did admire his clothes. Even if she didn't have her heart set on Andrew, admiring the prince's clothes was all a girl like her could do. One only had to look at him, so confident, so handsome, so *male*, and then look at her to know she never stood a chance. She wasn't the type who caught princes. She was too odd. London had taught her that in the most brutal way possible.

'Miss Milham, good day.' The Prince gave a short bow in greeting. 'What a pleasure to encounter you.' Evie was aware of Beatrice and May exchanging quiet looks. Her usually confident friends seemed daunted by his presence.

Evie dipped a curtsy. 'Your Highness, may I introduce my friends? This is Miss May Worth and Miss Beatrice Penrose.'

He greeted each in turn, taking their hands and smiling at them, his eyes as warm and genuine as they'd been last night, proof that she'd been right. These rituals were mere politeness to him. They meant nothing. He asked how they were enjoying the weather and enquired about their errands, making small talk, doing the work of putting them at ease. He must do it all the time, Evie realised, watching the interaction. Everywhere he went, people were probably in awe of him, in awe of being in the company of a royal prince. Did he ever get tired of the effort?

Then he was talking to her and she forgot her speculations. 'It's quite fortuitous that I've run into you, Miss Milham. I was hoping to take you up on the offer to view your tapestry. I regret we did not get to speak of it more in depth last night.'

Evie blushed under the weight of Bea's and May's stares. They were wondering what she hadn't told them. 'You are welcome to view it any time. Someone is always at home,' Evie managed. Beside her, May straightened, her posture becoming alert. *That* worried her. Apparently, May had overcome any self-consciousness.

'Tomorrow,' May interjected with a smile to the Prince. 'You should come tomorrow to view the tapestry. Evie is always home on Tuesdays in the afternoon and the light in the tapestry room is very good around one o'clock.' Oh, sweet heavens, May had invited the Prince to her house! Had, in fact, all but *begged* him to come over. Even for May, this bordered on mortifying. Evie was suddenly wishing the Prince had been a little more awe-inspiring.

'May——' Evie tried to mitigate her friend's boldness. The poor man would feel trapped. 'He might be busy.'

But the Prince took May's boldness in his stride. He didn't *sound* trapped. 'One o'clock it is.' He looked in her direction. 'If that is acceptable to you, Miss Milham?'

May's foot came down on hers under their skirts before she could think of politely refusing. Evie heard herself squeak, 'One o'clock would be fine,' before the Prince smiled once more and continued down the street.

'What do you think you're doing?' Evie whirled on May the moment the Prince was out of sight. 'You invited a foreign dignitary to my house! *My* house. You don't even live there. Since when do you invite guests to *other* people's homes?'

May gave a smug laugh, unfazed by the outburst. Evie was envious of that laugh, that confidence. Nothing bothered May, not even a flagrant disregard for the rules. 'Since *you* started passing up perfectly good opportunities to spend time with handsome men.' May pulled her into a quiet side street. 'He was angling for an invitation and you were prevaricating with your generic responses. "Come over any time,"' May mimicked.

'I didn't want him to feel coerced.' Evie folded her arms over her chest in defence.

'Oh, I assure you, he wasn't feeling coerced. He was running wild and free with no fences in sight,' May replied, blowing out a frustrated breath. 'Evie, a handsome man who is also a royal, foreign prince wanted to come to your house. How many times do you think that happens, especially in West Sussex?'

'To see a tapestry,' Evie reminded her.

May was undaunted. 'Who cares about the reason why? He's still coming.'

'I'm not interested in him that way,' Evie explained patiently. 'I'm interested in Andrew.' She didn't need to catch a prince, nor did she want to. Her sights were firmly set on Andrew Adair. Besides, what would a man like the Prince—a dashing, well-travelled, sensual man—do with a girl like her who'd never been out of England? It seemed an exercise in futility to even imagine it; a very *warm* exercise that she had no business entertaining in broad daylight on a village street.

'Let me try, May.' Beatrice stepped up. 'Evie, dear, you can use the Prince as leverage. Men are competitive creatures.

'Once Andrew sees another man interested in you, it will pique his own curiosity, especially if that man is a royal prince and a friend. Andrew will wonder what he's been missing.'

'And he'll make the effort to find out?' Evie supplied the rest. She beamed at her friends. Perhaps May's plan was pure genius after all. 'What would I do without you? I'm so glad you're here.' She paused and gasped as a sudden thought hit her. 'You will come tomorrow, won't you? Both of you? You'll know what to say, what to do. You know what my father will be like. He'll go on and on about King Arthur and all of his books far longer than is decent and my mother will be so overset about a prince coming to visit, she'll spend the afternoon on the fainting couch or pestering the cook for perfection.' Her parents were good people, but they were not social people. Entertaining was not their strong suit. 'I can't possibly face the Prince alone.'

There was no rush of assurances. She had the sense again that something was wrong. Bea and May exchanged another of those looks between them. They'd been doing that a lot today. May took her hand, her blue eyes serious. 'We'd love to be there, but I'm afraid we can't make it.' She flicked a glance at Bea and Beatrice nodded. 'We are leaving tomorrow for Scotland.'

'Tomorrow!' Evie protested. 'But you've barely arrived?' She looked at Bea. 'What has happened? We were supposed to have two weeks.'

Bea's hand went protectively to her stomach. When she pressed like that, catching the fabric so that it was flat against her body, her stomach looked larger, the pregnancy more advanced. 'I'm showing sooner than expected.' She bit her lip.

Evie felt immediately selfish. 'I can let out some more dresses for you. We can do it this afternoon.' She'd been altering Bea's clothes for her since the spring, using her needle to keep Bea's pregnancy discreet.

'That's sweet of you, Evie, but no.' Bea gave a sad smile and shook her head. 'My parents would be more comfortable knowing I'm safe in Scotland before any speculation begins.' That was putting a polite trim on it, Evie thought. Beatrice's parents were worried about scandal more than they were worried about their daughter's safety.

Beatrice put a brave face on. 'Besides, if I'm showing so soon the baby might be early, it might be twins. It will be good to be away and settled before too much longer.' She meant before November, when the baby was due. Late autumn didn't seem so far away when one looked at it like that. In less than four months Beatrice would be a mother. Alone. Evie glanced at May. No, not alone. 'You're going with her?'

'Yes.' May's eyes met hers in a silent plea for understanding. Evie nodded. Beatrice needed May more now than she did.

'I'm glad you'll be with her.' It was the truth. Beatrice shouldn't be alone. If her family refused to be there to help her through the birth, then her friends definitely should be. She wasn't sure how May had arranged it, but it did bring her a sense of comfort to know May would be there.

Beatrice reached for her other hand. 'We *are* sorry to leave you, Evie. But I think May has set you on a path towards success.' The words offered a new light to May's bold gesture. It had been a parting gift. May had pushed her towards her future with the invitation to the Prince.

The import of that didn't escape her. They weren't the Left Behind Girls Club any more. Claire had Jonathon. Beatrice would have May and the new baby. Everyone was moving forward. For the first time since their childhood days, Evie was on her own.

Chapter Four

Dimitri strolled promptly down Evie's drive at half-past one the next day, admiring the haphazard compilation of bricks and time that was the Milhams' house. Definitely Elizabethan, he concluded, in its initial construction. He could make out the symmetry of the era in the roofline. He squinted up against the sun to take a more professional interest in the house. An archaeologist was part-historian, part-architect and part-expert in a host of other subjects as well. He picked out a few themes with his keen eye. There was a nod to early Georgian in the pediment above the front door.

That pediment was likely the most recent addition to the house's eclectic architecture. From the state of the front gardens, the latest generation hadn't paid much attention to the external state of the house. He strode along a gravel drive where flowers grew in wild anarchy alongside, having long ago given up any adherence to the limits of the beds they'd been planted in. There were no boundaries here, none of the order of the organised, ornamental gardens of Kuban, modelled on the tamed excellence of Versailles. There were no pruned hedges or carefully shaped bushes. Yet, the look suited the place much better. Many back home would disagree with him, would give such wild nature a disparaging glance. He found it charming, a peaceful haven. He wondered what the Kuban nobility would do if he replicated such a style at his home.

The housekeeper answered his knock and he stepped inside, his senses taking it all in with the astute eye of an archaeologist trained to look for patterns and behaviours: books stacked on consoles in the hallway, books lining shelves in every room the housekeeper took him past, some books lying open. The interior matching the exterior perfectly. The occupants of this house had far more important priorities than landscaping. They lived an internal life of the mind.

'I'll let Miss Milham know you're here.' The housekeeper left him in a cheery yellow sitting room, where more books populated the walls and a small, cosy cluster of furniture upholstered in yellow-and-rose chintz resided in the wide bow of the windows.

A housekeeper. Dimitri smiled at her departure. No stodgy butlers here. A housekeeper had received a Prince of Kuban and had no true notion of who had just walked into the house. He liked the novelty of that anonymity. Everyone fussed over him as if he were more special than the next man. But here, in the Milhams' household, he sensed he might be able to move past that. Andrew's words drifted back to him: *She's not rich enough.* The Milhams did not keep a full complement of staff, perhaps for multiple reasons. Perhaps it was financial, or perhaps they understood every servant was another responsibility, one more acquired burden, an anchor against freedom. Dependents were both a blessing and a curse.

'You came.'

He turned, catching the sound of surprise in Evie's voice. She looked cool and fresh in a white summer muslin sprigged with tiny blue forget-me-nots. Blue was definitely her colour. It brought out the auburn highlights in her hair, turning it more chestnut than brown. They'd not been obvious at the assembly. Dimitri smiled. 'Did you think I wouldn't?' He spoke the words without thinking, the teasing, flirtatious response coming easily to his practised wit. This was how urbane princes interacted with women. He was curious as to how Evie Milham would respond. How would his hypothesis play out now that they were alone, away from a crowd where she felt self-conscious? He told himself it was no more than simply his usual 'excavation' of a person, of taking their measure, yet a part of him was on edge, wanting her to make a certain response, wanting her to come alive for him.

She blushed a little, but she did not shrink from being direct. 'I didn't want you to feel trapped. I feared May pushed the appointment on you.'

'I wouldn't miss it.' He was touched. She'd been advocating for him. She'd been trying to *protect* him. It was a very small protection to be sure. In a life spent protecting others he simply wasn't used to it being the other way around. 'Many people would not hesitate to use any means necessary to capture a prince's time.' He probed carefully. It was true. One woman had followed him to the privy and locked the door.

'I think you'll find I'm not like most people.' Another sort of woman would have made the line into a not so cleverly veiled invitation. Not Miss Milham. Was that a warning? A hint of regret? Why ever would she want to be like others?

He was counting on her assessment to be correct. 'I find the "usual" holds little fascination for me.' His own voice was low, issuing a private invitation of his own, his eyes holding hers, daring her not to look away. He should not wish for such a thing. Nothing but trouble could come from it. But he couldn't stop himself from wanting it anyway. *Come to life for me, Evie Milham. I know you're in there. Don't be afraid.*

There it was. Her steady gaze, her answer. She did not look away. He gestured to the wall of books, looking for a subject to put her at ease. Now that he had her this far, he didn't want her intimidated. 'Have you read all of these?'

'Some.'

He was going to have to work harder. He wanted to assure her his title meant nothing. He was as ordinary as the next man, at least he wanted to be. No one needed to stand on ceremony with him. He'd never get to know her secrets otherwise, secrets he had no business knowing, no need to know.

'Which ones? Which ones have you read?' He grinned. It was a preposterous question. There were over a hundred books right in front of him. He plucked a book at random from the shelf. 'How about this one? *A History of the West Country* by Pieter von Alpers? He's not even a good Englishman from the sounds of his name.' The comment made her laugh and that was what he intended.

'He's Dutch.' Evie smiled, letting it light her face.

'Sometimes it helps to see one's own history through the eyes of another. My father says it brings new perspective. But, no, I haven't read that one.'

She was starting to relax. He could see now that she wasn't shy as he'd first thought, but merely wary. This was a learned behaviour, acquired at some point. This was her attempt to protect herself. From what? From whom? He tucked the new piece of information away.

Evie ran her hand over the book spines on the shelves, coming to stop on one of them. 'I've read this one.' She handed it to him. 'He has an especially interesting interpretation of early Saxon history.' He smiled appreciatively. Evie Milham was a historian. How intriguing. He didn't meet many women who were or who would admit to it.

'Like father like daughter? I'd like to meet your father some time. I could use a local historian's help on my project. I was surprised Andrew didn't include him in the initial circle of investors for the site. By the way, is he joining us today?' Was *anyone* joining them? He could hardly believe someone *wasn't* chaperoning and yet it appeared the Milhams' casual approach to living extended to their daughter, who was apparently allowed to meet men unattended. He thought it seemed somehow disrespectful of them to leave her alone no matter how honourable his intentions were.

'Are you worried for your reputation?' There was a shade of worry in her eyes that was entirely sincere. Other women would have delivered the line with a flirty laugh. He knew plenty of those women. But Evie Milham was not one of them. She was genuinely sympathetic. 'Shall I call someone?' She was flustered again and it was his fault. In an attempt to honour her, he'd managed to insult her.

Dimitri chuckled, trying to put her at ease. He'd not meant to upset her any more than he'd meant to insult her. 'Are *you* worried for *yours*?'

'You're here to view a tapestry, not ravish me.' Evie scoffed. He heard the hint of sorrow, or was that resignation, again?

'Are you sure about that?' he teased, although he wasn't sure it was entirely a joke on his part. Evie Milham was ravish-worthy, with her glorious hair and that carefully guarded smile, especially when she wasn't doubting herself, when she was letting her real self out to play as she had when they'd discussed the history books.

She smiled, but there was a shadow in her eyes now. 'I've had years to be quite sure of that, Your Highness.' He understood. She thought *he* was embarrassed to be alone with her, maybe even ashamed to be seen with her. The realisation gave him pause. Where had she ever acquired such a belief about herself? Was this where the wariness came from? He would have to work harder to put her at ease, to convince her she had nothing to fear from him.

'Call me Dimitri. Please,' he urged, refusing to remark on that shadow for fear she would see any encouragement he offered as pity. 'We're a thousand miles from Kuban. I hardly feel like a prince this far from home.' He liked it that way. The further from Kuban he got, the easier it was to forget he was a prince, the easier it was to live simply, to be a man only, not a title he'd acquired by an accident of birth. If only others felt that way too. Unfortunately, they were all too keen to remind him of the chasm that separated him from other men.

Evie took the invitation as he'd hoped. 'All right, then, *Dimitri*, the tapestry is this way.' She led them through a warren of hallways to a gallery that ran the length of the back of the house. The tapestry was easy to spot. It was of considerable size and hung in the centre of the left wall in a large glass frame. Even with the glass protecting it, Dimitri could tell it was of fine and authentic quality. He stepped towards it, unable to resist doing anything else, drawn to the vibrant hues of blue, red and orange. 'This is remarkably well preserved...' he breathed in real appreciation, letting his eyes roam the story of the tapestry. 'Arthur's wedding to Guinevere, if I'm not mistaken.'

'Yes, my father has spent considerable amounts of time researching it. He's in the final stages of writing a book about the tapestry,' Evie offered. He stared at it a while longer, asking questions, before turning his attention to other artefacts in the room. The gallery was a repository of history. There were other, smaller, tapestries hanging from the walls, unprotected. He wandered over to one depicting a unicorn set against a blue-flowered field.

'This one is quite fine as well. Is it of some import?' He wondered why it wasn't under glass too. It seemed familiar, as if he'd seen it somewhere before.

Evie shook her head. 'No. It's one of mine. It's merely a copy of a famous French tapestry.'

Dimitri peered closer, studying the stitches. 'You did this? It is marvellously well made.'

Evie shrugged off the praise. 'I drew the pattern from a piece of art. I like to work with cloth, sewing, weaving. I draw my own patterns.' That was interesting indeed; a historian and a seamstress, although that seemed too menial of a word for what she'd done here, and an artist. Evie Milham was a trove of hidden talents.

He spied a framed collection of ink work hanging on the wall. 'Are these some of your patterns?'

'Yes. I drew them for one of my father's books, but he liked some of them so much he wanted to frame them.' Evie blushed. 'A father's prerogative, I suppose. Some would say he's biased.'

Dimitri looked closer. The work was exquisitely done, meticulous and clean. 'I don't think he's biased at all.' An idea came to him. He could use someone with a decent artistic eye at the site.

They strolled the perimeter of the room, he asking questions and Evie answering, each answer a revelation. Evie Milham might appear to be somewhat quiet and unassuming, but beneath that exterior, there was much of her waiting to be unwrapped, waiting to be discovered. She was knowledgeable about history, able to answer his questions with impressive intellect; she could replicate medieval tapestries with an expert's skill; she was sensitive to others' feelings, perhaps too much so.

Did she make a habit of casting herself in the subordinate role in conversation? He'd seen it at the assembly. She'd put herself forward when Andrew had failed to introduce her, but the moment she perceived she was an interloper, she'd withdrawn, content to defer to the wishes of others. But today he'd applied considerable skill in drawing her out, in making her an equal in the discussion, and she had blossomed.

He could not remember enjoying a conversation this much. There was no pressure to perform, to be the Prince. He had only to be himself.

They passed out into the gardens off the gallery and into the sun. There was more order to these gardens than the ones in front of the house, probably because these gardens were designed to show off statuary. Most of the statuary were broken. There wasn't a whole statue among them, but that only reinforced their authenticity. 'Shards my father has picked up over a lifetime,' Evie explained with a rueful smile. 'These are from Italy, from his Grand Tour twenty-eight years ago.' She gestured to a twin set of partial busts.

Dimitri made noises of suitable impressment. He was more interested in how the sun caught Evie's hair, the auburn flame of it flickering in the smooth brown depths. The statues couldn't compete. Her hair was beautiful, even coiled in a tight braid that wound neatly about her head. He imagined for a moment undoing that braid and combing his fingers through it. Undone, her hair would be long, and straight, the smoothness of it falling through his fingers like Chinese silk. It made him wonder what Evie Milham would be like undone in other ways. What other secrets lay beneath her unassuming exterior? What would she reveal to the man who uncovered those secrets? What would she discover about herself? He felt a flicker of regret that he couldn't be that man.

'Miss.' The housekeeper caught up to them on the gravel path, breaking his attention on Evie's hair. The woman was huffing from the exertion. 'Mr Adair is here, shall I send him out?'

Evie's face split into a smile. 'He can join us. Please, bring some lemonade and the little cakes Cook baked this morning, if it's not too much trouble. The lemon seed are his favourite.'

Evie's gaze moved to a point over his shoulder, her smile widening, lighting up her whole face. Dimitri didn't need to turn to know it was Andrew striding down the path. A fierce little spark of competitive maleness lit in him. He wanted that smile for himself, not for Andrew, who didn't want it, and didn't appreciate it. His friend's boldness bordered on arrogant. Andrew hadn't waited for permission to join them. He'd *assumed* he'd be welcomed and the presumption was irrationally annoying. Why did he care if Andrew joined them?

They sat for lemonade and cakes at a table under a shade tree and Dimitri knew why he cared. Evie, who had become relaxed during their tour of the gallery, had suddenly become self-conscious and tense, too eager to please: Was the lemonade sweet enough? The cakes fresh enough? The whole while, Andrew took the demure obsequiousness as his due, oblivious to Evie's efforts once more.

'I must get the recipe from your cook.' Dimitri reached for another lemon seed cake, easily his fourth. 'These are delicious.'

'Too simple for the court of Kuban, though.' Andrew threw out the thoughtless insult and helped himself to a fifth cake. 'Can you imagine these plain little things on a tea tray along with those frosted delicacies of yours?' Andrew glanced over at Evie, the first real look he'd given her since he arrived. 'You haven't seen a tea until you've had tea Kubanian style.'

Dimitri watched Evie brighten at the comment directed at her, willing to overlook the insult delivered to the cakes Andrew claimed to prefer and which she'd especially thought of serving on his behalf. Didn't she see the comment wasn't for her benefit, but for Andrew's? This was a chance for Andrew to show off. His suspicion was confirmed when Andrew launched into a detailed description of the one time he'd experienced a Kubanian tea at Dimitri's apartments in Naples where they'd met.

Evie listened, enrapt. Dimitri wanted to kick Andrew. Andrew had adopted quite the superior attitude since they'd arrived in Sussex. It was not something that had stood out to him in their travels.

'Is that how you met? Over tea?' Evie turned her attention his direction, playing the polite hostess who recognised one guest had dominated the conversation for too long. 'I had no idea Andrew had made it as far as Kuban.'

'He didn't,' Dimitri put in quickly. Maybe it was selfish, but he wanted to disabuse her of the notion that Andrew had been to the remote Russian kingdom in the steppes. In fact, Andrew had not strayed from the conventional path that made up every Englishman's Grand Tour. 'We met in Naples. I was hosting a gathering for expatriates around Europe to celebrate work I'd completed at Herculaneum. My team and I had uncovered a mosaic destroyed by the eruption of Vesuvius. We spent that spring restoring it.'

'Wonderful stuff. What the Prince was doing in Herculaneum rekindled my love for ancient history.' Andrew leaned forward, ready to take up the reins of conversation again.

Evie smiled. 'My father would enjoy hearing about your experiences.'

Andrew cut her off with a wave of his hand. '*Ancient* history, Evie, not medieval. There's quite a difference. Centuries, in fact.' His tone bordered on patronising as he laughed. Was Evie going to sit there and let his remark go unchallenged? Of course she was. She wasn't going to pick an argument with the object of her affections.

Dimitri couldn't help himself. After all, Andrew wasn't the object of *his* affections. 'I think she knows the difference, Andrew. Miss Milham and I were having the most enjoyable afternoon. She showed me the Arthur tapestry and some that she's done as well. Miss Milham is very talented and *exceedingly* knowledgeable on several subjects.'

Andrew's gaze fixed on him, sharp with curiosity. 'Ah, the tapestry. I remember now. I had wondered why you'd come.'

Dimitri heard the veiled slander—that Evie alone couldn't possibly be attraction enough. He hoped Evie hadn't heard it. It would hurt her. Perhaps it was remarks like that which had led to her self-consciousness. Such remarks were nothing to him, but she had not cut her social teeth in a royal court. He met Andrew's gaze with his own, unwavering, his sense of protectiveness rising instinctively on Evie's behalf. 'Well, then you have your answer. I am still looking for mine. What exactly brings *you* here this afternoon?'

What had just happened? Evie glanced from Andrew to Dimitri. Were they fighting over *her*? It was too preposterous to believe; the golden-haired Andrew Adair and a Russian prince, sparring over her while they sipped lemonade in the garden. It was ridiculous in the extreme and yet she wasn't sure what else to make of it. Oh, how she wished Beatrice and May were here! They would know for certain.

'More lemonade?' Evie groped for something to say that would relieve the tension. She was not equipped to handle such a situation. She passed around the dwindling tray of cakes to give herself something to do. Dimitri took two, Andrew took three, shooting the Prince a triumphant look designed to make a point. At this rate, the two of them were going to eat themselves sick. She gingerly picked up the threads of the original conversation. 'You met in Naples, and then what?'

'The Prince made a fortune on the mosaic, selling it to a museum in Naples,' Andrew supplied drily. 'He was moving on to Greece, to a temple excavation on the peninsula. I was intrigued so I tagged along. We did the temple and another small dig near Athens, then worked our way home.' Andrew sat back in his chair and folded his hands across his stomach with smug victory. 'I told him about our local Roman villa, which has never quite got off the ground in terms of a full excavation, and the rest is history.' He laughed at his joke. The tension eased and Evie was almost convinced she'd imagined it to begin with. The visit concluded amiably, the gentlemen polishing off the last cakes and the remainder of the lemonade before rising to leave.

The Prince bowed over her hand as he had at the assembly room. She was struck once more by the intensity of his gaze and the heat generated by his touch.

It still didn't mean anything, she reminded herself, but silly as it was, she liked how her stomach fluttered when he touched her. 'I was wondering, Miss Milham, if you would consider helping on the villa excavation? You mentioned you draw your own tapestry patterns and I need someone to do a catalogue of drawings for any artefacts we might uncover.'

Her pulse sped up at the prospect, flattered that he'd acknowledged her skills. What an honour, an honour far beyond any she'd ever expected. For a moment she couldn't find any words. She settled on 'I would like that very much.' When he touched her, looked at her with those dark eyes, spoke to her in that low voice with its dentalised 'th's and hard 'r's, she felt like a princess. Almost.

'Come to the site tomorrow.' He released her hand with a smile and the magic was gone. She was once more merely Evie Milham, plain and quiet, the sort who admired men on their pedestals, not one who was put up on a pedestal of her own. She certainly wasn't the sort of girl those men fought over. Not the sort of girl a prince would pay serious attentions to, but for a moment she had been.

Chapter Five

The walk back to Andrew's was…different. For once, it was silent. Usually, most of their walks were filled with Andrew's talk. Andrew liked to think out loud. Normally, Dimitri didn't mind. Today, however, Andrew was silent except for the occasional swish of his walking stick cutting through the high grass in the meadow. Dimitri opted to wait. When Andrew was done processing he would talk.

'What happened back there?' Andrew gave the grass a hard thwack with his stick. Apparently, he was done processing. 'For a moment, I thought we were going to quarrel over Evie Milham.' He said the last as if the notion was insane. Dimitri didn't think it was in the least preposterous. Didn't Andrew see it? The beauty beneath the simple attire and the simple hair; the devotion she was waiting to lavish on him? As for himself, he was thinking far too much about that hidden beauty. When she'd spoken of tapestries and stitchery, he'd wanted to take her hair down pin by pin, pull it loose from its tight *coiffure* and spread it through his fingers like so much embroidery silk.

'I was unaware there was anything to quarrel about.' Dimitri shot Andrew a wry smile. 'She is quite solidly yours by her own design.' Perhaps Andrew needed a little push in Evie's direction, something to drag him out of his oblivion. Maybe he could help with that. Maybe *Evie* could use some help with that. She was making it too easy for Andrew, catering to his every whim. Andrew would never respect a woman like that. He would, however, use that woman. Dimitri's stomach gave a small twist. He hardly knew her, but it sat poorly with him to think of Evie Milham being used in that manner.

Andrew lifted a brow. 'Do I sense a wager coming on? There was a time when you could turn a lowly country girl's head like that!' He snapped his fingers and tossed a smug grin at Dimitri. 'Or, are you losing your touch? I admit I have a head start. She's known me her entire life. But you're a prince,' he goaded. 'Surely that evens the playing field.'

'Those games are fine with ladies of the court,' Dimitri offered warily. He wasn't sure he liked the idea of pushing Andrew towards Evie any more. Last night, it had seemed like the right thing to do, a way to help out Miss Milham. His stomach twisted again. 'I think those games are rather cruel, however, when played with unsuspecting country ladies.' Dimitri's stomach twisted harder, more violently than before. This time he didn't think it had anything to do with Evie and everything to do with seed cakes. Too many seed cakes.

All things in moderation, his old *nyanya* had told him more than once growing up, always *after* he'd over-indulged. Some day he'd learn, but apparently not today. His covert eating contest with Andrew had been petty. From the hitch in Andrew's step, it looked like he might be feeling the effects as well. They'd behaved childishly and they'd got their just desserts in the most literal way possible. Andrew let out a burp and a sigh that set them both to laughing. 'That's better.'

The tension between them eased and Andrew slung an arm about his shoulders, having already forgotten Evie Milham and his silly wager. It was for the best. Dimitri knew he certainly had no business involving himself in careless games regarding a young woman's affections. There could be no entanglements for him. He would be returning to Kuban. Taking Andrew's wager would require deliberately breaking an unsuspecting girl's heart. The best he could do for her would be to help her understand her own value, to see her own beauty. She didn't need to settle for a man like Andrew.

Dimitri shot a sideways glance at Andrew, only half-listening to a story about Evie's seed cakes. Andrew was golden and laughing in the sun. It was easy to see why Evie would be taken with him. But Andrew was also entirely self-absorbed. Even now, with just the two of them present, he was 'performing' the story for an audience. Usually, Dimitri was impressed with Andrew's showmanship. On the road, Andrew's glib tongue had talked them into a few prime situations such as the dig in Greece. But here in England, his 'showmanship' seemed rehearsed to the point of narcissism. It reaffirmed Dimitri's premise: There was no doubt Miss Milham would be good for his sometimes high-handed and arrogant new friend. She would love him in spite of himself, and, given time, perhaps she would help him see what was truly important in life. But at what cost to herself? The real question to ask was: Was Andrew good for Evie?

Dimitri laughed out loud at the direction of his thoughts. Andrew would think the laughter was for the story. In reality Dimitri was laughing at himself. Who was he to decide their future, or even be interested in it? He hardly knew Evie Milham and he'd barely known Andrew for a year. He had no business interfering. Aside from his curiosity over the quiet Miss Milham with her russet hair and her hidden hobbies, he wasn't even sure what had sparked his attentions in the first place. Maybe it was a sign after all that he was ready to return to Kuban, settle down and live the life he'd been destined for since birth, the life his family *needed* him to live.

Perhaps it was for the best he felt that way, since his return, even his marriage, was inevitable. Dimitri shook his head to clear his thoughts. He wouldn't think of that, not yet. There was still some time left to him. He needed to focus on the immediate future first. What came next would take care of itself. Until then, he had one last excavation to oversee and to enjoy.

The excavation site was bustling with organised activity when Evie and her father arrived the next morning. The scale of that activity was quite impressive. Workers, hired from local labour, hauled carts of rocks and debris away, others whisked dust from slabs to see what was hidden beneath, while still others were engaged in the process of sifting rubble through sieves searching for shards of artefacts. The industry was punctuated by an occasional shout—some of them in Russian, a reminder that not all the effort on site was local.

'The Prince has brought his own team,' her father commented as they picked their way through the site, trying to stay out of the way. 'He's very methodical, very efficient. He'll have his men oversee various aspects of the project so he doesn't have to train new foremen.' It was a reminder of what she'd forgotten so easily yesterday. Dimitri Petrovich was a prince, a man who was used to being served, used to commanding and directing others. Travelling with a retinue was to be expected.

From across the site, Dimitri waved to them, beckoning them over. 'Ah, there he is,' her father remarked with a chuckle. 'Good thing he spotted us. I might not have recognised him today.' Evie privately disagreed. Dimitri might be dressed like everyone else in durable trousers tucked into dusty boots and a loose cotton shirt of off-white homespun, the clothes of a labourer, not a prince, but she'd know him anywhere. He couldn't disguise those cheekbones or those eyes.

'Sir Hollis, Miss Milham, welcome!' He strode towards them, stripping off working gloves as he greeted them. His shirt was open at the neck, showing a patch of tanned skin, and already splotched with sweat and dirt. He'd not only been working, he'd been working *hard*.

'You must pardon my appearance; we have great hopes for today. We're excavating the dining room, or what we hope is the dining room.' He smiled broadly and his enthusiasm was infectious. 'Let me show you. We have something of a map to work from.' He led them over to a table set off to the side, an informal work station where papers were weighted down with rocks.

He picked up a book and turned to a well-marked page. 'There's a two-page description of a villa that matches this one in location and there's a reference to a west-facing dining area to catch the setting sun. If we're right, we've found the villa of General Lucius Artorious.' The air around him fairly crackled with his excitement and Evie felt her own excitement rise, stoked to its own height by the prospect of the project and by his nearness.

He passed the book to her father. 'The account is short, but it's very detailed. It even names some specific items that were in the home. If we could find them, it would ensure the authenticity of the site.' He smiled at Evie. 'We've already found some items— nothing that's listed, of course, but items that suggest a man of social standing and his family were here. Are you ready to draw? I have a workspace set up for you in the cataloguing department.' His wink was just for her. 'We use the term "department" very loosely here. I hope our working conditions aren't too rustic for you, just canvas and some tables, but my assistant, Stefon, is brilliant and he can show you anything you need.' Some of her excitement defused. An assistant, of course. It wasn't as if the Prince could work privately with her. It was probably for the best. However would she concentrate on drawing if he was hovering nearby with his smiles and touches? She really had to get over this silliness.

He took them through the site, gesturing to points of interest as they went. 'To the left are the cooking facilities. We feed the workers three meals a day. To the right is the "museum" where we keep the items that are already catalogued.' The site was truly impressive. This place was a little self-contained city. She'd not realised all the services necessary to support such a project. He made an off-hand motion to the left. 'That tent out there is my private quarters.'

Tent? Evie stopped to gape. It looked more like a pavilion. It was big and white, and set back from the site, perhaps for privacy. 'You live out here?' She quickened her step to keep up with her father and the Prince.

The Prince nodded. 'It's a necessity. One must be vigilant or sites like this are easily vandalised. I've found there's nothing like human presence to deter unwanted attentions.' He threw an entirely manly glance at her father. 'It helps that I'm a pretty good shot.' The two of them laughed together. They seemed to have established an instant rapport that transcended their stations.

Vandalism? She was still trying to wrap her mind around the fact the Prince was *camping* like a soldier on campaign. No matter how large the tent, outdoor living required a certain amount of concessions, especially if a man was used to living amid royal luxuries.

'This is your workspace, Miss Milham.' The Prince ushered her under a wide triangular expanse of heavy canvas tied between three trees. Beneath it sat desks and tables with boxes next to them, writing and drawing supplies on them. One other clerk was already busy at work. The Prince held out her chair. 'The items to draw are here in this box. There are notes attached, I can't guarantee all the handwriting is legible. The information will have to be recopied with the drawings and we'll need three copies of each drawing.'

Evie nodded, sitting down in the chair and taking in her workspace, her mind already organising the task in her head. She was eager to begin. This was no different than the work she did for her father. She surveyed the supplies, assuring the Prince she had all she needed.

'Very well, I will leave you to it, Miss Milham. Again, let me tell you how very grateful I am to have someone of your skills assisting on the project.' He turned to her father. 'If I might borrow your expertise as well, Sir Hollis? I have a few questions.' She watched them go with a smile. When Dimitri had visited, Evie had worried her family would be too casual for him, but now that she'd witnessed on two occasions just how hard he worked to put others at ease, to help them forget he was a prince, she was glad for her father's easy-going nature. Dimitri seemed to like that her father extended that easy companionship to him. Her father enjoyed a quiet life and offered his hospitality and friendship to all those around him regardless of status. It seemed Dimitri responded to that. Just as she'd responded to his genuine appreciation of her work. Evie shook her head as if to refocus her thoughts. She needed to prove herself, she needed to show Dimitri his confidence in her hadn't been misplaced. She couldn't do that if she spent the day staring after him.

It only took a few minutes to become entirely immersed in the task. There were pencils to sharpen and the pages of fresh journals to cut. Then all was ready. Evie took a deep breath. This was peaceful work, work

that was both useful and relaxing. She could lose herself in the drawing just as she did with sewing, her
mind absorbed by the process of bringing something
to life with a stitch of thread, the shading of a pencil.
The first item was a jewelled comb. Evie laid it on
her table and began.

Sketching in the morning was pleasant. There was
a light breeze that filtered in regularly, enough to keep
the workspace cool without ruffling the papers. Drawing in the afternoon, however, was less pleasant. The
breeze had stopped and the heat had increased. So too
had the flies. Nothing horrendous, she told herself,
swiping at the pesky fly for the hundredth time, merely
inconvenient. This wasn't the desert after all. And she
had only to look across the work site to appreciate the
comforts of her space. Out in the direct August sun,
men laboured with carts and rocks, brushing, sifting,
hauling, while they strained and sweated, the Prince
among them. Archaeology was dirty labour. His hair
had come loose, his shirt untucked. He didn't look ter-
ribly royal at the moment, just a man. Perhaps that was
why he liked his work so much...

'Evie!' A shadow fell across her table, startling
her. 'What are you doing here? I would have thought
you'd have left by now.' Andrew moved some papers
aside so he could sit on the table's edge.

'Careful! The ink isn't quite dry!' she squawked,
appalled at his thoughtlessness.

Andrew jumped up and stepped back, glancing
down at his trousers. 'Thanks for the warning, I
wouldn't have wanted to stain these trousers. They're
new.'

'I was thinking about the paintings,' Evie said

crossly, still alarmed at how close she'd come to losing the afternoon's work to a careless gesture. 'They took hours to complete.' His trousers! Hah! The drawings were much more important. Andrew had at least *twenty* pairs of trousers. The man was a clotheshorse. Usually she admired that.

'Why, Evie,' Andrew drawled, looking at her with more careful consideration than he'd given the drawings. 'I do believe you're put out with me.' A boyish grin teased at his mouth and he looked devilishly handsome in his clean, creased buff trousers and coat of blue summer superfine.

He looked immaculate and cool, not a speck of dust on him. Quite the opposite of herself. Suddenly self-conscious, Evie pushed a loose strand of hair behind her ear, hoping she didn't look as hot as she felt. Of course Andrew would see her now when she wasn't looking her best or apparently acting it.

She really had behaved like a shrew and to Andrew of all people. Surely that wasn't how one got a man's attention. 'I'm sorry. It's just that these drawings are one of a kind and they took hours.' Andrew wasn't an artist. He couldn't be expected to appreciate things like wet ink.

Andrew studied the drawings, seeing them for the first time. He held a few of them up, while she cringed and hoped they'd dried sufficiently to be touched without smudging. 'Evie, these are good, really good.'

'Thank you.' She could feel herself blush. When had Andrew *ever* complimented her? This was a first.

'We should be thanking you.' Andrew put the drawings back down on the pile. 'Dimitri will be pleased. Speaking of which, did he find anything of

interest today?' He gave her a wide smile, his blue
eyes twinkling.

'Nothing from the dining room yet, they're still
working.'

'That's too bad. I know he has high hopes for it.'
Andrew reached for the box of catalogued artefacts.
'What's in here?'

'There is a jewelled comb.' Evie flipped through
the pages of her drawings. 'It was the first one I did
today.' She handed it to Andrew, pleased that his eyes
lit up. She'd thought it the best she'd done all day. It
had been a challenge to portray the tiny pieces of em-
erald that were still embedded on the comb's edge.

'Lovely. Museums are always interested in pieces
like this.' Andrew considered the drawing thoughtfully. 'Where's the comb itself?'

'It's already been taken over to the "museum".'
Evie gestured towards the canvas collection centre,
where Dimitri planned to store the artefacts.

'Hmm.' Andrew muttered more to himself. 'Do you
think you could make me a copy of the drawing? I'd
love to have it for myself, a souvenir of this project.'

'I'll do it tomorrow.' Evie beamed, pleased.

The Prince strode up and Andrew stepped away
from the table. 'Ah, there you are. It's about time you
showed up now that it's nearly supper,' the Prince
joked, slapping Andrew on the back before turning
to more serious business. 'How did it go today? Were
you able to secure the supplies we need?'

'Yes. Your small army of workers will have food,
starting tomorrow. Plenty of vegetables, just how you
like,' Andrew assured him. He winked at Evie and explained. 'While you have all been playing in the dirt

here today, I've been in negotiations for food supplies.'
He picked up a drawing. 'Evie has outdone herself on
these.' He handed one to the Prince and Evie found
herself anxious. It was rather disconcerting to have
someone look over her work right in front of her. She
would have preferred Dimitri look at her work privately once she was home. She hardly dared to breathe
while she waited for him to pass judgement.

'Excellent,' the Prince declared with a smile.
'You've earned the right to go home.' He shot a glance
at Andrew. 'Perhaps you might be so good as to escort her home?' Her heart began to pound. This was
almost too good to be true; Andrew had acknowledged her talent and now he was going to drive her
home. So why was she spending more time staring
at Dimitri, who was hot, dirty and tired from a day's
hard work, when there was immaculate, charming
Andrew to stare at?

'I would like nothing better.' Andrew offered her
his arm, drawing her attention through the effort. 'I
am parked just over here, Evie.'

'Miss Milham,' the Prince called after them, 'we'll
see you in the morning?' He had the manners to make
it a question, not a command.

'I wouldn't miss it for the world,' Evie called back,
cheerfully. Today had been one of the best days she'd
had in a long while and that wasn't even counting the
carriage ride to come.

Chapter Six

Which was just as well, Evie reflected, the curricle
jolting to a halt outside her house in the summer twilight. The drive wasn't nearly as exciting as it should
have been. It was, in fact, something of a disappointment. Perhaps it was simply that the rest of the day
had been far more exciting than *it* should have been
and all else paled by comparison. After all, it wasn't
every day a girl got to catalogue and draw items that
were a thousand years old. A few centuries old, that
was one thing. She'd done that plenty of times for her
father, even for herself when she drew her tapestry
patterns. But a thousand? That was *incredible* and she
had the ink stains to prove it. She clenched her hands
into fists, hoping Andrew wouldn't notice, not when
he looked like perfection itself handling the reins on
the seat beside her, his hair burning gold in the sinking sunlight, his clothes the height of summer fashion, straight from London. He, like most gentlemen
of her acquaintance, would find it odd for a girl to get
excited about artefacts and ink.

Andrew set the brake and she let herself engage in

a moment of fantasy. Would this be what life would be like with Andrew? What if they were pulling up to *their* house after a day spent engaged in the pursuit of history? Would they go inside and sip cool lemonade before dinner? Would they talk through the finds of the day on a back veranda, a candlelit dinner laid before them? Would they watch the sun sink together before he took her hand and led her up to the bedroom?

It occurred to her that when she'd thought of Andrew in the past, it had never been with an eye to finding any intellectual fulfilment with him. Andrew drew a woman with his looks, with the way he carried himself. Those were always the things she noticed about him first. She wasn't alone. They were the things every girl in the parish talked about when they talked about handsome Andrew Adair. But now that she knew he loved history too, it seemed more important than ever that she win him. They would have so much in common, so much to build a life on. It proved her instincts had been right all these years of gazing at him from afar. She and Andrew belonged together, no matter what reservations Beatrice might hold.

Andrew came around to her side, reaching to help her down. His hands were at her waist, swinging her to the ground and breaking her out of her daydream. She stumbled a little as he set her down. Andrew laughed as he steadied her. 'Evie, where are you? You're miles from here.' She loved his blue eyes when he laughed, all sparks and lights. Today, they were laughing for her. That should be a victory of sorts. How long had she waited for such a reaction?

'Just enjoying the scenery.' Evie dared the flirtatious line before she could think better of it. She smiled up at him. He was tall, nearly as tall as the Prince, who was more than six feet. She got a beaming smile in return, but nothing more. What had she expected? Andrew was a gentleman.

Andrew ushered her up the steps to the front door, his hand skimming the small of her back, a gesture her body and mind barely registered. She waited for more: for heat, for recognition. Nothing came. Perhaps the touch was too insignificant. It wasn't as if the front steps of her home was a setting designed to coax any intimacy. But the lack of *any* registration left her strangely let down. She felt as if she was waiting for something that had not yet arrived and she was loath to let Andrew leave on such a low note because of it.

'Would you like to come in? I'm sure my father would love to talk about the project. The Prince gave him a thorough tour this morning.' She tried not to hold her breath, tried not to appear too wistful. It was just a casual invitation issued to a long-time neighbour.

Andrew gave her another broad smile. For a moment she thought he'd say yes. Then he shook his head. 'I appreciate the offer, but I must decline. I've had a long day and another early start tomorrow. You do too. The Prince is lucky to have you assisting us in this endeavour.' He held her eyes for an extended moment. 'I will look forward to my drawing, Evie.'

He strode back down the steps and drove away, leaving her still waiting. Still wanting *something*.

It wasn't until the end of dinner with her parents, over the cheese and fruit course, that she understood what she'd been waiting for and why. She'd wanted her body to register his touch as it had registered the Prince's; with a rush of heat and sharp awareness.

Evie nearly choked on a slice of pear. What did she think she was doing? Comparing the Prince and Andrew? That was a piece of wanton madness if ever there was one. She tried to rationalise the direction of her thoughts. Was it too much to expect that she feel something at Andrew's touch? And why not? After all, the Prince had only touched her amid a crowd in a public venue. His touch had been nothing more than what politeness demanded, yet she'd come *alive* at it. Both times. It had been much the same when he'd come to view the tapestry.

'Are you feeling all right, dear?' Her mother gave her a concerned look. She had to be careful here or her high-strung mother would pester her all night if she thought anything was wrong.

Evie answered with a sip of her water. She couldn't plausibly conceive of answering that question with any amount of truth. It would give her mother a fit if she knew what Evie had spent dinner thinking about. Evie had learned long ago to keep her imagination to herself.

Her mother rose from the table and smiled at her father. 'Why don't we all move into the sitting room? Mrs Brooks has left the doors open to catch the breeze.' To Evie, she said, 'I have a letter from one of your sisters.' She retrieved a letter from a pocket in her skirt and smiled as if she held a great prize. If it was from Diana, maybe she did. Diana had married two years ago to an earl in Cornwall and promptly popped out an heir. Evie would bet money the contents of the letter held news of a spare arriving in the spring. If the letter was from her other sister, Gwen, perhaps the letter was less of a prize. Gwen had married a baronet's second son who aspired to be a don at Oxford. Evie had sewn both of their wedding gowns.

This had become the routine of their evenings since her sisters had gone. The three of them would eat, would go into the sitting room. Her father would read to them from one of his current history interests, her mother would read any interesting letters and Evie would stitch on her latest project. Tonight it wasn't enough. How could she go from the heat, the dust, the masculinity of the excavation site to her mother's sitting room? To letters about someone else's life? How could she, when her head was full of Andrew and a Russian Prince with a hot touch? Her life had suddenly become interesting on its own without any help from her sisters.

She made her excuses at the stairs. 'I think I will go up instead. I am tired,' she lied with a wan smile. 'I might write a note to May before I go to bed.' That part was true. May and Beatrice would know what to make of her mind's tendency to compare the two men.

But it was difficult to concentrate on writing the letter. Her mind kept drifting back to the day and all she'd seen—a thousand-year-old comb and a white pavilion where even now, as the summer moon rose, a dark-haired man might be preparing for bed. It did not occur to her until she climbed into her own bed that she hadn't once wondered about Andrew in his. Those feelings would come, she told herself. Of course they would come. How could they not? She'd been infatuated with Andrew for ages. It was entirely different with the Prince. Dimitri was exciting and new, she'd not had time to think about him, to adjust to him, to get used to him. She didn't know what to expect, whereas her infatuation with Andrew was a well-travelled path.

There was likely no harm in finding Dimitri exciting and new. She might as well enjoy the novelty of such a fantasy while it lasted. He would leave and, besides, he was a prince and she was Evie. There was certainly no future there no matter how rousing his touch or how hot his eyes. But for a little while, Madame Fortune was finally smiling on her.

Fortune was finally favouring him. Andrew poured himself a brandy in the dark quiet of his study. He was treating himself to a glass of the good stuff tonight. He'd known from the start, uniting himself with Dimitri Petrovich would be a good idea and now he could turn that association into a cash crop of artefacts. The comb Evie had told him about was a good start, a sign of more to come.

He took up his seat in front of the cold hearth, content to sit in the dark and think. He'd been staggered by the amount of money a museum had paid the Prince for that mosaic in Herculaneum and again when the Prince had sold some of the artefacts from the excavation outside Athens.

The money was pocket change to a man of the Prince's wealth, but Andrew had a broader vision in mind. If a museum would pay those sums, how much more would *private* buyers pay for the privilege to possess a piece of authentic history? That was the real market, in Andrew's mind. The Prince was rankly opposed to that option. Private collections kept artefacts hidden from the public. In the Prince's mind, museums were the public's gateway to understanding and accessing their past. Andrew didn't care. Everything had a price, even the past, and he would sell to the highest bidder.

History could be very lucrative, as long as the Prince dug up something of merit. That was the risk. But it was a risk that cost him nothing but time. The site might not prove to be fertile. He had great faith in the Prince. The Prince understood what to look for and the Prince knew why certain items had value, why they appealed to people. Once the Prince dug up something of merit, the next step would be to get the right clientele out to the site. That's where Evie's drawings came in to play. He could use them as advertising to the right clientele, powerful, rich men. After that, he had another plan for those drawings that would further line his pockets. All he had to do was flirt a little with Evie, keep her dangling, keep her willing to please, which shouldn't be hard to do if the Prince was right about her affections—and he had to make sure the Prince didn't find out about his plans until it was too late. Once the Prince returned to Kuban, there would be nothing he could do about it. Andrew just had to wait him out until October. Andrew smiled in the dark. This was turning out well, better than expected.

Things were going better than expected, but that didn't mean they were easy. Dimitri stood and stretched, rolling his shoulders to get the kinks out of his neck. He'd spent most of the day on his hands and knees painstakingly brushing off what he hoped were tiles in General Lucius Artorious's dining room. It was looking promising. Now that they'd made it to the centre of the room, an elegant mosaic was starting to emerge in the shape of a rose embedded in the floor and the team had found pieces of pottery that had been taken over to Evie with hastily scribbled notes for cataloguing.

Ah. Evie. She'd been a godsend. He let his gaze linger on her at a distance, her head bent over her work, her hand moving tirelessly, her concentration unbreakable. Did she know he spent far too much of his days watching her? Far too much of his time wondering about her—about her life in West Sussex? Aside from his growing intrigue with her, bringing her on to draw had been a good business decision. Her work was excellent, her attention to detail as focused as her drawings had led him to believe. And there were actually items for her to draw. Progress was being made that bore out his research. Andrew had not been wrong when he'd suggested a Roman general's villa was here in the rolling hills of West Sussex and that information was paying off in spades.

His gaze found Evie at her table and he smiled. Evie's pile of drawings grew by the day, drawings that would serve as illustrations in the book he would put together on the excavation, as well as drawings he would archive for the museum in Kuban. She made not just one copy, but three of the same item, each one a brilliant replica, each one a product of her patience. She had an aptitude for the art and for the organisation of it. Stefon, impressed, had told him how Evie had overhauled their usual organisation system and made it more efficient.

She made his own days more efficient too in ways she probably didn't realise. Did she know how much he looked forward to their brief conferences that started and ended each day? He liked the routine of that—of looking forward to talking with her at the beginning of the day when everything was fresh and new. They would talk about the prospects for the day, what he hoped to find, hoped to do. To speak his hopes out loud gave his day structure. They would end the day much the same way: a brief discussion of whether or not those hopes had materialised. It was a good way to put the day to bed.

Bed wasn't exactly the best way to conceptualise that thought. It brought on the idea of other things, other people that needed putting to bed. One person in particular. Evie was not immune to him. He'd noticed the way her eyes would follow him when she thought he wouldn't see, the telltale leap of her pulse at the base of her neck when he was near. He'd been looking, of course, for the proof of attraction. He was a hot-blooded male after all.

But he also wasn't entirely self-centred. He noticed how alive she became, how each day she relaxed a little further in his presence, how her eyes sparkled, how her words rushed out as she argued her point, how she teased him about his hurried handwriting on the little notes he sent over every day attached to potential artefacts. When she was with him, it wasn't that she was a *different* person, but she became a *real* person. He wondered how long Evie Milham had projected only a shell of herself to the outside world and how it was that no one seemed to have noticed when he, a stranger, had noticed from the start.

The idea that her real self only shone in his presence carried its own intoxication. She was like a rare jewel, unveiled only on special occasion, shown and known only to very few. He liked being in that exclusive company even though he couldn't pursue certain avenues. *You can be her friend. You don't have to seduce her.* It was a convenient argument he'd been making with himself all week, an argument he'd been alternately winning and losing. Friends would be easy, convenient, but it wouldn't change the chemistry brewing between them. They were both aware of it. Evie, with her leaping pulse and fade-away gazes that couldn't quite meet his eyes, and he with his eyes drifting towards her work station more often than they should. It confirmed for him that it wasn't Dimitri the Prince that made her nervous, she'd got over that once she'd had work to do. It was Dimitri the man that prompted her blushes and slide-away looks, proof that he was occupying too much of her time too.

Dimitri handed his brush to an assistant, issuing instructions to finish the corner. It was getting late. It was time to call it a day and take stock of what they'd found. He strode towards Evie's table, eager for their conference, to see her exquisite drawings, to see *her*. In the distance, the dinner bell rang and workers put away their tools. Within minutes, the site was empty.

She glanced up as he approached, rising from her seat, already reaching for the day's pictures, anticipating his questions. 'There isn't much to show you today,' she said apologetically.

'Of course not.' He smiled easily. He hadn't expected much. Today had been focused on the dining-room floor, hardly something that could be carted over to Evie's station. 'Tomorrow, when the floor is uncovered, I will need you to come out to draw it.' He paused, noting how she kept herself busy, her eyes focused on the task of cleaning up her workspace. 'May I ask you something, Evie?'

That got direct eye contact. He'd used her name for precisely that reason. Dimitri enjoyed the rise of colour that came to her cheeks. Whenever he looked over here during the day, she was a paragon of efficiency, always busy, her head bent just so as she drew. Then, he'd approach and she would not meet his eyes. He wanted her to, though, not just because he wanted to see her desire clear, but for her sake too. He wanted her to own her feelings, to declare them without hesitation. Desire was nothing to be ashamed of. It took courage to own one's feelings and it took confidence to stand by those convictions. Evie had those things even if she didn't know it. Yet. 'I would like you to show me your cataloguing system. Stefon has been bragging about it.'

'What? Now?' She looked about, maybe taking in for the first time how empty the site had become, the long purple shadows on the site making it difficult to see much. They would need a place with light and she was probably hungry. He could satisfy on both accounts.

Be careful you don't do this for selfish reasons, his conscience warned. It would be too easy to convince himself he did this for purely objective reasons—this would be a working dinner, nothing more. That wasn't quite true. He did want to learn about her cataloguing system. But he also wasn't ready to let her go for the day. Perhaps he was merely lonely. In that case, anyone's company would do. He could ride into town and drink a pint at the tavern or drop in on Andrew. No, to be honest, it was Evie's company he wanted and he was willing to use the cataloguing system as an excuse to help himself to her company. She wouldn't come otherwise.

'We could go over the system in my tent. I'll send for dinner. This way we won't be interrupted. During the day there are a hundred things demanding my attention all at once. I'd never be able to digest a cataloguing system with all the distractions.' He had to stop talking. He was rationalising too much. She'd think he had other motives and maybe he did if he was honest with himself. He wanted to spend some time with her. He saw her hesitate. At least she hadn't refused him out of hand. In this case, hesitation was good. She was considering it.

He offered her a persuasive smile. 'You're not worried for your reputation, are you?' he teased. 'We're discussing how to catalogue artefacts with a veritable herd of assistants around, hardly the best circumstances for ravishing.'

She smiled, revealing a hidden dimple along with the inner daredevil; the woman who would risk dinner alone with a man in his exotic tent. 'Well, when you put it like that, how can a girl refuse?'

Chapter Seven

She should have refused. One step into the pavilion and she knew this had been a mistake. Now, here she was about to eat dinner with a prince, in his pavilion, alone, no matter how he tried to argue to the contrary. His team was across the site, eating at long wooden trestle tables. They would come back and retire to their own tents within shouting distance of an alarm, but no one would actually be inside the Prince's pavilion with them. Not that one person would be all that noticeable.

The pavilion was enormous, as luxurious, as decadent as any eastern sultan's. Her original idea that the Prince was camping on site was definitely erroneous. No one 'camped' like this. There were no deprivations here. The long dining table, with elegantly curved legs complete with matching chairs for twelve, running through the centre of the pavilion, dispelled any notion of deprivation. Just in case it didn't, the chandelier of Venetian glass hanging overhead did. Every inch of the pavilion was furnished expensively. One corner housed an active workspace with a polished walnut desk and a matching glass-fronted bookcase that rivalled any gentleman's study in England. Those things might draw the eye, but it was the heavy damask curtain, partially drawn back with thick gold rope partitioning off the pavilion and the curved Venetian divan set in front of it, draped in silk throws and rich-hued pillows, that held Evie's attention.

'The fabrics are magnificent...' Evie breathed, unaware she'd moved towards them until her fingers brushed the silken surfaces. *Lovely.* They felt like rose petals beneath her touch. She fingered the damask of the curtain, noting the quality of the weft. 'Italian?'

'Yes, I had the curtain done in Florence several years ago. The silks are from China.' Her mind was interested in the answer, but her gaze was already drifting beyond the damask, catching a peek of a sleigh bed heaped with silk and pillows.

She could hardly drag her eyes away from that tantalising glimpse of bed. Worse, he caught her staring. 'My private quarters,' he answered her wandering gaze and Evie flushed.

The Prince came up behind her. She could feel the heat of his body at her back, making her entirely aware of him. *His private quarters.* Yet another reminder of how foolish she'd been to accept his invitation. What had she been thinking? They were entirely alone except for his silk pillows and decadently dressed divan.

'Please, come.' His hand skimmed her back, ushering her forward through the curtain, and she nearly jumped from the contact. Surely he didn't mean for her to go *into* those private quarters? And do what? 'There's water for washing if you'd like to refresh before dinner.'

It took a moment for her to drag her mind back from a more prurient train of thought. Washing up. Of course. 'Water would be lovely,' she managed. The colder the better. The silk had really got to her. Dear Lord, her cheeks were going to start a fire if she blushed any more.

The water did help. She splashed some on her face, but its cooling effects were offset by the dominating presence of the bed, which was more magnificent up close and fully revealed. It begged the question: what sort of a man slept in such a bed? Her rather fertile imagination knew the answer: A tactile man, a sensual man who would want the slide of silk, the caress of fine cotton, against his bare skin. A man who would do more than sleep in that magnificent bed.

Evie reached for a cloth, the fine quality of the linen a matter of fact. Dimitri Petrovich was surrounded by the best of everything. She ran the damp cloth down her neck, heat flaring low and sudden in her belly with intimate insight. The Prince did not come to that bed clothed. Neither would he come to that bed alone.

She swallowed hard, her imagination running riot about what might happen in such a bed, with such a man. To be that woman! It made her previous fantasies of sipping lemonade and talking over the day with Andrew appear positively lukewarm, insipid even, when there was such passion to be had in the dark, to lay naked, entangled in silk and man—that was decadence at its finest. Such images begged the question: were they inspired by silk or by the man himself?

Evie laid aside the towel and smoothed her skirts, checking her face for smudges in the small mirror. Ink had a rather regular talent for showing up in the most inopportune places like cheeks and chins. She pulled the pins out of her hair and shook it down, running her hands through its tangles. It had become messy over the course of the day. She twisted long auburn lengths into a simple bun at the back of her neck and re-pinned it. There. She looked as neat as she could after a day of sketching in the August heat. Did it really matter how she looked? She needed to keep a practical head on her shoulders even if her imagination wanted to run away with her. This was only dinner for the express purpose of discussing her catalogue system, not a grand ball, and the Prince had already made it abundantly clear the dinner was strictly business. She hoped thinking of him as the Prince would help take the edge off the butterflies. Thinking of him as *Dimitri* only encouraged them and a host of other hot emotions.

Evie stepped into the main room, butterflies fluttering just a bit anyway in her stomach. May would say, 'Business or not, a girl didn't have dinner with a prince any night of the week', and Evie's stomach agreed. The main room was empty, no sign of the Prince. But the flap at the entrance was drawn back and there were sounds of someone outside.

Evie moved towards the noise, but she'd barely stepped out of doors before she wished her curiosity hadn't been so insistent—or not. Dimitri stood with his back to her—his *bare* back, that was. Washing. She was entirely unprepared for the sight of a half-naked prince, especially this one, although perhaps she shouldn't have been. Common sense should have been her first warning. She should have guessed he'd want to get clean as well. The sounds should have been her second. Water usually meant washing.

Evie knew what she ought to do. She ought to step back before he noticed her. But her feet, her eyes, the rest of her, had other ideas. They were determined to stay. Even performing this simple act, he was beautiful to watch. Water streamed down the lengths of dark hair; back muscles flexed, rivulets slipping over muscled planes as he raised his arms and ran a cloth over his body, wiping away the dirt of the day. Oh, those arms! How she wanted to be that cloth, how she wanted to run her hands over that body, feel the ripple of muscle beneath her fingers, trace the breadth of those shoulders.

Such thoughts were definitely proof she really should step back. To stumble upon him by accident was forgivable. Accidents happened. But to stand here and *knowingly* watch him bathe was a flagrant breach of his privacy. To see him half-naked and not retreat was an even more grievous sin—or so she had been taught. At the moment, though, Evie couldn't think why. This was not sinful, it was beautiful. Her eyes were glued to his back, memorising every inch of him; how those broad shoulders gave way to a back tanned from countless hours spent shovelling, hauling, lifting. Prince he might be, but he was no stranger to hard work. Labour had honed every muscle hewn plane of him.

Her eyes gave in to the final temptation, dropping lower, to where his back tapered to a lean waist before disappearing into trousers. He was gorgeously made even out of his clothes. His tailor might be a genius, but the man had quite the body to work with. Genius would be easy.

Such thoughts prodded her conscience. She really ought to go back inside now. At the very least, she ought to look away, but there were a lot of things she *ought* to have done today—she ought to have gone home, ought to have refused the invitation to dine alone even if it was just to discuss cataloguing techniques. What she ought to do had already lost several battles today and it was about to lose one more. Ought was no match for that back. She'd look just a few seconds longer.

He reached for the clean shirt and Evie knew a moment's panic. The gesture was too casual. She'd pushed her luck and retreat was no longer an option. She'd been caught. His next words confirmed it. 'Have you seen enough?'

'I didn't mean to intrude,' she began to apologise. He was going to make her take responsibility for her actions and she probably deserved it. She *had* been staring. But he was not entirely blameless. He'd *known* and he'd done nothing to stop her, to interrupt her. 'You knew I was there?' It came out as part-question, part-accusation.

Heat prickled low in her stomach as she realised what his knowledge meant. He'd encouraged her voyeurism, the act taking on a higher element of intimacy because it had been shared. He'd been her accomplice, abetting her curiosity the whole while. The best defence she could manage was modest chagrin. 'What sort of man lets a woman look at him like that?'

She knew. The man who slept in that decadent bed. The man who was striding towards her, hands smoothing back his hair into a sleek, damp tail as he came, a friendly smile on his lips even while his eyes burned like hot coals. She was not ready for his response as he stopped before her. 'I could ask you the same.' His voice was low, sensual, the sort of voice a man used when he wanted to seduce a woman. He was... aroused? By *her*? Had she read that right? His next words had her entirely at sea. 'What sort of woman looks, Evie?'

A woman who thinks you're a pagan god come to life, a woman who wants to touch you, who wants to be touched by you in return, a woman who would willingly go to that silk bed of yours and learn all that she doesn't know if only you would show her. She hadn't the skill to dissemble, to flirt, to call upon womanly subterfuge. She only had the truth at her disposal and that would not do at all, but she needed an answer. His eyes held hers and this time she could not look away. He was prepared to wait her out, to wait for that answer. What would happen if she uttered those words out loud? Would he grant her fantasy? Would he laugh? Would he remind her that she had reached so far above herself she tried for Olympus itself?

Dinner saved her. Dimitri shot the arriving dishes a disapproving glance before flashing her a wry smile. 'Apparently, supper is served. Shall we?'

To call dinner a 'reprieve' would have been errone-ous. Evie had only to step inside the pavilion to know it was more a case of out of the frying pan and into the fire. She'd traded the hot flirtation of words for the spicy sensuality of exotic foods eaten in an equally exotic setting. The Queen Anne dining table went unused as Dimitri ushered her towards a low round table set before the curved divan. 'I much prefer this to a formal table,' he explained, pulling out piles of silken cushions to sit upon. 'We get the custom from our Turkish ancestors.' He helped her to sit, the press of his hand sending a hot rush of awareness to her stomach. 'In Kuban, we were not always Russian.'

He sat down beside her, not opposite her. 'I hope you won't think I am completely barbaric.' He wasn't entirely joking.

'Hardly...' Evie breathed, her eyes riveted on the array of food set before them. 'This is...' she paused, casting about for the right word '...exciting.' A proper lady would regret the use of that word and its naughty implications, but as proper as Evie was, she couldn't regret this—the chance to partake of exotic dishes, to eat with this intriguing man. 'What is it all called?' A proper lady would eat in moderation too, but there was no way she was going to be able to manage that, not with all this possibility set in front of her.

Dimitri smiled. 'We'll start with *shchi.* It's cabbage soup. Everyone eats it, rich and poor alike.' She felt herself beginning to relax, falling into the ease she'd felt when they'd looked at the tapestry. This time, it was his turn to be the teacher as he led her through the dishes. There was *okoshkra,* a salad done with boiled beef and vegetables, which he told her had to be very specific. 'Not any vegetable will do.' He gave her another of his endearing winks. 'One must be a spicy herb, the other a neutral taste like turnips.'

'And the fish?' Evie rolled the flavor around on her tongue, familiar and unfamiliar. 'Carp?' she guessed.

'Similar.' He smiled his approval. 'Tench.' He reached for another dish. 'If you like fish, try this.'

'Oh! Cold smoked salmon!' Evie gasped. 'My favourite. We hardly ever have it.' A luxury indeed and these slices were cut so thinly as to be nearly transparent, a sure sign of its excellent quality.

Dimitri used a tiny spoon to scoop up a portion of small black balls and spread them on a piece of flatbread. 'Caviar? We like to think ours is the best in the world.' Evie thought she would have eaten snakes if he'd offered them to her from his own hand, his dark eyes soft chocolate with amber lights. He was having a good time, with *her*. The thought was extraordinary to comprehend. Simple Evie Milham, who hadn't had a beau in her life, was eating dinner, not with a prince necessarily, that wasn't the important part, but that she was eating with a man who enjoyed her company.

'It's good.' Evie swallowed. Liking it pleased him. She could see it in those eyes. He was proud of his country and he wanted her to like it too. She looked away, their gazes lingering too long over the caviar. 'You must miss your home. I imagine it's hard being away.'

Dimitri made one of his customary gestures towards the food and the room beyond. She was getting used to those movements. His body was so much more expressive than an Englishman's. 'Kuban is with me wherever I go. It keeps me from missing it too much.'

She cocked her head and studied him, seeing him, seeing his pavilion, in a new light. The silks, the low table, the divan, the dinner were so much more than furniture and food. They were an extension of who *he* was. The dining table was merely a concession to the world outside of Kuban. 'Your country must be lovely.'

He reached to the centre of the table and lit a candle, his long fingers flicking out the match flame. The candlelight was a subtle reminder of how late it had become, but Evie could not bring herself to go. *Just a few more minutes*, she promised herself.

'It is beautiful, in a wild fashion. One has to know where to look. Kuban is full of rivers and mountains, and grassland too. We grow wheat, and rye. We fish in our rivers. We mine gems in our mountains. It's a rich land, a diverse land.' He poured her another glass of wine. Was this her second or her third? She never had more than two glasses at home and never more than one in public.

The room was starting to take on soft, fuzzy edges as the evening deepened. Beside her, the Prince warmed to his subject, stretching out on his pillows as he told her about Kuban; the cold snows in the mountains, the coast of the Black Sea, how Kuban geographically and culturally straddled European Russia, and the infidel influences of the Ottoman Empire. Kuban might be just outside their pavilion, England a thousand miles away, so immersive were his tales, his voice hypnotically low, his eyes starting to burn again, flames of dark agate. This time, Evie could not, would not, look away for fear she'd miss something vital.

Perhaps those stories even explained the man himself—those high cheekbones, the dark eyes, the beautiful smoothness of his olive skin a genetic memory of shared ancestry with Turkish sultans. Evie sipped her wine, letting the stories sweep her away, her mind painting imaginary pictures, mentally sketching patterns. What a fabulous tapestry these stories would make.

'But for all that, it's sparsely populated. In the winter, it's easy to believe there are more wolves than men. It's too bad the wolves can't be recruited to help us. Our lack of population has made it difficult militarily to hold it against the Turks.' His voice was a velvet caress in the growing darkness. 'We are searching for alternative solutions besides wars we are ill equipped to win despite our material wealth.'

'I want to see it.' Her words came slow and sincere in the dark. In that moment, she wanted more than anything to see this wild land, wolves and all. 'Do you have a picture of it? I want to see it some time.' An idea started to take hazy shape. She yawned, her words beginning to slur with drowsiness, with wine. 'I have to go.'

Dimitri straightened up. 'You can't go yet, we haven't had our vodka. No Kubanian meal is complete without it.' He reached for a bottle of clear liquid. It looked like water as he poured it into two small glasses.

He raised his glass, letting the candlelight catch the liquid and turn it to dancing prisms. 'To a lovely meal, Evie, and even lovelier company.' He swallowed his all at once and Evie followed suit. She'd been prepared for it to burn. May and Bea had got drunk once on brandy. They'd said it tasted like fire. But this was smooth. Until it hit her stomach.

'Oh!' Evie gasped. An explosion of heat unfurled in her abdomen. 'That has quite the, um…'

'Kick?' he supplied, and they both laughed. 'I should have warned you.' She didn't mind. She liked this feeling, not all of it due to the vodka. She felt warm, relaxed. Nothing mattered except what was happening right here. She hated to leave. All of this would evaporate as soon as she stepped outside. This was her

Cinderella moment, but even Cinderella had to leave the ball. Too bad. But girls like her didn't stay out all night with handsome men. Good girls, quiet girls, didn't invite scandal. Evie stifled a yawn. Of course, it wasn't a scandal unless one got caught. Still, she wished she could stay.

Evie put aside notions of staying. She had to leave now while she had the strength and will power to do it. She made to stand, but her feet caught in her skirts. She stumbled, taking a staggering step towards the low round table and bumping her knee.

Dimitri reached out a hand to steady her and came to his feet. 'Whoa, Evie. I don't think you're fit to go anywhere.' He had both arms about her now, a safe haven. She let him take her weight. She hadn't realised how tired, how boneless she felt, how *right* he felt, or was that how right *she* felt with his arms about her? How would she manage to get home now? Somewhere in the back of her mind came the thought she might get what she wished for.

Chapter Eight

'I have to go to bed,' Evie yawned, but it was a weak protest. Even she knew she'd given up the fight. There would be no going home. She'd have been happy to sleep right here, standing up in Dimitri's arms. She could smell the lingering remnants of his soap with its unique notes of cloves and vanilla, she could feel the masculine heat of his body against hers. She felt warm and safe, a very delightful combination of feelings, a very *dangerous* combination of feelings. It had her wondering what he would do if she reached up and put her arms around his neck, if she drew him to her, closing the little distance between them. They were so close already, surely it would be the easiest thing in the world to brush her lips against his. So easy, in fact, she was doing it before she could think twice.

It felt natural, right. Her lips skimmed over his, a light feathering touch that lasted a fraction of a second, but it was long enough to send a shot of pure bliss straight through her. Bliss was warm, alluring, drawing her in. She wanted more; more feather brushes of lips on lips, more warm bliss.

She'd not bargained on that, on being the hand-maiden of her own addiction. She had only wanted to feel what it might be like to touch him. She had never dreamed she'd want to keep touching him, tasting him. Her lips found his again. She heard him sigh, heard him breathe her name, 'Evie.' A caution and an invitation all in one simple word.

'Dimitri,' she murmured. 'Kissing you is like drinking vodka. Warm and soft at first, but with a hidden kick.'

He gave a low growl of a laugh, his eyes dark. 'I think you're the one with the hidden kick.' His mouth hovered just over hers. Her pulse raced, recognising he was in no hurry to move away and she didn't want him to. She'd barely formed what she wanted in her mind before he did it; his hand cupping her jaw, sliding to the back of her neck, slipping beneath the heavy weight of her hair to cradle her head in his palm; all the better to kiss her, all the better to angle his mouth over hers, to take not just her lips but her mouth in his possession, no feathering passes for him. Nor for her either. They would no longer be enough. He might as well have set her on fire. How could she be content with a mere brushing of lips when all this awaited?

He coaxed her with his tongue, encouraging her to respond in kind, showing her that kissing was a full, tactile experience. Not just mouths met when they kissed, but tongues and bodies. She understood now why people kissed with their eyes shut; it heightened the other senses. She could smell him, taste him, feel him, his hands on her, his body against her. He was warm and hard, all muscle and strength. Perhaps she should drink vodka all the time if it gave her boldness with such a reward.

The kiss changed, becoming more insistent. The finesse was falling away, replaced by something more ragged and hungry. Dimitri had changed it, not she, but she strained towards it none the less. Whatever the kiss demanded, she would give. Whatever Dimitri wanted, she wanted too.

'We have to stop.' Dimitri's voice was hoarse, his mouth, his body, breaking the kiss.

Apparently, she'd been wrong. She didn't want whatever Dimitri wanted. Her arms were still about his neck. She pressed against him, wanting to pull him down to her, wanting to start it all over again. 'I don't want to stop,' she murmured.

He resisted, unwrapping her arms from his neck. 'Don't, Evie. It is hard enough to be the voice of reason at the moment. We need to stop. It's late. We're tired, we've drank enough wine and vodka to forget our good sense. In the morning we'll thank ourselves for showing some restraint.' He smiled to ease the disappointment, she supposed. 'Let's put you to bed.'

He led her into the curtained alcove of his private chambers and turned back the silken covers of his bed, her heart leaping irrationally for a few beats. Surely he couldn't mean... She could barely put the thought into coherent words. Perhaps she had drunk more than she ought.

'You take the bed. I'll take the divan. I've travelled enough to know it's comfortable.' Her heartbeat fell back to normal. No, he didn't mean *that*. 'I'll send a note to your home and let everyone know you're safe.' He tucked the coverlet around her like a good friend, hardly at all like the lover who had plundered her mouth, whose body had strained against hers just moments ago. Fabulous. It hardly seemed fair. Vodka had turned her randy, but apparently it left him with a modicum of reason. But she hadn't the stamina to worry over it.

Evie closed her eyes. This was nice, being fussed over, and he was right: she was tired. Perhaps she would rest just a short while. She'd think about that kiss later. A thought came to her and her eyes flew open with a sudden burst of alertness. 'We forgot!'

'What did we forget, Evie?' He sat on the side of the bed, his tone humouring, but she was serious.

'We forgot to talk about cataloguing.' She closed her eyes, her voice already a murmur, her wakefulness already vanishing in the trail of his soft laughter, a most seductive sound to go to sleep by.

'Another night, Evie.' She felt his weight leave the bed, felt his body bend over hers. 'Sleep well.' She had the sensation he might kiss her again. And he did. This time on the forehead because even if she had gone and lost her head, he had kept his.

What had he been thinking? She'd given him the faintest of kisses and he'd gone and lost his head.

Dimitri stuffed a pillow behind his head, trying to get comfortable on the divan. He'd lied when he'd told Evie drink had driven them to carelessness. It might have driven her to a little boldness, but not him. He'd not drunk so much that he hadn't a clue what he was doing. He'd been very aware the whole time. By the saints, he'd been aware! His whole body had been damn well aware and she couldn't have failed to notice. Just as he hadn't failed to notice this had likely been her first kiss. But that hadn't stopped her from exploring, experimenting, throwing herself into it wholeheartedly.

There was something intoxicating about knowing he'd been her first kiss. His women, the women he had *affaires* with, were well past first kisses. He had no illusions there. He was the middle for them. As fine a lover as he might be, he wouldn't be their last. There would be men after him just as there'd been men before him.

Dimitri tucked his hands behind his head and stared at the pavilion ceiling. The idea of applying that logic to Evie sat poorly with him. The problem with first kisses was that they raised a protective urge. First kisses implied next kisses, last kisses. He didn't like thinking of not being the next kiss, the last kiss. He didn't like thinking of who might *be* next. Andrew. Would she kiss Andrew the way she'd kissed him? Would she respond to Andrew the way she'd responded to him, with all her heart and body?

You're being ridiculous. She can't be a nun for you just because you kissed her first. No, Evie wasn't meant to be a nun. She was meant for passion and for love. She was meant for a family, a husband and children of her own to lavish her kindness, her smiles, her wit on. He could picture her in a house not that different from her parents' home, with its wild gardens and hotch-potch architecture, out on the lawn playing with children, laughing, while something delicious baked in the kitchen.

It was too easy to imagine her on the lawns of his summer palace, laughing and playing with children.

She would like his summer palace. It wasn't too big by Kubanian standards. It was surrounded by woods and there was a lake for rowing. She would like his library. But that would be all she'd like about Kuban. She wouldn't like court, where he spent most of his time. She wouldn't play those games, wouldn't know how to and it would destroy her. Even if he was free to do so, he'd never take Evie to Kuban. She would be very much the classic bird in a gilded cage.

Like him.

It was not a fate he would wish on anyone. It was his destiny because he'd chosen it and it was for a good cause: His sister, so much younger than he, so beautiful, so in need of his protection. For her, he would go home and meet the deadline of his thirtieth birthday. For her, he would marry the border sultan's daughter under the guise of doing his patriotic duty. His marriage would keep the peace. His marriage would ensure Anna-Maria would not have to leave her home.

He conjured up a mental image of his sister, Anna-Maria, thrust into his twelve-year-old arms moments after her birth by a desperate nurse who hadn't the presence of mind to tell him to leave the room while his mother died. He'd loved his baby sister on sight.

Love was a double-edged sword if ever there was one, making a man powerful in one moment and weak in the next. Even at twelve, he'd felt powerful holding Anna-Maria, buoyed by a surge of protectiveness that had taken up residence in him that day and had never left. But he'd seen his father's weakness that day too; a man who he'd always looked upon as invincible. His mother's death had changed his father, nearly broken him. Those had been his first lessons about love. He'd been very careful since then.

To date, he'd never been in love. One could have extraordinary affairs without it, thankfully. Love would not be a commodity in his marriage to the sultan's daughter. If he was cautious, he might escape this mortal coil without further experience in the pain of love.

He turned to his side, pushing thoughts away. He didn't *want* to think about Kuban and the future—quite the piece of sexual dissuasion, that. His erection was nearly gone now and it had taken his mind off Evie—beautiful, innocent, untried Evie, who kissed with great enthusiasm if not experience; Evie, who was sleeping just a few feet away; Evie, who of a certainty would expect love in exchange for any more kisses.

Chapter Nine

She'd kissed Dimitri! It was her first thought upon waking. The second being, *he* had kissed her in return. She lay quiet, letting herself remember how the evening had ended—his lips on hers, their mouths tangled, their bodies flush up against each other. She'd been hungry for him—it was an entirely new, unfamiliar and delicious sensation. She'd never been with anyone who conjured up such a depth of feeling. She shivered beneath the blankets, her body remembering his touch even now hours later. She remembered every touch, every word. Oh, sweet heavens, had she really said *that*? Had she told him kissing him was like drinking vodka? She must have. She remembered it far too clearly. Ugh. At the time it had seemed profound, witty even. This morning it just sounded half-cracked.

Evie groaned and reality began to settle. She felt awful. Now that the initial pleasure of waking to a pleasant memory had faded, practicalities set in. There was a dull throbbing behind her eyes and the brightness of the room kept them shut. Her tongue felt thick and the rest of her felt less than fresh. How would she ever face Dimitri like *this*?

There would be no escaping it. She groaned again, this time for a different reason. She pried her eyes open to confirm it hadn't been a dream. She had indeed spent the night in Dimitri's pavilion. How was she to walk out of the tent and explain that to anyone who saw her? She had only the clothes she slept in and none of her toiletries. There was no way her appearance would persuade anyone she hadn't been here all night. She needed to be more careful with what she wished for.

Evie sighed. She'd best get on with it. The longer she put it off, the worse it would be. With luck, it was still early enough to go to her work station without encountering too many questioning glances. Evie sat up carefully, cautious of her aching head. A small piece of paper lay on the coverlet. It was an effort to reach out for it, but the note made her smile. Bold, flowing black script that matched the tags she spent her days reading, informed her all she needed was laid out on his trunk. It was signed with a big 'D' at the bottom. Dimitri. The single initial seemed intimate, an echo of the evening. Below it was a postscript: 'breakfast will be waiting'.

She glanced over at the trunk. A dress of hers lay out with a small valise packed next to it. She could guess what was inside. He must have asked for those things when he'd sent the note so her parents didn't worry. Not that they would. They'd been scheduled to play cards at the Ramseys' last night and would have been out late themselves. They might not have even missed her.

The thought took some of the delight out of the surprise of finding her things here. She'd spent the night alone in the company of a man, an act that was the very definition of scandal, and her parents hadn't noticed. She knew they loved her. They were good parents who indulged her pursuits, but she knew they'd given up on her. Oh, they'd let her live with them, they would support her, their single, spinster daughter, as long as they lived. But they'd despaired of her ever being more than that. They'd settled. After all, two out of three wasn't bad. Two girls had married, one decently and one very well. Surely that was respectable enough, especially when the third daughter wasn't nearly as pretty, wasn't nearly as witty with her conversation and who had 'quiet' skills. She didn't play the pianoforte at musicales like Diana, or sing like Gwen. Those were portable, public skills that could be demonstrated in polite company wherever one went. Not stitchery, not tapestry patterns, not making clothes. The former were not portable. One did not tote tapestries around to show off to eligible gentlemen. The latter was too much like being involved with trade, too much like work. A gentlewoman didn't *make* her own clothes.

Evie swung her legs out of bed and made her way carefully to the valise. She drew out a fresh chemise and stripped out of her clothes to wash. Dimitri's thoughtfulness had not ended with the clothes. Her own hairbrushes and ribbons had already been laid out on the bureau for her. The thought brought a blush to her face. To do that, he'd crept in here while she was sleeping. The act seemed private, intimate, somehow attached to their kisses of the night before, that their relationship had changed in some way.

She tried not to think about the kiss as she washed. She really had to reorganise her thoughts. She could not go on all day fantasising about that kiss. It might have upended her world, but it had not upended his. She'd have to get used to *not* thinking about that kiss. It could *not* be the centre of their relationship. She would only disappoint herself. The kiss had been a moment out of time, the product of a late night as Dimitri had put it and perhaps some vodka—a hypothesis that seemed more believable in morning light. It had been an enjoyable, rash moment, nothing more. And yet, it meant so much more to her. She'd never been kissed, she'd never been taken so much by surprise by her feelings, her body.

She'd been utterly unprepared for what had transpired. And yet she shouldn't have been. He'd warned her, hadn't he, in all their previous encounters? In his touch, in his eyes. She'd responded to those—why had she not extended that same expectation to something far more intimate? Now she knew. Now she would know for ever. Evie glanced over at the rumpled bed. Now she knew she'd been right about the kind of man who slept in that bed. Funny, the knowledge didn't satisfy her. It only served to make her more curious.

She forced herself to redirect her thoughts. She thought instead of all she would have to tell May and Bea: about the note, about the evening, about the washing incident, about the tapestry viewing and tea afterwards. There was so much to share and they'd only been gone a week. And it was all about Dimitri. The thought stayed with her as she tidied the bed, trying to be a good guest. It was Dimitri who had dominated this week, starting with his visit to her home and his invitation to come help at the site. Other than an uneventful and somewhat disappointing curricle drive home, this week most definitely had not been about Andrew. That was another complication to think about later.

She ran a brush through her hair and selected a rosy-pink ribbon that matched the tiny flowers of her dress. She might not be able to hide the fact that she was walking out of the Prince's tent, but at least she'd look decent doing it. She would wear her hair down today, though, out of a need to hurry. The faint scent of sausage wafted into the room, reminding her that breakfast was waiting. Dimitri Petrovich was waiting.

Chapter Ten

Not just waiting for her, Evie discovered as she stepped out into the sunny morning. He was *cooking* for her. Dimitri glanced up and gave her a look that bordered on a smoulder. Was he even aware he did that? Sensuality was so effortless for him. 'Good morning. I'd call you a sleepy head, but it's still early.'

Now that she was outside, Evie could feel the earliness. The sun was up, but a cool bite still lingered in the air, a reminder that while the afternoons were hot, autumn was coming. August was nearly done. She held out her hands to the flames, the warmth of his little cook fire a welcome contrast.

'What would you like? Sausage? Bread? There's smoked salmon left from last night.' He poked the sausages where they lay on a grill over the fire and laughed. 'We Russians are frugal, simple people at our core. Breakfast is hearty if not fancy. Most of the time, if it's not black bread for breakfast, it's left-overs from dinner the night before.'

'It all looks delicious.' Evie took a seat in one of the camp chairs, acutely aware that the food wasn't the only thing looking delicious. He had been up well in advance of her. He was shaved and dressed in clean work trousers and shirt. But his hair was still loose, falling forward as he turned the sausage. His long hair was fascinating to her. Men in England wore theirs far shorter, but his fell past his shoulders, sleek and dark and free. It gave him a primal look, the appearance of a fierce warrior from long-ago days when men were perhaps less refined creatures.

As if he read her thoughts, he straightened up and pushed his hands through his hair, catching it back in a smooth tail. Instantly, the fierce warrior was gone, replaced by the gentleman. 'Don't fuss on my account.' She had the impression smoothing back his hair was akin to putting on a jacket in a lady's presence, a means of hiding the masculinity within lest it be too disconcerting for the female mind. But he'd never quite be successful in hiding his maleness entirely. Thank goodness. She liked his hair loose. That was something she could not say to him without a firm understanding of their relationship. What were they to each other? Were they becoming friends? Would they remain only co-workers? Simply two people who shared a love of history and that love had brought them together for a short time?

'I didn't put my hair up for you,' she joked. Dark eyes lingered thoughtfully on her face, taking in all that hair she'd left down, and she swallowed hard. Maybe she should have put it up. Suddenly, loose hair had taken on an unexpected sensuality.

'But your hair is beautiful, a woman's crowning glory. It is a shame, I think, to confine such glory to

pins and braids, to hide it under hats.' He filled a plate
and passed it to her.

'My hair is too red,' she countered.

He shook his head in correction and gave her a
smile that filled her to her toes. 'Corundum. That's
the colour of your hair. It's a mineral mined in cen-
tral Russia.' He stood up. 'Wait here, I'll show you.'
He disappeared inside the tent and returned with a
small leather pouch. He knelt beside her chair, spill-
ing the contents into his hand. 'That's the one I want.'
He held up a rock chunk. The surface revealed a polished variegation of reds and browns that combined
to form a soft russet that was at once both hues. 'This
is corundum.'

He put it beside her ear and leaned back to take in
the match from a distance. 'Perfect. I knew it would
be.' Evie laughed. He looked so pleased with himself.
Dimitri laughed with her. He slipped all the rocks
back into the little bag except for the chunk of corundum. That piece he pressed into her hand and folded
her fingers around it. 'Keep it. So you'll remember
the colour of your hair.' The moment took on a keen
edge, silence overcoming their laughter. She would
remember far more than the colour of her hair. She
would remember him. She would remember a man
with dark eyes who could turn her hot with a glance,
who could make her question the assumptions of her
world in a touch. A man who could make her burn.
Perhaps he knew that.

She would remember too that he was a Russian
prince, a man far above her in all ways, station, looks,
and experience, as to be a god. Gods belonged on
their pedestals, not come to earth for the likes of her.

* * *

'Well, what do we have here? I swear I heard laughter, although it's far too early to find anything remotely funny. I say, Evie, you're out and about early.'

Evie's gaze darted past Dimitri's shoulder as Andrew strode into the campsite, his eyes drifting between them with sharp assessment. He looked immaculate but tired, as if it was indeed too early for him to be out of bed. She kept her fist tight around the rock chunk as if it had become a secret she had to protect. Guilt swamped her. She had the unmistakable feeling of having been caught out at something illicit, something that had to be hidden.

Dimitri scrambled to his feet, perhaps sharing her sudden awareness of how this scene might appear to an outsider; he squatting at her side, his hand closed over hers, her hair down. Truly, she ought to have put it up.

'Whatever is going on, I hope there's coffee,' Andrew groused, making himself comfortable in the other chair, but his gaze continued to study them. 'I'm not interrupting anything, am I?'

'No coffee. Black tea, strong,' Dimitri offered, overly cheerful, overly casual as he reached for a spare cup. 'Black tea is a true Russian drink for breakfast.' He ignored Andrew's pointed question.

Andrew took the cup and made a look of disgust. 'I like your Turkish side better. Coffee. Now, that's a breakfast drink.'

Dimitri pulled up a nearby crate and sat, unfazed by Andrew's gruffness. 'There's sausage, help yourself. I know you like that.' Evie had the impression this discussion had taken place before, on the road, in the midst of their fabulous adventures wandering Europe together. She envied Andrew that opportunity. How many dinners had he and Dimitri shared filled with stories of exotic Kuban with its wild steppes and wolves?

'It's early, Evie. What are you doing here so soon?' Andrew took a bite of sausage, his gaze narrowing again with hints of speculation as it passed from Dimitri to her.

This was the type of scrutiny she'd most wanted to avoid. 'We needed to discuss the cataloguing system,' she improvised, surprised at how fast the half-truth came to her. She glanced at Dimitri to encourage confirmation.

His eyes met Andrew's. 'We had meant to do it last night—' he made one of his wide gestures '—but time got away from us.' He left the interpretation up to Andrew. Challenge flared briefly in his eyes. Evie knew immediately where this was headed: battle of the seed cakes part two. It was a direction she didn't entirely understand. These were unlikely candidates to compete over her. She was plain Evie Milham and they were handsome men who could have any woman in any room anywhere.

Evie rose and set aside her plate. 'Thank you for the breakfast. I must get to work if we are sketching the dining room out of doors today.'

The two men stood. 'I'll drive you home tonight, Evie,' Andrew said quickly, making no effort to disguise the triumphant look he shot at Dimitri. Evie smiled her thanks, still clutching her piece of rock. Whatever the two of them needed to settle, they could do it without her. She had enough to settle on her own, starting with why Dimitri had said such a thing and left it wide open to interpretation. It was almost as if he'd wanted to invite Andrew's speculation.

'What the hell did you mean by that?' Andrew's voice was a growl once Evie was out of earshot. 'We would have talked about it last night but we ran out of time?'

Dimitri met Andrew's heat with cool detachment. He gathered up the breakfast dishes. 'I meant exactly that.'

'But *why*?' Andrew pressed. '*Why* did you run out of time?'

'Why does it matter?' Dimitri dumped the dishes in a bin to be washed later and wiped his hands on a towel. 'I thought you didn't care about Evie Milham. I believe she wasn't rich enough for your notice? Your words, not mine.' He *was* rather surprised Andrew cared that much. Andrew might speak callously, but the man's word was good. He meant what he said, even if it was sometimes cutting.

'I care if she's being taken advantage of.' Andrew stepped forward. 'I am her neighbour, her long-time acquaintance, if not friend. I will not stand by and let her be seduced.'

Dimitri chuckled. 'You have a very active imagination if you can get that much out of a single comment.' He had no intention of telling Andrew why they ran out of time; that he'd been too busy spinning tales of Kuban so he could watch her face become dreamy in the candlelight, so he could watch her mind come to life behind those blue eyes.

He added as censure, 'I don't think the nature of

your speculations do you or her any credit, by the way.' Never mind that Andrew's conjectures might be warranted in this case. He had kept Evie out too late, had put her to bed in his bed with all its silk and pillows, and that was after he had kissed her. Never mind she'd slept alone and fully clothed in his bed. Never mind that the kiss had kept him up half the night and had left him with no clearer answers this morning about the intensity of his response to Evie's untutored kiss.

Andrew put a hand on his forearm, his grip strong, his voice serious and low. 'Don't mess around with Evie. A man like you could never make her happy. You should know that better than anyone. She thinks you're a prince. How do you think she'd feel if she knew you were nothing more than a high-class sod sold to the highest bidder—your words, not mine.'

'Are you threatening me?' Dimitri threw off Andrew's hand. He'd been among the royal court long enough to recognise veiled blackmail when he heard it. He never should have told Andrew that juicy little secret. Back then, the revelation had been too new, too fresh, and their friendship had been new and fresh too when they couldn't see the flaws of the other, only the commonalities.

'Only if the truth is threatening,' Andrew responded, his face hard. He took a step back and his expression softened. It was like watching a master thespian at work. More often these days, he wondered how much of Andrew was an act and, if it was, what lurked beneath the surface of that carefully crafted veneer? What did Andrew need to hide? The man had the perfect life in his grasp, a life Dimitri would trade his own for.

Andrew held out his hands in apologetic surrender. 'I am sorry, old chap. I didn't mean to pick a quarrel. I just don't want to see Evie hurt.' He shook his head, but his sincerity did not ring true, not when he'd been thoroughly denouncing any interest in Evie just a few days ago. 'England is not Kuban, it's not even the Continent, where a woman of a certain age might sit alone with a man. Our rules are stricter, especially when it comes to young, virginal women. I don't want to see her or you forced to the altar for a marriage neither wants.'

Andrew pushed a hand through his blond hair, his brow knitted in a fairly good facsimile of consternation. 'Good Lord, just think of what would happen? You would lose everything, your title, your home, your wealth, and that's not even including what would happen to your country, your family, your beloved sister.' Andrew shook his head to indicate the consequences were beyond his comprehension. He stepped forward once more, placing a congenial hand on his arm this time. 'Can you just imagine what a disaster that would be for you?'

Dimitri *could* imagine it and while it would be a disaster, that wasn't the first word that came to mind. 'Disaster' wasn't precisely what he'd been thinking when Evie had walked out that morning, all fresh and sharp in that white muslin with the pink flowers, her hair down. He'd been speared by an errant thought: what if it could be like this every morning? Waking up with a lovely woman—no, not any lovely woman, *that* lovely woman. Waking up with Evie, sharing a simple breakfast before heading out to excavate, to discuss the site with her and what they had found or might find? And then Evie had smiled at him and he hadn't thought at all. She'd stolen his breath with her wide smile, her natural beauty as lovely in the morning as it had been in the candlelight.

She'd looked at him with genuine delight this morning and he'd been reminded of how she'd watched him wash. Had that been the look on her face then too? She'd had plenty of time to retreat, but she hadn't. Evie might be quiet, but she was curious too and bold as she'd demonstrated last night. He had no doubt now there was passion within her, waiting to be unleashed. He'd tasted a bit of that last night. Envy stabbed, sudden and unlooked for. He didn't want Andrew to be the one to pick up where he'd left off in making that discovery. He wanted to be the one to take her on that journey.

It had been the devil's own temptation to kiss her on the mouth, to see where a kiss and midnight vodka could lead. She'd been intoxicating in the candlelight, her soft words igniting him, prompting him to take advantage. One kiss had led to where he'd known it would and then to more exquisite liberties he'd fought hard not to take. He could give her nothing beyond those moments. Perhaps it had been that knowledge which had given him the will power last night to end it. Andrew was right about one thing: he knew better than to lead her on. And himself. Evie wasn't the only one he'd be fooling.

Chapter Eleven

She was leading them on. Evie looked at her letter to Bea and May with disgust. It read like a romance. She knew better. Would they? Evie re-read the letter again. She'd given herself a three-day cooling period before she'd put her ideas to paper to avoid any misleading embellishment and yet it still seemed to be there behind her words.

She sighed and set the letter aside. Even the bare facts painted a certain picture replete with dinner on silken pillows, a night spent in a silk-clad bed and a hand-cooked breakfast over an open fire. She hadn't even got to the part about the corundum. She glanced at the chunk sitting on her vanity. Her mind could still feel the warm intimacy of his hand when it had closed around hers. The memory was too personal. Maybe she'd leave that part out as she had the kisses.

Evie leaned out the open window of her room, letting the cool late evening air bathe her face. As vibrant as those images in her letter were, she knew with certainty the conclusion those images drew was preposterous. Dimitri was *not* courting her and he definitely wasn't seducing her. Was he? Surely not. He'd been the one to pull away from the kisses and he hadn't started them. But he'd also been the one to press the corundum into her hand and look at her so sincerely her heart had nearly stopped.

Regardless of his intentions, she could no longer deny that for whatever reason there was a slide towards intimacy between them, a closeness that had sprung up perhaps because of the work at the site, a closeness that might have sprung up anyway even if they hadn't shared an evening. Common interest bound people together. Look what it had done for her and Andrew. For the first time ever, she had his attention.

She should include that in her letter as well. It was a startling omission given that Andrew had driven her home every evening that week since he'd come upon her and Dimitri at breakfast. What did it mean that she'd forgotten to include such a detail? What did it mean that she'd found herself kissing Dimitri of her own volition, initiating it even, when she'd had her heart set on Andrew for years? It was a rather significant development in the grand scheme of her hopes. Just a few weeks ago, she'd been angling for just such an occurrence. She had his attention, but what was she doing with it?

Evie rested her head on her hands and stared up at the stars. She *could* imagine Bea and May reading about that development and nodding sagely to one another, concluding that their plan must have worked. Andrew had merely needed a chance to see Evie in her element and the presence of another male to move him to action. Evie smiled to herself as she pictured her two friends tucked away together in a cosy parlour stitching baby items and talking over her news.

From her friends' point of view, it would be all that simple. But Evie knew it wasn't. She did not intend, nor had she ever intended, to use Dimitri as a foil for Andrew. Neither had she intended to be attracted to Dimitri Petrovich, but she was. The attraction of him was too potent to be denied. She'd be lying to herself if she said she felt nothing for him. She'd be lying too if she limited that attraction to just his extraordinary looks. This attraction was rather multifaceted when she dissected it. She liked talking to him, liked his enthusiasm for his work, for history. She liked his enthusiasm for *her*. He praised her work, thanked her for her effort, enquired about her comfort. In short, he noticed her in ways people had not noticed her for a long time. As a consequence, it was hard to ignore him, hard to thrust him back up on the pedestal he belonged on. He kept climbing down and putting himself in her way.

But the attraction was uncomfortable for them. In the three days since he'd given her the corundum, they'd been careful with each other, limiting their interactions to their morning and evening discussions about the site. Those had been brief and she sensed Dimitri was deliberately keeping himself in check, holding himself back from her. She had only two answers for such a behaviour. Either he was embarrassed that he had kissed her and feared inviting another incident, or he'd liked kissing her and was too much of a gentleman to engage in such an activity again. She didn't need to be a genius to know there was nothing he could offer her. No matter how he tried to forget it, he was a prince—that alone made him unattainable. He'd leave and go back to his kingdom. Evie laughed a little at that, playing with words. Prince Impossible—that was Dimitri Petrovich.

Maybe that was another layer of her attraction. He was safe. She could expect nothing from him and she'd known it from the start. He would leave, he would require nothing from her; not her heart, not her soul, not even her affections. He couldn't hurt her. She could only hurt herself where Dimitri was concerned and that was something she could control.

Evie yawned. The long days at the excavation site made sleep easy in the evenings. She would add the part about Andrew tomorrow before she sent the letter. Tonight, there was one more task she wanted to do before she went to bed.

Evie pulled out the drawing tablet where she sketched her patterns and her box of embroidery silks. She wasn't quite done with the pattern yet and she still had to map it on thin tracing paper, but it was coming along. She wanted to make Dimitri a piece of needlework depicting Kuban in exchange for the corundum. It would be something he could hang in his pavilion wherever he went and, selfishly, maybe it would be like sending a piece of herself along on his journeys. He would look at it and remember Evie Milham of Little Westbury, who had come to life for a short while.

She'd based the drawing on his descriptions and tonight she wanted to check her colours. Evie laid out a vibrant cerulean blue, a rich dark brown, a deep forest-green and an emerald-green and then rummaged for a red. She discarded them one by one. This one was too orange. That one was too pink. The third one might be right. She studied it, unable to make a determination. Evie turned towards the mirror on her dressing table, holding the little skein next to her hair and then next to the chunk of rock. Ah, victory! The match was perfect. She'd found corundum. She smiled, feeling silly and pretty all at once, remembering the brush of Dimitri's hand at her ear as he'd held up the rock, the close of his hand around hers. But the remembrance only served to bring her thoughts full circle.

If he's not seducing you or courting you, what is he doing? came the naughty little thought. Evie piled the threads back into her box, trying to ignore the question, but it wouldn't go away and she couldn't answer it. She didn't know what Dimitri was doing. Perhaps nothing. Perhaps she was reading too much into it because she was so intent on winning Andrew's attentions. Not everyone thought about romance. Not everything between a man and a woman had to have romantic overtones.

Maybe the better question to ask was, what was she doing? Was she developing another impossible infatuation? First, Andrew, and now that he wasn't so unattainable, she'd turned her attentions to a prince. A prince of all people! If anyone was unattainable, it was he. After all, he would be leaving at some point in the near future. She couldn't hold him even if she somehow managed to catch him.

He wouldn't be here for ever. When the excavation was done, he'd move on and she'd still be here. Both thoughts made her sad. She had to remember Andrew would be staying behind too. He'd made it no secret in London this past spring that he was home to stay and home to marry. It was time he picked up the reins of his grandfather's estate. A few months ago, the news had alternately thrilled and panicked her to no end. Tonight, it was starting to feel like a consolation prize: she and Andrew left behind together while Dimitri Petrovich pitched his pavilion in a new, exotic location.

Evie climbed into bed and blew out the light with a determined breath. She needed to focus on the successes of the week. Andrew was driving her home and tomorrow he'd even offered to pick her up in the morning. They had twenty minutes each way to converse. In those twenty minutes, she had all of his attention. During those drives, he told her his plans for his grandfather's estate: plans for crops, plans for the gardens, for redoing the inside of the house, which hadn't been decorated for sixty years since his grandmother had come there as a bride. He'd smiled at her when he'd said that, his blue eyes twinkling with intimate implications. His bride would have the pleasure of doing the house to her tastes.

Was she supposed to have read something more personal into that message? Had he meant to imply she might consider herself in the role of being that bride? Why didn't that bring a certain thrill to her stomach? Why hadn't that made it into her letter? Surely, such a disclosure meant she was attaining not only his attentions, but his affections too. Why wasn't the realisation of that goal more exciting to her when it was what she'd wanted so much? It was one more thing she'd have to ask Bea and May before she closed her letter.

A gust of wind blew open the window and she got out of bed to latch it, leaning out once more to smell the air. They'd have some wet weather by tomorrow afternoon for certain. The scent of burgeoning rain was on the air and perhaps more. There was a summer storm coming.

Thunder rumbled, closer now than it had been half an hour ago. Dimitri pushed his hand through his hair and cast a frustrated glance overhead to the sky. They wouldn't get much work done this afternoon with the storm moving in. Ominous grey clouds had loomed all day in portent. Rain, *heavy* rain, was imminent but he was prepared. He'd sent the English work crews home after lunch. There were only his men left now and they were busily covering up key parts of the site with tarps, something that was becoming a struggle as the wind came up. Dimitri was eager to see the tarps secured. There was nothing more damaging to excavations than mud, the usual result of dust, dirt and water. There'd been a flash flood in Herculaneum that had nearly destroyed weeks of work.

A fat drop of water fell on his nose followed by another as the skies officially announced their opening. Dimitri strode across to help settle a tarp over the carefully dug-out mosaic floor of the dining room. They were close now to verifying the authenticity of the villa as Lucius Artorius's. He secured his end of the tarp with a firm rock and then added another. Not a moment too soon. Lightning flashed in the sky, followed by an immediate boom of thunder. There were shouts as the loud noise took his men by surprise, a horse whinnied in fright over the sound of men, its fear loud enough to rival nature's brontide, loud enough to draw Dimitri's attention.

He shaded his eyes from the rain drops and

searched the site for the horse—it was probably one of the horses used to pull the wagons. He couldn't see it at once, but he could hear it. Hooves pounded, generating thunder of their own. Dimitri turned in a circle, trying to sight the sound. He found it; the heavy draft horse had got loose from the rope corral and was plunging through the site, scared and heedless.

Dimitri scanned ahead, gauging the horse's trajectory, and caught the movement of a muslin skirt, a glint of corundum hair—Evie! His heart was in his throat. Good Lord, what was she still doing here? Why hadn't she gone home with the rest of the English? New fear gripped him. The horse was headed for the cataloguing department, for *her*. It wasn't concern for the precious, fragile artefacts that gripped him, but concern for Evie. *She* was in the horse's path and oblivious.

'Evie!' he shouted futilely and began to run. He hoped to cut off the horse, hoped he could turn the crazed animal from his path towards the open space beyond the canvas. He shouted her name as he ran, waving his arms, but it was no use. All of her attention was fixed on securing the papers and boxes beneath the billowing canvas. If the horse reached the workspace, he'd tear right through it, not caring if Evie stood in his way. One strike from those hooves would finish a grown man. Even if she escaped the horse, there would be collateral danger in the form of falling boxes and overturned tables left in the horse's wake. Dimitri ran faster, vaulting half-walls and altering his path, no longer concerned about swerving the horse. He had to get Evie out of there.

He closed in on the workspace, coming from the

left as the horse came on the right. 'Evie! Evie! Run!' Surely she could hear the horse by now, even over the wind.

She looked up, saw him and then as if in slow motion, turned to look behind her, back at him and then down at something on the table. Her face was pale, her body paralysed with indecision. 'Evie, run!' he called again, but she reached for a stack of drawings instead, determined to save the work.

It was a race between him and the horse, Evie the prize. Running wasn't enough. He wouldn't make it in time by foot. He needed to fly. At the last moment, he launched himself the remaining distance, taking Evie to the ground, pushing her out of the way of the horse, covering her with his body as they landed in the newborn mud, filthy and safe. An upturned table just feet from them emphasised how close their call with true disaster had been as the horse ran past.

'Evie, are you all right?' Dimitri pushed to his feet and offered her a hand, drawing her up out of the muck. They were both covered in it. He raised a hand to wipe a clump of mud from her cheek, only to make it worse. His hand was muddy too, courtesy of his rather ignoble leap. He was talking in a rush, all of his words running in relief to have her safe, unharmed and only dirty. 'We'll get you cleaned up. Let's get you to the pavilion, there's hot tea and water and towels.'

His own hands were starting to shake as he refused to let go of her arm. She was pale, so pale. She looked as if she might faint if he let her go. Despite his protests to get to the pavilion, he just stood there and wrapped her in his arms. If he could just hold her, perhaps he could steady the both of them. The pavilion seemed miles away at the moment.

'I'm fine. I'm fine,' she repeated, her words muffled against his shoulder. He could feel her hands dig into his back through his shirt. Unhurt, but not unshaken. He heard the tremor in her voice. 'But the work…' she murmured against him. 'The day's drawings are ruined. I'll have to do them again.'

'Don't think about it. It's ink and paper.' Most women he knew wouldn't have spared a thought for the work when they stood in the rain covered in mud. 'Everything can be retrieved,' he assured her, trying to move her away towards shelter. He wanted her safe and dry, away from the wind and falling objects and racing horses, away from startling lightning and thunder. 'The artefacts have survived centuries in the dirt, they'll survive a little more weather.' Most of them were sealed in crates already anyway. The only ones not truly secure were the ones being sorted today. They were packed carefully enough in straw to perhaps even survive a wild horse. But the two of them needed to get inside. The rain was pounding and they were soaked through. Dimitri put a strong arm about her, urging her to follow his lead, which she did reluctantly.

Evie was still protesting when they stepped inside the dry sanctuary of his pavilion. 'We can't just leave everything!'

'Yes, we can. It's a storm out there and it's not exactly safe for humans.' He heard the irritability in his own tone. 'Perhaps you are oblivious to the thunder and the lightning, but I am not. I have no desire to be fried.' One never knew with lightning, where it would strike next or even when. Out in the open, flat plain, they were exposed, prime targets even if the odds were in their favour.

He draped a robe around Evie's shoulders. 'Here, get dry and put this on. I'll make some tea.' He gave her a gentle push towards his private chamber.

'What about you?' She sounded mollified now, penitent even.

'I'll survive a little longer. It's not the first time I've been caught in a sudden storm.' He'd been caught in worse, like the time the Kuban river had flooded and he'd had to ford it with a caravan. But today had been a special kind of fear when he'd looked over and seen Evie nearly trapped by the whirling dervish of a canvas.

He started the little cook stove, trying to keep his mind off what was happening just feet away behind the curtain: Evie slipping out of her wet dress, wet chemise, her nakedness covered by nothing except his robe. Her hair would be wet, a loose russet flame. She would look decadent.

'All right, your turn. I can take over the tea from here.' The words drew his eyes up from the fire. Evie stood before him, dressed in his robe, a paisley silk trimmed in a wide band of black satin. Even knowing she'd look decadent, even having a pre-existing picture in his mind, was not enough to protect him against the jolt of white heat that went through him, as sizzling as any bolt of lightning. This was what he'd been trying to avoid all week since he'd kissed her. He'd held himself apart, determined to act honourably, determined he wouldn't suffer another lapse in judgement. It didn't seem to matter. Temptation was as determined to find him as he was to avoid it.

The robe was belted tightly at the waist, which only served to emphasise the full swell of her breasts above and the curve of her waist below. Did Evie have any idea how provocative she looked? No, of course not. If anything, she was self-conscious of the overlong sleeves she had to push up, the length of the robe she had to be careful not to trip over. But she was provocative none the less. The vee of the robe begged for a man's hand to part it, to slip inside the silk barrier and possess the bounty within. Perhaps even to do more, to part the robe and reveal all of her.

His groin tightened, giving him another reason to get out of his wet trousers before Evie got a look. The storm wouldn't last more than a few hours. That was the nature of summer storms. They blew in fast and strong, determined to make trouble. This one was proving to be no different.

Chapter Twelve

The trouble with robes was that they made one think about what was underneath them, which was most likely nothing. Evie wrapped her hands around the thick ceramic mug, letting the heat of the tea warm her. Thinking about the tea, about being warm and dry, was definitely preferable to thinking about the man seated across from her on silken pillows in nothing more than a robe—a robe that showed off an expanse of bare chest now that he'd had a chance to change too.

No, not 'preferable', Evie amended. It wasn't 'more preferable' to think about being warm and dry, it was merely more decent. Who wouldn't want to think about a nearly naked handsome man? She could hear May's words in her head: how many times did a man like that come to the remote corners of West Sussex? May would tell her not to waste the opportunity. More to the point, hadn't that been her own exact advice to Claire? Hadn't she advised Claire that if Jonathon didn't kiss her, she should kiss him?

Evie felt her cheeks heat and she hastily dropped

her eyes. When had staring become kissing? Is that what she wanted? More kisses? Did she want more than kissing? And he might too. Wasn't that the issue they'd been dancing around all week with their careful manners and avoidance?

Evie shifted on the pillows, tucking the long robe beneath her. Maybe she didn't want to know what Dimitri's intentions were, given that there were probably no intentions at all. Perhaps it would be best to remember the potential than to test it and find it was an illusion.

The silence was starting to stretch towards awkwardness. She needed to hold a conversation with *him* instead of her thoughts. She could talk to them all night, and she probably would, alone in her bed. 'Tell me about your life in Kuban. What's it like to be a prince?'

It seemed like a fairly innocuous question, not all that different from what she would ask at a dinner party. What gentleman didn't want to talk about himself? But Dimitri was reluctant to answer. She thought there was a glimpse of sadness in his eyes, a shadow of resignation on his face. 'There are two Kubans actually,' he began. 'There is the Kuban I told you of, the land itself with its mountains and rivers. That land is beautiful and wild. Then there is the kingdom of Kuban, high in the mountains. That is my Kuban.'

'Where you will be King some day?' Evie sipped at her tea.

He surprised her with a shake of his head. 'Oh, no, I will never be King. Our peerage doesn't work that way. In Kuban, I'm more like your royal dukes here. I'm related to the royal house, but I'm not in direct line.' He gave a wry smile. 'Thank goodness. I content myself with that piece of knowledge every day. I remind myself to be thankful for small graces that have spared me the throne.' He arched a dark eyebrow. 'Does that disappoint you?'

Evie understood the question at once. He was really asking if *he* disappointed her. Was she somehow offended by his lack of royal ambition? Evie cocked her head and studied him, sensing the challenge in the question. He was testing her. But to what? To agree or to disagree? These sorts of games were beyond her. She could do nothing but speak her thoughts. 'It pleases me more than it surprises me. Most men I know are hungry for ambition. They'd want to be King even if they didn't have the talent for it.'

'Most women I know want to be Queen.' The words were said cynically and Evie saw the hard truth behind them. This man who was intelligent and well travelled, who was handsome and engaging, was seldom taken on those merits.

'No wonder you like life on the road.' How sad, not only for him but for others that no one looked past his title to see the man within who devoted his life to the preservation of history. They were missing the man for the Prince. In truth, she couldn't imagine this vibrant nomad of a man chained to a throne. She was glad he wouldn't be. 'Kingship is hard work, leading a country, deciding its fate.' Evie made a face. 'It's thankless work too, I suspect. Few kings in history have been appreciated in their time or even after. Historians aren't always kind. I think we forget that kings are merely men and sometimes we expect them to be more.' She paused. 'I would not want to be King.'

'Life at court can be…stifling,' Dimitri confided. His eyes were on her, softer now, the sadness lifting. 'Your viewpoint is very, ah, refreshing. What about you, Evie? Is life in West Sussex all you'd hoped?'

She laughed. 'It can be. But it can also be…stifling.'

Dimitri looked quizzical as if he didn't quite believe the truth of it. Evie rushed to explain. 'It's beautiful here, of course, in a bucolic sort of way and the sea is just a few miles off where it's more rugged when you get bored of farmland and rolling hills. But, nothing changes. Everything remains the same. Neighbours have been neighbours for generations. Their children grow up together as their grandfathers did and even their great-grandfathers before them. Everyone knows everyone. There aren't many surprises.' She gave Dimitri a glance over the rim of her mug. 'Until you came along.'

He chuckled. 'Now I better understand my appeal with the female half of the Little Westbury population. I thought it might have been my good looks,' he joked. 'I see now that it is merely the presence of a stranger, any stranger.' He inclined his head. 'Thank you for so humbly enlightening me.'

She laughed, too caught up in the teasing fun of being with him to rethink the words. 'Stop it, you know your looks have quite a lot to do with it. I doubt women would turn out for just any archaeological talk.'

His voice dropped, low and sensual, the atmosphere between them crackling with something electric and unexplored. 'Is that why you came? To listen or to look? Did you come to see the handsome Prince of Kuban?' There was a hint of derision in his tone, derision for himself, and she did not understand it. Neither did she understand it when he looked at her like that—all dark smoke and smoulder in his gaze. She *did* understand its general intent, of course, even a woman destined for spinsterhood recognised desire when she saw it, she simply didn't believe it. How was it conceivable that it be aimed at her? Suddenly it was too much. What did he want from her? What did she want for herself? This limbo of uncertainty was pure purgatory.

'Please don't do that.' She couldn't bear it if he was toying with her. She was enjoying his company far too much, especially after having been denied it for a few days. She knew intuitively he was being himself in these moments, not the polite façade she'd seen all week.

'Do what?' He leaned close, his knuckles skimming her jaw in a light caress for which there was no other explanation but the most improbable.

'Act as though you're seducing me.' She clapped her hand over her mouth. She could hardly believe she'd let that thought escape. Surely he would laugh at her now. But he didn't laugh.

His hand sifted the wet strands of her hair. 'Maybe it's not an act. Why do you find it so hard to believe? Why do you doubt your appeal, Evie? You're quite beautiful when you allow it.'

'I don't doubt myself,' she countered, instinctively defensive.

'No?' he argued with a smile. 'Maybe "doubt" isn't the right word. Perhaps the word I want is "hide". You like to hide. I saw it the first night, in your hairstyle, your gown.'

'My gown?' Evie interrupted.

'Yes, the hem of your gown was where the gorgeous embroidery was, not up around the bodice where everyone would see. You, Evie Milham, specialise in being discreet.'

'I specialise in *knowing* myself. I don't like being the centre of attention.' Just like now. She wasn't sure what to make of the undivided attention of his dark gaze and it made her uncomfortable. She wasn't sure what came next, what *would* come next. His hand was still in her hair.

'And in all that self-knowing, Evie, do you think you're not capable of rousing a man?' His brow knit, as if he found the very question perplexing, an unbelievable hypothesis. 'You rouse *me*, Evie. Very much.' He drew his knuckles gently down her cheek, their heads close together. She could feel heat coming off him. 'Tell me, Evie, should I act on that attraction? Would you like it if I did? No, never mind, it's a useless question.' The pad of his thumb ran across her lips, raising a shiver of delight on her skin. Never had she been touched like this. 'I already know you would. You are made for passion, did you know *that* about yourself?' His hand dropped to the column of her neck, his fingers over the hard beat of her pulse. 'Let me show you. Let me show you what you were made for, let me show you what you do to me.'

She licked her lips. Their faces, their mouths, inches apart. Evie had never been any good at lying even when her pride was at stake. There was only one possible answer she could give him. 'Yes.'

He moved into her then, his hand cradling her jaw, his mouth taking full possession of hers, and it was as delicious as she remembered. Perhaps sin was always delicious and Dimitri did not disappoint. She gave herself over to him, her mouth open, her body willing and warm against him, honest in its hunger, proving their first kiss had not been entirely driven by the external factors of a late night and drink and a surge of boldness on her part. This was his kiss, this time *he'd* started it. She could no longer doubt the attraction. Her tongue answered his, exploring and tasting on its own with a frankness she did not question.

Nor did she question it when he pressed her back against the silk cushions, his body covering her, her hands busy at his shoulders, her arms wrapping around his neck, her robe escaping the confines of its sash in her efforts to be close to him. She was aware of his warm hands parting the loose vee of her robe, of her body exposed. She heard his breath snag with desire as his palms ran over the contours of her body. She knew that her response spurred him on, that he revelled in the gasps that escaped her, that the arch of her body answered his caress. She had power too in these moments. This was not his seduction alone.

'Evie, you *are* beautiful.' He began to move down her, his mouth and hands making a slow trail, each kiss burning hotter than the last. He kissed her breasts, his tongue flicking over the peaks of her nipples until a moan escaped her and her body arched up, begging for more, more of him, more of his magical mouth. Had anything ever felt so exquisite? But it was just the beginning. A thrill of excitement ran through her, her body recognising he had no intentions of stopping.

He moved to her navel, feathering it with a kiss before journeying lower, his hands framing her hips, fingers wide-set where they spanned her belly. His mouth graced the nest between her legs with a kiss, an appeal. He was asking for entrance into her most sacred core. Evie shifted beneath him, instinctively parting her thighs, instinctively granting access. She was well past the point of denying him anything.

He kissed the inside of her thigh, his thumb running the length of her, parting her with a wicked caress. His touch made her tremble, but it was nothing except mere preparation for the real onslaught that came next; the descent of his mouth, the flick of his tongue, not just once to tantalise, but twice, thrice, and more until she was oblivious to anything but the sensations of pleasure washing over her. She was aware her hands had locked themselves in his hair, to steady herself, to keep him there, heaven forbid he leave her now when her body throbbed, when it looked for release, torn between wanting this to end and wanting this to last for ever.

How much pleasure could one body take? She was going to splinter, positively break apart at this rate and in the next moment she did, her body rearing up, thrusting against his mouth as she came apart with a pleasure so raw, so wild, she couldn't help but cry out, couldn't help but let it take all of her.

It was a while before she could move again, think again, aware that Dimitri lay sated between her thighs, unmoving as well, the silence punctuated by the returning rhythm of his breathing. When reason did come, it was with one thought: This experience was both complete and incomplete. She was not meant to be alone in this. An idea came to her, surely she could reciprocate in kind. She moved a hand down her body and rested it on his head. After a while, she spoke. 'I think pleasure is best when shared. Come lay down beside me.'

The words brought him up from between her legs, his hair falling around his shoulders like an ancient warrior, his eyes dark and glittering as they searched her face. She let her expression reflect her intentions, gratified when a slow, wicked smile took his mouth. He understood that she meant it.

He stretched out his long body beside her, his words an invitation to access what lay beneath the loose robe he wore. 'Touch me, Evie.'

Oh, sweet heavens, yes. It was exactly what she wanted to do. She wanted to touch him. She slid her hand beneath his robe, pushing it aside, revealing the muscled expanse of chest she'd caught glimpses of in his workman's shirt. He was a feast for her eyes, for her hands, the planes of muscles an atlas leading her ever downward to the hot male core of him until her hand wrapped about the thick centre of him, feeling his heat, his hardness. She ran her hand up to his apex and down to his base, taking in the contradictions of him.

He covered her hand with his where she grasped him. 'Stroke me.' Together, they moved up and down, once, twice, and then she was on her own. She experimented, finding her own rhythm in the journey of her hand up and down his length again and again.

His head was thrown back, his neck arched to expose the taut cords of his neck as he moaned with pleasure, his eyes closed as he lost himself. She was losing herself in this too. There was potency in knowing one could render such a man powerless, but more than that there was a kind of joy in knowing she could bring him this release, this pleasure. She felt his body gather itself, heard the gathering in his moans.

'Evie.' The single hoarse word was meant as a warning, a caution to let go her hold on him, but Evie held on, her eyes meeting his as they shared this intimacy together—but as wonderful as the moment was, it raised more questions than it answered. Not just for her, but for him too. She saw it in his gaze too when he looked at her, the relief of his release still fresh on his face. This afternoon they had opened a beautiful, horrible Pandora's box that could not be shut. Until now she had not realised there were two sides to pleasure.

Chapter Thirteen

He had her reeling. He could see it in her eyes, could feel it in the reluctance of her hand to let him go; not because she was a virgin, but because he'd got inside her defences, subconscious as he expected they were, and now she didn't know what to do. *He* was pursuing *her*, not the other way around where the pursuit had always been her choice—a choice she used to chase the unattainable—like Andrew Adair who wouldn't truly notice her in a proverbial million years. Such a pursuit carried no risk, the outcome assured before the pursuit even started. Did she understand that about herself yet? That she set herself up for failure? No wonder she was reeling now. She had found success with him.

To be honest, she was not the only one reeling. He reached for his trousers, fumbling for the handkerchief he carried, and handed it to her. It was the first of the little steps they would take to restore their afternoon to normalcy. She would wipe off her hands, get up, get dressed and he would do the same. Outward order sustained.

But she would carry her inner turmoil with her as would he. He was quite undone by this unexpected turn of events. The only edge he had on her was that he understood his defences, understood the reasons he was so undone. His defences were not that different than hers. The women he allowed himself access to required nothing of him beyond the physical. They kept his heart safe. They did not require his feelings to be engaged. It was the very reason he sought them out. They didn't disrupt his carefully laid plans, nor did they threaten the armour he'd built around his heart.

Evie would not settle for such a man and he didn't want her to. She needed a man who could give her both his body and his soul. He could no more be that man than Andrew could. He could give her no more than a few moments and hope those moments would transform her, help her to see herself as a person of value, who didn't need to be discreet, who didn't need to hide.

This afternoon hadn't been for him, it had been for her. At least that's what he told himself. It was the only way he could justify it. If there was one thing he wanted to give Evie, it was to erase the self-doubt, to prove to her that she was desire personified, a flame of passion come to life. That was something he had to *show* her, something he could do for *her*. For a few moments, he could allow himself to set aside his own burdens and limitations for the greater good of Evie Milham without threatening the world he'd created for himself.

He watched Evie rise, getting one last glimpse of the russet triangle between her legs, the pink tips of her breasts. She gathered the folds of her robe about

"FAST FIVE" READER SURVEY

Your participation entitles you to:
✳ 4 Thank-You Gifts Worth Over $20!

Complete the survey in minutes.

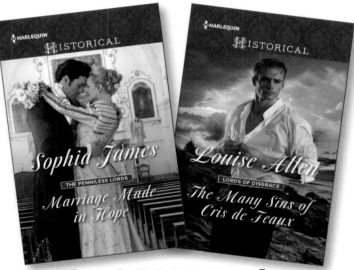

Get 2 FREE Books

See inside for details.

Dear Reader,

Since you are a lover of our books, your opinions are important to us... and so is your time.

That's why we made sure your **"FAST FIVE" READER SURVEY** can be completed in just a few minutes. Your answers to the five questions will help us remain at the forefront of women's fiction.

And, as a thank-you for participating, we'd like to send you **4 FREE THANK-YOU GIFTS!**

Enjoy your gifts with our appreciation,

Pam Powers

To get your
4 FREE THANK-YOU GIFTS:

✱ Quickly complete the "Fast Five" Reader Survey
and return the insert.

"FAST FIVE" READER SURVEY

1. Do you sometimes read a book a second or third time? ○ Yes ○ No

2. Do you often choose reading over other forms of entertainment such as television? ○ Yes ○ No

3. When you were a child, did someone regularly read aloud to you? ○ Yes ○ No

4. Do you sometimes take a book with you when you travel outside the home? ○ Yes ○ No

5. In addition to books, do you regularly read newspapers and magazines? ○ Yes ○ No

YES! I have completed the above Reader Survey. Please send me my 4 FREE GIFTS (gifts worth over $20 retail). I understand that I am under no obligation to buy anything, as explained on the back of this card.

246/349 HDL GLDA

FIRST NAME

LAST NAME

ADDRESS

APT.#

CITY

STATE/PROV.

ZIP/POSTAL CODE

▲ If offer card is missing write to: Reader Service, P.O. Box 1867, Buffalo, NY 14240-1867 or visit www.ReaderService.com ▲

BUSINESS REPLY MAIL
FIRST-CLASS MAIL   PERMIT NO. 717   BUFFALO, NY

POSTAGE WILL BE PAID BY ADDRESSEE

READER SERVICE
PO BOX 1867
BUFFALO NY 14240-9952

NO POSTAGE
NECESSARY
IF MAILED
IN THE
UNITED STATES

her, suddenly conscious of how revealed she'd been. 'You don't have to cover up, not for me, Evie,' he admonished. 'You're beautiful.' After all they'd done this afternoon, those words were the ones that made her blush.

'You still don't believe me?' He rose too, deliberately letting his own robe gape, exposing his nude body in all of its natural glory. He didn't dare touch her for fear of starting something that would take them past the middle ground of passion where they'd played this afternoon. Today's play had been safe, physically. It had ruined no one.

Evie managed a half-smile. 'Is that what this was? An exercise in boosting a poor girl's confidence?'

That was when he knew he'd lied to himself. He could not admit to it because it simply wasn't true. He'd done this for him because he wanted her, beautiful, intelligent, hidden, Evie Milham. 'Is that what you think?'

Evie gave a sad shrug. 'It's the only explanation that makes any sense.' She gestured towards him, her hand motioning the length of his body. 'Whatever would you be doing with me? Just look at you. You're handsome and well-travelled, and perfect in every way possible.'

'And you're not?' Dimitri countered. He was suddenly not interested in getting dressed, not interested in restoring normalcy. Normalcy was his enemy. If they put on their clothes, they'd be burying more than the afternoon, more than their nakedness. He reached for her hands. 'Don't you think I ask myself those same questions? You have this fabulous life with a family you're close to in a beautiful part of the world and a chance to do the things you love, your sewing, your drawing, your weaving. With all that at your disposal, what are you doing with me?'

He watched the irony of that statement reflect in her eyes as she puzzled out the answer. 'You have everything, and I have nothing to offer you, Evie. All I can do is take from you and leave you.' He dropped his voice, recognising the hard truth of that. For all that he wanted to give her, he could give her very little beyond memories when it came down to it. He could tell her this much at least. 'I'll be leaving, going home.'

'I know,' was all Evie said, her blue eyes solemn as they held his, her fingers tightening in his as if she could keep him a little longer.

She didn't know the reasons for it, though. He wouldn't tell her today. Telling her the rest made him feel like a cad and he wasn't ready to have her hate him yet. He'd save the last for when he truly needed it to drive a final wedge between them so that she'd let him go if she hadn't done so already.

'It's not my choice to make.' He shook his head. He wanted her to understand leaving was inevitable. He could do that much at least without incriminating himself. 'Kubanian law requires that all royal males return at the age of thirty to serve the kingdom in whatever capacity the kingdom feels they are best suited to serve.' In his case, it was with his body. He would marry Ayfer Hanimsultan, breed beautiful sons and keep the border peace. He was a cad of the lowest order to think he could set that aside for an afternoon and seduce Evie. He should apologise, but he wasn't sorry, not for a moment of it, and that was very hard indeed to reconcile.

'What happens if you don't go back?' Evie asked softly.

'The unthinkable.' His own voice was low, as if uttering the words was a sacrilege. He hardly dared to let himself imagine such a scenario, let alone put it into words. But with Evie's blue eyes holding him, Evie's hands touching him, the remembrance of pleasure still lingering in the air between them, he *wanted* to tell her. 'I would be renounced. I would lose my title, my wealth, my lands.' None of which mattered nearly as much as the other items at stake. 'I have a sister...'

Oh, God. It was horrible and exquisite all at once. They were sinking in single accord to the silk pillows, to their knees, their hands gripped in the other's grasp and she could not look away for fear he'd stop talking. She had become his lifeline and in these moments, his soul was open as his tale poured out: the Kubanian requirement to return home, to serve the country, the consequences for failing to comply— his young sister forced to wed a border sultan's son, taken from her home to never return, to live in a foreign culture with a foreign faith to secure the country if he didn't come home.

His sister needn't worry. Dimitri would not fail her. Evie swallowed, understanding what that meant. Saving his sister meant she would lose him definitively. She'd never had any hope of keeping him, hadn't even aspired to letting her thoughts follow that path. So why did the thought of him going leave an ache in her stomach?

'So you see what a roué I've been. I've been the worst of men when it comes to you, Evie. I cannot stay, I cannot promise you anything and yet I put you in a compromising position today. A gentleman would never have behaved as I did, never have encouraged what I did.'

Evie shook her head. 'Do you want to apologise for what we did? Do you regret the pleasure?' The bold words came surprisingly easy, but she'd become a bold woman this afternoon, sitting with a man in nothing but a borrowed robe, engaging in giving and receiving intimacy beyond her imagining. A man had put his head between her legs, his tongue up against her most private places, she'd put her hand about his member and stroked it. 'Or do you only regret the circumstances in which they occurred?' Did she really want to know the answer? She would die if he regretted what they had done, what they had found.

'I do not regret you, Evie. I will never apologise for what we did. But it has created a circumstance in which I don't know what comes next. We're both wondering what happens now and I don't know, Evie.'

But she did. She knew what came next. He *had* to go home. They couldn't change that. She didn't *want* to change that. There was too much depending on his return. She would never want to be responsible for any single consequence he'd enumerated today. His commitment to family, to country, was beyond admirable. They both knew what came next, it just didn't, *couldn't*, include her. And that wouldn't change until she did. She could not have him for the long term, but what about for the present? Was that what she wanted? It would need some thinking about.

Outside, a horse harness jangled and Evie leapt up in a panic. 'It's Andrew come to pick me up!' Was it that late already? Here she was in a man's robe, her hair undone. A hand flew to her cheek. Did she look like she'd been pleasured?

Dimitri was on his feet, all calm reassurance in the wake of her urgency. 'You have a dress here from the night we had dinner.' He gestured to his private chambers. 'Go, get changed. I'll stall him and I'll explain we were caught in the deluge.' She flashed him a grateful smile. They were suddenly co-conspirators in this little deception. It occurred to her as she checked her appearance in Dimitri's mirror that perhaps she ought to feel guilty about what had happened, that she should feel as though she'd cheated on Andrew. But she couldn't summon an ounce of remorse, and why should she? Andrew had done nothing over the past three years but drive her home a handful of days. Anything that had been done, had been done on her part and most of that had been only in her head.

She paused and studied her reflection. Who was this woman in the mirror who shared intimacies with a foreign prince, this woman who listened to his confession, this woman who had thrown over a long-standing infatuation for one man after twenty-one days with another? She didn't know that woman. Or perhaps that woman had been there all along and only just now dared to show her face. Had she really changed? Or had she simply fixed her attentions on Dimitri because the situation with Andrew had become possible instead of impossible? May had once accused her of such behaviour, of pursuing Andrew because there was no hope of catching him. Impossibility kept her safe, it made neither rejection nor acceptance likely.

Evie pushed the notion aside and attacked her hair

with the brush. She didn't want to believe she was capable of using Dimitri as a replacement for Andrew. Such a tactic made her no different than many of the other catty girls of the *ton*, Cecilia Northam, in particular. Cecilia was a chief antagonist of the Left Behind Girls Club, although Claire had temporarily routed her. No, she wasn't using Dimitri as a buffer against reality. She liked him too much for that. Which begged the question, what was she doing with him? What did she hope for, especially knowing what she knew now?

Beyond the curtain she heard Andrew's voice, slightly higher, and louder than Dimitri's. She had to hurry before Andrew had too much time to think through what she was doing here. Perhaps she should try harder with Andrew, make sure she wasn't displacing her affections. After all, it would be she and Andrew who would be left here when Dimitri went. She smoothed her dress and stepped from behind the curtain.

'Andrew, I wasn't sure you'd come.' She smiled as if she was glad to see him, casting a quick glance in Dimitri's direction to make sure he'd had the foresight to at least tie his robe.

'Of course, I came when I discovered you hadn't returned home. Besides, I wanted to tell Dimitri my news. Lord Belvoir and some of his cronies are coming over the day after next to see the site—well, primarily to see the artefacts, they're the real draw. Belvoir's bringing his daughter, the two of you know each other, I believe.' Andrew grinned, pleased with himself, oblivious to how poorly the news sat with her.

Evie's stomach went cold. Lord Belvoir. Cecilia

Northam's father. The one thing she liked about the countryside was that Cecilia wasn't in it. In Little Westbury, she was safe from Cecilia's cutting remarks and false sugar. Now, Andrew had managed to bring her most-feared adversary here at a time when she didn't have Bea and May or Claire beside her. She glanced at Dimitri and understood immediately why Cecilia would lower herself to come to the country. Cecilia, reigning Diamond of the First Water for three Seasons running, wouldn't miss a chance to align herself with a prince.

'Well, Evie, let's get you away.' Andrew coughed in the silence, his gaze drifting between her and Dimitri. 'It's hardly seemly for you to be in the company of a barely dressed man.' There was a scold in that for Dimitri, she noted. Andrew did not approve. That was fine with her. He could disapprove all he liked as long as he didn't suspect anything.

And that was that. By the time she was settled beside Andrew on his curricle seat, the afternoon had returned to normal. What had happened between her and Dimitri in the pavilion seemed like something out of time, the disaster of the charging horse seemed far away. Even the weather conspired to reinforce the fantasy of it all. The dark skies had cleared to blue, the rain had stopped, leaving behind a few puddles and a rainbow. The wind was gone and it was a summer day once more. Dimitri and his crew were already at work repairing the rampaged catalogue tent and here she was seated beside Andrew, travelling home as she did every day. Normal hurt.

'Is everything all right, Evie? You're quiet today.'

Andrew tooled the horses through a muddy curve in the road.

She was always quiet. There was nothing new in that except that he chose today to notice, the one day when she'd rather he'd not. 'I'm fine.' Lie. She wasn't fine, she was changed. Something had happened today and she suspected Andrew thought so too. *He'd* been quiet, which was probably what he was noticing more than her silence. Usually, their rides were filled with his talk of the day and all the things he'd accomplished.

'I hope the storm didn't inconvenience you,' Andrew began. 'I came as soon as I could. I was still in town when the weather changed. There was nothing I could do.'

'It was no trouble. I was well taken care of.'

'Oh, I am sure you were. He's a dab hand with the ladies.' She did not care for Andrew's tone. He cleared his throat. 'About that, Evie. You and Dimitri are getting on fabulously. I love that two of my friends have found a friendship of their own. But I would caution you. You don't know him all that well.'

Evie looked at her hands, decidedly uncomfortable. 'What is there to know? He is your friend after all.' Perhaps Andrew needed a reminder that friends didn't throw friends under carriage wheels. True friends were loyal. 'I am sure I can trust your judgement.' She was certain Andrew would never bring a scoundrel into their midst and turn him loose on the unsuspecting, staid population of Little Westbury. That was what he was implying wasn't it? That Dimitri Petrovich, who cooked her breakfast and saw to her every need, was indeed a scoundrel? But that Dimitri

Petrovich had also lain naked with her and declared himself a rogue. Maybe Andrew wasn't wrong? There was no rule that stated rogues couldn't be likeable.

'He is a fine friend for any man,' Andrew acceded. 'But for a woman it is different. He's a foreigner. His ways are not our ways.'

'I haven't your experience travelling the world. I'm afraid you'll have to explain.' The remark was acerbic. Old Evie, not the Evie who had indulged herself this afternoon, would have said the line with a note of deference. But New Evie was spoiling for a fight. If he was going to malign his friend, he'd have to be more specific. She wasn't going to sell out Dimitri for a vague reference.

'It's hardly the sort of thing a gentleman talks about with a lady.' Andrew gave her a quelling glance. He transferred the reins into one hand, his face softening as he touched her on the arm. 'I don't want to see you hurt, Evie. Dimitri could hurt you and not even realise it.' He shook his head. 'He's a *prince*, Evie. He has palaces and servants and untold wealth. He is used to having anything, anyone he wants, when he wants them. He's not like us.'

'Don't you think he could be, though?' It was the first time he'd ever touched her voluntarily, the first time he'd ever shown such regard, and yet her concern for Dimitri overrode those attentions. What had Dimitri said today—that she had a perfect life?

Andrew gave a laugh, not an entirely kind one. 'He's a prince. Why would he want to be like us?'

Evie shrugged, part of her feeling a little silly for having said the words out loud, but she wouldn't back down. 'I think he's a man who is not entirely happy with who he has become.' It was the best she could do without repeating all Dimitri had shared with her. It felt like a betrayal to blurt all that out to Andrew. Besides, it might call into question *how* she knew.

'Do you know him so well, then?' Andrew's tone was sharp as they pulled up to Evie's home.

'Probably not.' She was going to have to concede the argument before she incriminated herself and Dimitri.

Andrew's smile softened at her concession. 'Of course you don't. How could you? You've known him for a handful of weeks and spoken to him on only a few occasions.' He jumped down and came around to her side. 'Beware, Evie, it's part of his charm. He has a way of binding people to him quicker than is prudent. It's easy to fall for him.' Her cheeks started to burn. Is that what she was doing? Falling for the Prince?

He swung her down, his hands lingering at her waist, his eyes on her face, his voice gentle. 'He'll leave, Evie. He has no choice. He has to go home, where he belongs. He'll leave and we'll still be here.' Much was implied in that statement; that Dimitri was the interloper; that somehow she and Andrew were in this together and would be left behind *together* to a quiet life in Little Westbury. His thoughts mirrored the ones she'd had so closely, she ought to be trembling with delight. Why wasn't she?

Empirically, all the reasons to do some trembling were there: his touch, his gaze, his confession, his concern. It was a picture-perfect moment and the best she could muster was warm gratitude. She managed a smile and a demure downcasting of her gaze. 'I can handle myself with D—the Prince,' she hurriedly corrected. 'I appreciate your concern, truly I do. Thank you for the ride home.' She stepped back. It was time to say goodbye. Anyone looking out the window might misunderstand the nature of their conversation. While that might not have bothered her a few weeks ago, it inexplicably did now.

Andrew gave her wide smile. 'I should be thanking you, Evie.' He gestured to a leather portfolio under the seat. 'Your drawings are exquisite and I know it's an extra effort for you. I've acquired quite the collection of your work now.'

He stepped forward, trying to capitalise on the compliment, but she backed up once more, uncomfortable with the nearness. Thankfully, he did not press his point or his distance again, but she was aware that he watched her go in and that he didn't drive off until she was well inside. Was Andrew declaring himself at last? It seemed a cruel bit of irony to think he'd finally found his interest in her at a time when her attentions were engaged elsewhere. What was wrong with her that she couldn't celebrate such a momentous step forward towards her dream?

Chapter Fourteen

What the hell was wrong with her? Andrew chirped to the horses. He had a few miles to go to make his next meeting. He'd not planned on going back for Evie this afternoon, but he'd forgotten the portfolio with the drawings and it had added an hour to his day. It had been worth it. He thought about the small artefacts hidden beneath the seat: the emerald-studded comb and the ladies' matching hair clips Dimitri had dug up later. The usually bustling site had been deserted when he'd arrived, a perfect opportunity to get his hands on a few items that might appeal to the man he was meeting today, if he could ever get there.

The storm would provide a convenient alibi. Surely it would be easy enough to believe a few artefacts had gone missing amid the wind, mud and overturned boxes. He was counting on the artefacts to make up for his tardiness, a little something to soften his customer's disposition.

If not, that would be twice today he'd failed to soften someone's disposition, the first being Evie's. Usually, he was quite good at disposition softening.

But Evie had not swooned at his attentions. It was rather odd given that Evie was supposed to be interested in him, something he'd taken as matter of fact long before Dimitri had pointed it out. He'd not lied to Dimitri. His interest in Evie could only go so far. He had bigger ambitions for himself than marriage to a baronet's daughter could provide for.

He needed a rich bride with a big dowry. Restoring his grandfather's estate was just the beginning. He didn't love history as much as he loved the money history could make. A gentleman might dabble in historical pursuits and make money respectably if one knew the right outlets. There might also be greatness associated with it in the form of a title. Recovering special artefacts might be one way to attract royal attention. He was banking on it. In the meanwhile, there were some potentially lucrative black markets to pursue with his artefacts as well.

Andrew slowed the horses and swore under his breath at the muddy road. He wouldn't risk the horses just to be on time, he wasn't rich enough yet to afford new teams whenever he felt like it. But he would be. Pairing up with Dimitri Petrovich had been one of his more brilliant ideas, even if he did find the Prince a prosing, ethical bore. Once he'd seen how much money the Prince had made with some of their excavation projects by selling artefacts to museums he'd seen his way clear. He wouldn't limit himself to museums.

The outskirts of the little town where their meeting was to be held came into view. It was an obscure place to meet, but his customer preferred it that way. No witnesses. Andrew pulled into the yard of the tavern, a dingy-looking place, but this would take no more than a few minutes. He checked the pocket pistol he carried, just in case—a habit, he told himself, from the Grand Tour when a gentleman couldn't be too careful—it had nothing at all to do with the disreputable nature of his business. After all, the man he was doing business with was a reputable publisher in London. There was nothing illegal about what he was doing. He was just doing it without permission.

Andrew took the portfolio out from under the seat. He wasn't doing anything wrong. He would make sure Evie's name was mentioned too as the illustrator. This dig was as much his as it was the Prince's. He was the one who'd suggested the idea, who had brought the Prince here. He had just as much right to take credit for the effort and for disposing of the dig's products as he saw fit.

Inside, the tavern was dark. He scanned the room, letting his eyes adjust. He found his man sitting in the back at a private table, although most tables were 'private' this time of day given that men were still at work and the rainstorm had probably cut down on traffic. Andrew straightened his shoulders and adjusted his coat. This was important. He had to seal this deal. He pasted on his best business smile. It was show time.

A half an hour later he walked out of the tavern two hundred pounds richer. The man had indeed been impressed with the hair clips and comb. He'd also been interested in purchasing a few more items. That's where Evie's drawings came in handy. Andrew could use them as a purchaser's catalogue of sorts. Interested buyers could look through them and make an offer.

Later, when he was done with the drawings, the publisher had offered to buy them. In fact, the man had already paid him an advance on a book containing those drawings and the descriptions that went with them. All Andrew had to do was write an introduction about the project.

Just the thought put a spring in his step. A book was the key to respectability and to a genteel lecture circuit. All the great explorers put out books about their journeys. Books would lead to talks, only he wouldn't give talks to common folks in assembly rooms. He'd talk to people who mattered. He leapt up into the carriage seat, already imagining the great nobles he'd present his findings to—lords who would fund larger projects like the men coming out to the site tomorrow.

Archaeology was a lot like mining actually, only he was digging for artefacts instead of gold. England's history was rich. There must be millions of things beneath the surface waiting to be discovered. And he would discover them, just as soon as Dimitri was gone. He was growing impatient to have the site to himself. Of course, it would be easier with Evie on his side. He'd need to find a way to keep her on it. He needed her drawings until he had enough for the book and she would know how to manage all the cataloguing.

Evie's interest in Dimitri was becoming something of a concern. Andrew didn't need Dimitri convincing her that archaeology was something a community should participate in since it ran contrary to his own plans. She'd been rather adamant in her defence of the Prince today. Such fire had surprised him actually.

Evie was usually subdued in her opinions. It made him wonder what had transpired to make her so willing to defend Dimitri. What could Dimitri have said or done to inspire such a show in Evie? He worried most about the latter. Was Dimitri seducing Evie? Giving her false hopes? Normally, he wouldn't care. Dimitri could seduce whomever he liked. But he needed Evie to be on his side. And really, what could Dimitri be thinking? It was hardly honourable for Dimitri to toy with her affections. The man could offer Evie nothing and he knew it.

But Evie didn't. It would be so easy for a man like Dimitri to turn her head. Unless there was someone else who could turn it back. Evie was ultimately a practical girl. Perhaps it was time to 'help' her understand Dimitri's limits before things went too far. If she knew what he knew about the Prince, she might be a little less inclined to champion him. Dimitri could use some reminders too, in the guise of friendly advice. Dimitri needed to know it was not acceptable to receive a woman in his pavilion wearing only his robe, nor was it acceptable to cook her breakfast so early in the morning. That scene in particular still niggled at him. Something wasn't quite right there.

Perhaps too it was time for him to start moving a supposed courtship forward before it was too late. Clearly, it would take more effort than he'd given it today. If a touch at the waist, a lingering look into her eyes, a soft show of concern wasn't enough to hold Evie's attention, perhaps a kiss would be, and if that wasn't enough, he could always make her promises he didn't intend to keep.

* * *

Dimitri spared yet another glance for the cataloguing department, busy under the restrung canvas. It was the twentieth or so glance he'd 'spared' that direction all morning, although it could quite possibly be more. It was entirely possible that he'd lost count. The point was, he'd been looking a lot, looking so much, in fact, that he'd nearly crunched a bowl beneath his foot, and not just any bowl, but a bowl a thousand years old and broken neatly into two large pieces, a bowl that could be easily glued together. Such 'complete' finds were rare and they were impressive.

At first, he told himself he was checking on the canvas, to make sure that the rigging was tied tightly after yesterday's debacle of a horse running through the area and tearing everything down. But after the fifth glance and the fact that there was only a light breeze that wouldn't challenge even the poorest rigging, he had to acknowledge the truth: he was watching *Evie*. Today, she wore her usual wide white apron over a plain, durable dress to shield it from ink and dirt as she and a few others dug out their work from the residue of the storm. Her hair was done up in a tight bun. There was nothing about her reminiscent of the temptress she'd been yesterday in his pavilion. She was like a secret. *His* secret. He smiled at the thought, liking the notion of having the privilege to know the real Evie. Liking even more the notion that she'd given that secret into his care. He would cherish it, he would protect it.

He couldn't help wishing her hair was loose as it had been in the tent, surrounding her like an autumn halo. Even now, his hands twitched at the memory of her hair, wet and soft beneath his fingers. Other parts of his body twitched too at the memory. His robe had smelled of her after she'd left, all lemon and lavender, a soft womanly scent. It had tormented him most of the night. He hadn't slept well. Not merely because of the reminders of her presence in his tent—a place she'd spent too much time recently between dinner and the storm—but because of what it all meant, or didn't mean.

Dimitri hefted a large chunk of rock into a wheelbarrow and motioned that it be taken away. He brushed his gloved hands on his trousers and pushed back his hair, starting to sweat as the day approached noon. He wasn't in the market for a relationship, certainly not one that transcended a physical liaison. He would be going home soon. Yet, despite that understanding, she'd drawn him; the quiet beauty of her face, the intelligence of her blue eyes that veiled hotter depths, the quality of her conversation, which was thoughtful, and at times unguarded—that was when she was at her best. He wanted more of those times. Part of him looked forward to each day to see if there would be another glimpse—could he provoke another glimpse? What could he do or say that might give him one more look into that part of Evie? Why did she guard it? What other secrets did she hold? It was somewhat comforting to understand the roots of his attraction. But that didn't resolve it. He feared nothing would. It was the wrong time, the wrong place in his life to have met Evie.

He looked up towards her one more time and she waved to him, gesturing for him to come over. Dimitri put down his shovel, hurrying across the distance.

'How is everything?' he asked, surveying the neat, organised domain of cataloguing. After Evie's morning efforts, it hardly looked as if the place had been hit by a storm just a day before.

'The comb and the hair clips are missing.' Evie didn't mince words. 'I've been through the collection twice. They aren't here.' She waved a hand to indicate the workspace. 'They must have fallen out of a box when the crates tipped over yesterday, they could have been dragged some distance by the horse, or buried by churned-up mud. They're tiny, easily displaced.' She shook her head, despairing. 'I can't find them. I feel like it's my fault, but I was careful. I don't know how it could have happened. They were wrapped in cloth, protected and packed away. It would have been unlikely they'd have got loose.'

'They'll turn up.' He wanted to console her, but looking at the workspace, he wasn't sure they would. 'Nothing else is missing? Nothing else from the same box?' He thought it strange, if the box had tipped over, if the contents had come loose and been trampled or spread around, that nothing else in that box had suffered.

'No. The box is quite intact,' Evie confirmed.

A suspicion born of experience began to take shape. Theft, perhaps. It happened often enough. He'd seen it on several of his digs. A worker, not part of his usual crew, would pocket a small artefact thinking no one would notice a small item gone missing amid hundreds of others. This was bolder, however. The hair clips and comb were more significant than a pottery shard. It did, however, make motives clear. Someone taking them would be looking to make money.

That could be almost anyone. Plenty of the English labourers might be tempted to take something. The sum it would bring would be worth five years' salary to some.

Dimitri kept his thoughts to himself. 'Theft' was a dangerous word. He would not throw it around without proof. He also didn't want to start a panic or create a negative impression of the work that went on here, especially not with Andrew's lords coming out tomorrow. He pushed a hand through his hair. He wished Andrew hadn't invited the men without his permission. He'd have to be the Prince tomorrow, have to play the part of the aristocrat. Evie hadn't looked thrilled about the visit either when Andrew had mentioned it. Well, that made two of them.

He smiled at Evie. 'Don't worry. I'm sure we'll find them.' In the meanwhile, he would take precautions to make sure if there was a thief, the man wouldn't be able to take anything of worth. He had a man on his crew for just this reason who created excellent replicas, a very useful talent to have when it came to stopping thievery, if indeed that was what had happened. This problem was solved easily. Too bad other difficulties weren't solved with the same efficiency. How did one solve a problem like Evie Milham when the only solution that presented itself was suddenly quite unsatisfactory? It was the dilemma that had faced mankind since time immemorial: how did one manage to have one's cake and eat it too?

Chapter Fifteen

Yesterday she'd forgotten to be self-conscious around him and she hadn't realised it until she'd been getting ready for bed. She'd been so concerned about the missing artefacts, she hadn't been nervous about facing Dimitri the day after the storm, also known as the day after *The Acts*. It was much easier to think of it as the day after the storm. She was less inclined to blush spontaneously. But when she'd spoken with him, she hadn't blushed at all.

Evie puttered around the cataloguing 'tent', keeping busy with little tasks. She was too distracted to draw. Evie wished she would forget to be nervous today too, but she knew she wouldn't. Andrew's lords were coming to visit, led by Lord Belvoir and his catty daughter, Cecilia. Already, she could feel her stomach was tight with nerves. She did not want Cecilia in Little Westbury. She told herself Cecilia's remarks couldn't hurt her any more. She wasn't a young girl, first out on the town, naïve and eager to make friends. She'd rather not have to test that hypothesis. But that wasn't the only reason she didn't want Cecilia in Little

Westbury. A jealous little space deep inside her didn't want Cecilia anywhere near Dimitri, not after yesterday afternoon. She wasn't ready yet to let Dimitri go. She wanted to enjoy the thought of him as 'hers' for just a little while longer, even if the thought was more fantasy than reality.

Just how much, though, was open for discussion. The line between fantasy and reality was a blurry one. She could no longer discount the feeling that there was *something* between her and Dimitri, that it wasn't all just her. Yesterday wasn't an isolated incident. There'd been something that had sparked between them from the start. Dimitri cared for her. The thought brought a smile to her face as she worked. It didn't matter that nothing could come of that caring in the long term. It was just nice to know he *liked* her and maybe even more than liked her, because she more than liked him. For the first time in her life, she was in a reciprocated relationship. That was enough.

At least it was until she saw a cloud of dust on the horizon. The knot in her stomach, which had loosened just a little, tightened again. Andrew's lordly cavalcade was here. On cue, Dimitri strode out with Andrew beside him to meet the carriages. He was dressed as an English gentleman today, complete with a blue jacket, pristine linen and buckskin breeches, and tall boots polished to perfection. Everything about him was perfection. Even at a distance, she could tell he'd taken care with his *toilette*. His jaw was smooth, his hair was drawn back tight with a silver clasp done in the shape of a bear, the great Russian symbol. He looked every inch the Prince and less like the man she'd come to know.

Four carriages pulled up and disgorged their passengers, their voices floating to Evie's work station as everyone exchanged greetings. Dimitri's voice stood out above the rest, with its hard 'r's and low tones, contrasting with Andrew's enthusiastic tenor. Dimitri seemed polished, relaxed, while Andrew appeared over-excited.

Belvoir and Cecilia were the last ones out of the carriages. Evie had hoped that perhaps they'd not come after all. She should have guessed Cecilia would want to make an entrance. Her father handed her down and Andrew introduced her to Dimitri. 'Your Highness.' Cecilia's lilting voice carried on the breeze as she dipped a pretty curtsy, flashing a beatific smile. She looked stunning with her gold curls and pale skin, both of which were set off to advantage in a pink summer gown, her signature colour, with a pert straw hat with matching ribbon to keep off the sun, even though she carried a lacy parasol too. Cecilia Northam took no chances with the alabaster perfection of her skin. Evie looked down at her own ink-stained hands. Not like her. She had freckles in the summer and ink was her constant companion.

Dimitri bowed gallantly over Cecilia's hand and raised her up. Cecilia took advantage, tucking her hand through his arm and not letting him go. It was clear she was ready for the tour to commence with her on the Prince's arm and in the lead. Dimitri smiled at Cecilia and Evie wished he didn't look so pleased about it even if it was 'just business'.

She glanced at her desk. Maybe she should draw after all. She couldn't spend the whole day fuming and wondering. If she wasn't among them, it was her fault. Dimitri had invited her, saying she was a vital part of the work they'd done, but she had declined. She didn't want to spend the day waiting in trepidation for Cecilia to make a cutting remark or, worst of all, to bring up her most embarrassing moment in front of Dimitri. Distance would be her strategy today. With luck, she'd escape Cecilia's notice entirely.

She was absorbed in the drawing of a goblet when the group came past her station. The goblet took a certain level of skill because it had to be drawn from all angles, even the bottom of the base, in order to show off the insignia stamped into it that denoted it belonged to Lucius Artorious. It was one of the most important finds they had that linked the villa to his ownership.

'This is where the magic happens.' Dimitri walked the group up to her table with a sweep of his free hand, one of his big gestures. Evie would have liked to have stopped him. She wished he'd taken her at her word last night when she'd said she'd wanted no part of the 'festivities' today. But he hadn't listened, so now she pasted a smile on her face and set down her pen, rising to greet the guests.

Cecilia was still on Dimitri's arm, but his eyes lingered on Evie as he made the introductions. 'Some of you may already know her, this is Miss Evaine Milham, our resident artist, who is in charge of drawing and cataloguing each of our finds no matter how small. Thanks to her, our work is recorded.'

'Oh, Evie! It is you,' Cecilia gushed with a bonhomie Evie had come not to trust. 'I hardly recognised you.' She laughed and fluttered a hand. 'One never expects to see someone out of context. Normally, you're wandering ballrooms, but here you are, *working* away.'

Evie would have given anything for Beatrice and May to suddenly emerge. Beatrice knew just how to handle Cecilia but Evie was on her own now. All handling would be left up to her. She decided not to dignify Cecilia's doubly-pointed jab with a response. Instead, she directed attention towards the goblet. 'Let me tell you about one of our most important finds,' she began, catching a flicker of approval in Dimitri's eye and a flash of apology too. She was glad when they left, but Andrew lingered behind, fingering the goblet.

'I wish you wouldn't touch that,' Evie snapped. 'It's at least a thousand years old.'

Andrew withdrew his fingers. 'You're waspish today,' he commented, studying her carefully. What was he looking for? The way he watched her with Dimitri these days was making her uncomfortable. 'I don't suppose your temper has anything to do with Dimitri fawning all over Cecilia?'

'It looks more to me like it's Cecilia fawning all over Dimitri. Besides, what do I care who he fawns over?' Evie replied coolly.

'They are handsome together, two very good-looking people always are,' Andrew remarked. She tried not to let it sting. How could she compete with beautiful Cecilia Northam? She'd never been able to compete, but she hated being reminded of it. Cecilia was the beginning of all her woes.

'I have work to do, if you would excuse me?' Evie sat down and picked up her pen, her dismissal obvious.

Andrew didn't leave immediately. Instead, he

squatted down level with the table, level with her. His voice was soft. 'Evie, look at me. He's going to leave. I don't want you to throw yourself away on a man who won't appreciate you, not when there's a man who does, perhaps even a man who is very nearby.'

Only then did he leave her. She waited for her heart to pound, her blood to race. Andrew had all but declared himself. Coupled with his talk of restoring his grandfather's estate, and all the time he dedicated to driving her home, this was as close to direct declaration as it came. And she didn't want it. Didn't want him.

Evie stared into the distance, seeing nothing but her own thoughts. So the world didn't end with a bang after all, but instead a quiet whisper of truth, arrived at after years of consideration. She would have thought such a momentous truth would be heralded with more fanfare. She didn't want Andrew. She wanted Dimitri. But it wasn't just that Dimitri was a trade-off, a better substitute for Andrew. She didn't want Andrew regardless. Dimitri had merely helped her see it. And in helping her, she had come to want him with an intensity that rocked her to her core. She'd not realised how intense until she'd seen Cecilia standing with him, a reminder of how unattainable he truly was, how he wasn't the sort of man meant for her even if he had all the time in the world. And it hurt. She didn't want to give him up, not to time, not to the Cecilia Northams of the world. There were a lot of things perhaps she could change, but she couldn't change that.

A shadow fell across her desk, large and male. She looked up to find Dimitri standing there looking penitent. He'd taken his coat off and it was slung over his arm. 'I'm sorry.'

Evie rose and smoothed her hands on her apron, feeling self-conscious for the first time in a while in his presence. 'For what? There's nothing to be sorry for.'

'I disagree. I wronged you today. I didn't respect your request.' He held out his hand. 'Would you come walk with me?'

'Tell me about Cecilia Northam. Tell me what she did to you,' Dimitri asked quietly as they strolled in the little copse of trees to the west of the site. The animosity between the two women had been palpable today and Evie had handled the situation like a champion, but he still regretted putting her in that position and he was furious with Andrew, who ought to have known better.

'There's not much to tell…' Evie began hesitantly. 'She came out the same year we did, we being my friends, the ones you met that day in the street. She went on to be popular and we did not.'

'And yet she's not married,' Dimitri commented. All the girls had been out three Seasons. Popular or not, Cecilia was no further along in her pursuit of a husband than Evie was arguably.

Evie gave a small laugh. 'That's thanks to my friend Claire. They were both angling after the same gentleman, only Claire loved him and Cecilia did not. Cecilia just wanted him as a trophy on her arm. Her father even offered to buy him a diplomatic post.'

'Ah—' Dimitri chuckled '—that explains why she was so taken with me.' He tried for some self-deprecating humour. Cecilia was lovely, but to a man who had been schooled in the royal court of Kuban, she was untutored in the true art of subtlety. She'd been angling for him the moment she'd stepped out of the carriage and he'd known it. He was not interested.

Evie didn't find it funny. 'Of course she found you worth her attentions. She can't stand for anyone to have anything more beautiful than she. She once copied a dress of Claire's and wore it the same night to make sure everyone knew she was prettier in it.'

Dimitri went carefully here. They were getting closer to the heart of the matter. 'And you, Evie? What did she do to you?'

Evie turned to face him, her sweet face set with a hardness he was not used to seeing on her and certainly didn't like. The urge to protect surged strong as the simple sentence came out. 'She exposed me, showed everyone what I was and that I wasn't good enough for London society.'

Dimitri nodded, saying nothing. Sometimes silence was the best encourager. He squeezed her hand. Silence and touch. Evie bit her lip. 'I was eager to be friends with all the new girls I met in London. Cecilia and her mother came to tea one afternoon and I showed Cecilia my sketch book full of drawings for dresses. I had always shown Claire and Bea and May. We all grew up together. I thought nothing of it.' She paused here, blushing. 'My friends were always so complimentary about my drawings that I thought Cecilia would be too. I even offered to make her something, as a gesture of friendship. I was always making things for Claire and the girls. It was prideful of me. I had sought to impress her. Perhaps I got my just desserts.' Evie looked down.

'She took my sketch book. I didn't notice it was gone until later. She showed it to the other girls out that Season and made fun of the drawings and then made fun of me, in public. At balls she'd ask me if I was wearing a dress I had made myself and it was never done in a nice way. She nicknamed me the "seamstress". The best way to deter her attentions was to not call attention to myself. It was horrible.'

He could imagine. He didn't need any more details. He could imagine too how Evie had made the choice to slide away, withdrawing month by month until she was only surrounded by what was comfortable to her. Dimitri saw the knee-jerk logic of that, and the pain. He hurt for her, for the Evie who was ridiculed for her talents and then shunned.

'I am doubly sorry, then, that I allowed her to be here.'

'It's all right. She's everywhere. I have to deal with her.' Evie shrugged and offered him a half-smile. 'It's enough to know that Andrew was wrong.'

'Wrong?' Dimitri was wary.

'He said you were interested in her.'

What was Andrew playing at now? Dimitri feared he knew. There was only one reason a man would say something like that. Andrew wanted to drive a wedge between him and Evie. This was the second time Andrew had tried to do so. This time he'd gone after Evie. But he knew better than to malign Andrew to her.

Dimitri turned to face her. 'How could I be interested in her when all my interest is fixed on you? The question is, are you still interested in him?'

He held his breath. He hadn't known how much her answer mattered to him. This had been on the periphery of his thoughts, a little haze of guilt. He'd been wrong to kiss her, wrong to introduce her to passion's delights if she still cared for another. This was probably something that should have been resolved beforehand, but it had seemed not to matter to either of them in the heat of the moment. It had been, in fact, easily forgotten by them both.

Evie reached up a hand and stroked the long line of his jaw. 'I want *you*.'

He smiled, releasing his breath, aware how much her words mattered. He turned his cheek and pressed a kiss into her palm. 'Dear Lord, Evie, be careful what you say. You'd make a blancmange hard.' To say nothing of a man already experiencing the stirrings of arousal. He should not let her want him. He had to try and warn her. 'You know I can't stay.' And yet when he looked at Evie, he wished he could. Evie wanted *him*, Dimitri Petrovich the man, not the Prince.

He'd not ever been with a woman who had wanted that man, who looked at him and saw that man. It was wonderful and awful all at once. Women who wanted the Prince were easy to walk away from. They did not offer love in return, just their bodies. But Evie was on the brink of loving him.

'I know.' Their eyes locked and he read the unspoken message that passed between them. *I want you for as long as I can have you.* There was some hope here. Perhaps if they both understood the temporary nature of their association, they could find temporary happiness together. Maybe that would be enough.

'What does wanting me mean, Evie?' His voice was hoarse with hope and desire. She blushed. She understood what he meant. How far could the wanting go? Was it to be chaste if not pure? Holding hands, exchanging kisses, touches, or was it to be bold and illicit, involving his bed and naked bodies entwined in acts that could not be retracted? His body hoped for the latter while his code of honour knew he had to restrict it to the former. He would not ruin her for his pleasure or even for hers. She would come to hate him for it even if he would be a thousand miles away before she realised it.

She searched his face, perceiving the dilemma behind his words. 'We'll figure it out together,' she whispered, rising up on her tiptoes to press her mouth against his, 'one kiss at a time.'

Chapter Sixteen

One kiss led to dinner. At Evie's. With her parents. A bucolic temptation if ever there was one. An English summer dinner surrounded by reminders of what was possible if he turned his back on Kuban, on his family and Anna-Maria. Andrew called such a choice a disaster. Dimitri called it inevitable. He had no choice except to go back but that didn't stop him from dreaming and this—sitting across from Evie, her father presiding over the table at one end, smiling at her mother at the other end—was *the* dream.

This was life in ordinary time. No royal court to navigate, no bride of convenience waiting in his royal apartments, no *fear*. He was starting to realise that his life was full of fear. Fear for Anna-Maria, for his family if he failed to fulfil his Kubanian-ordained destiny.

He sipped cool white wine from his glass, Evie flashing him a covert smile over the candles as her father went on about his latest book. 'It will be a legacy to Little Westbury. In this area, we can trace our origins back to the Domesday Book,' Sir Hollis said proudly. Dimitri liked Sir Hollis Milham. He'd en-

joyed their talks the very first day Sir Hollis had visited the site. This was a man whom he could come to
respect the more he got to know him. Dimitri understood the pride Sir Hollis felt for his work. He understood the magnitude of such a gift to a community.
To understand one's heritage was an integral part to
understanding one's self. Evie's mother had beamed
at her husband, proud too of what he'd accomplished.

Evie's mother was a fluttery woman, who tended
towards nervousness over the littlest thing in her effort to please, but anyone could see her efforts were
honest and well meant even if those efforts bordered
on stifling. She'd asked him three times if he had
enough vinaigrette for his summer greens. Evie might
take after her in looks, but she took after her father
in temperament. Sir Hollis Milham was level-headed
and quiet, perhaps because her mother wasn't. Between the two of them, they counterbalanced Isobel
Milham perfectly. He learned that Evie had sisters,
two of them. Already married. It explained, perhaps,
why her parents were content to have her stay with
them, unwilling to have their nest emptied entirely.

*There could be more evenings like this if you
stayed*, whispered the very temptation he'd spent most
of the evening trying to avoid. More evenings of cold
meats, bread, a salad of sweet summer greens with
a tangy raspberry vinaigrette—of which there was
apparently an abundance—evenings of listening to
Hollis's insights, being fussed over by Isobel and Evie
flirting with him across the table, her eyes promising him pleasure once they were alone. Did she know
she did that? He shouldn't even allow himself to think

such traitorous thoughts, shouldn't allow himself to
conjure up such temptations.

To stay meant he had to admit certain truths to
himself—one truth in particular: He was falling for
Evie Milham. He had to be careful with his words.
'Falling' was as close as he'd let his vocabulary get.
He didn't dare describe what he was falling into. He
didn't dare use the word 'love'. He knew what love
was. Knew he should guard against it as much as
possible. Loving his family came with duty, it came
with fear. A man could only live with so much of that
before it crushed him. He'd seen it happen to his father. Love, protection, fear, duty—they were all inter-
twined. Loving Evie would be more of it, a different
version of it. He wasn't sure he was strong enough.
If love had broken his fortress of a father, surely his
own odds weren't any better. And yet, the urge to
tempt fate was strong.

'Sir—' the housekeeper bustled in, addressing Sir
Hollis '—Mr Adair is here. Shall I tell him to join
you?'

Sir Hollis raised his eyebrows at the surprise. Dimitri wasn't sure if Sir Hollis thought it a good surprise
or a bad one. Dimitri shot Evie a look, but she was
as perplexed as her father. 'It's quite the night for unexpected guests,' Sir Hollis joked in friendly tones.
'Send him out and bring the cheese. He can join us
for dessert.' Then in low tones, he said something to
the housekeeper that sounded remarkably like, 'No
seed cakes, though, or the man will never leave.' *Ah*,
Dimitri thought. *Not a good surprise.* Sir Hollis Milham didn't like Andrew Adair as much as everyone
else in Little Westbury. Interesting.

The atmosphere around the table changed with Andrew's arrival. The relaxation seeped away. But Andrew didn't notice. He was too busy dominating the conversation, full of easy smiles. 'We had a splendid day at the site today. The visit with Lord Belvoir and his friends was excellent. They were impressed with what we've done at the site.'

What *we've* done? Dimitri wanted to correct him. Andrew hadn't spent a single day on his knees in the dirt excavating anything. True, he'd been the one to bring him here and he'd been the one to see to the external arrangements like food and inviting the lords out, but he hadn't done any actual work on the site. Andrew's next words, though, were fighting words.

'I think a few of them would be interested in purchasing some artefacts, especially that bowl you found the other day.'

Dimitri shook his head. 'We are not selling the artefacts. We'd agreed. Anything from this dig will be displayed in a museum here in Little Westbury.' True, he didn't have an actual museum yet, but he had his eye on an empty office space next to the bakery near the village green. It would be one of the last tasks he did before leaving, the final task that would launch Little Westbury into completely taking over the project.

Andrew laughed. 'It's easy for you. You're a prince, you don't have to think about money. You can give it all away. I don't know the rest of us can afford to think like that. The dig has to support itself. Surely it won't hurt to sell some of the items. Don't you agree, Sir Hollis?' He flashed Evie's father a smile, hoping to engage an ally. Dimitri sat back and waited. He already knew what Evie's father would say.

'Frankly, I agree with the Prince.' Sir Hollis did not hesitate to take issue with Andrew. 'It's the principle of the matter. A heritage isn't for sale. It's one of the few things in this world that should not have a price put on it.' He winked at his wife. 'Love would be another.' Isobel Milham blushed, looking much like her daughter, and Dimitri admired the way Sir Hollis had negotiated Andrew's question with levity.

Andrew threw up his hands with an easy laugh. 'Save me from high-minded fools!' But Dimitri didn't think it truly was a joke to him. 'Well, never mind,' Andrew continued, leaning forward. 'They might invest anyway. They have deep pockets and we'll need them when you leave.' Andrew was speaking directly to him although there were others present. He'd effectively blocked the Milhams out of the conversation. It was entirely disrespectful. 'I had an idea. I stopped by your pavilion, but your assistant said you'd come here for dinner.' There was a question of accusation in the statement. 'I was thinking we might throw a party at the end of September, invite them out again, invite the locals, make it a celebration, a "passing the torch" ceremony, and a farewell party for you. You're leaving the first of October. It will be perfect.'

Dimitri felt his jaw tighten. He hazarded a glance at Evie to see how she'd taken the mention of a departure date. He'd said nothing concrete to her about exactly when he'd leave, only that he had to be home by February. But Evie had averted her eyes and was concentrating on her hands in her lap.

'I was thinking Miss Northam could plan it,' Andrew concluded the lay out of his plan. 'If she's in- vested time in the project, I'm sure her father would follow suit.'

'No,' Dimitri put in quickly. It might be sound logic, but he'd already foisted Miss Northam's un- comfortable company on Evie once. He wasn't going to do it again, especially after what Evie had shared with him this afternoon. No person like that was going to align herself with his projects if he could help it. What was the point, after all, of an apology, if he made the mistake again?

'No?' Andrew was taken aback. 'Is that a royal edict, Your Highness?' Dimitri didn't care for the snide tone of Andrew's voice, which went far be- yond teasing.

'It is simply, no,' Dimitri repeated. 'I think Evie and Lady Milham should plan it.'

'I beg your pardon?' It was Evie this time who broke in. 'I sew gowns and draw patterns.'

Dimitri argued with a smile, 'I disagree with your assumption that all you're good for is stitchery and drawing. I think you and your mother are perfectly placed to plan this party. You are a high-ranking local family. People look to you to set the tone.' He hoped Evie's level-headedness, though, would balance out her mother's tendency to overthink things.

'The Worths do that,' Evie argued back.

'They are not in residence currently.' Dimitri didn't hesitate and pressed on, laying out his case. 'Your fa- ther is highly thought of when it comes to history and you've been helping me. You understand what this project is about. You're the perfect bridge between Little Westbury and the excavation.'

Evie switched tactics. Good heavens, arguing with her was like arguing with a hydra. 'That doesn't mean I can organise a party. Under your criteria, Andrew would be the perfect party organiser. Isn't Andrew the one who arranges for all the supplies that come out to the site? He already knows how to order for a large group.'

Dimitri gave a loud laugh. 'He can order potatoes and sausage for a hundred men. That is not the same at all as planning a party. There are decorations to consider, seating arrangements, music, atmosphere.'

Evie opened her mouth for another protest, but it was too late. Dimitri had an ally. He'd thought he might.

Isobel Milham came to life at the mention of music and decorations. 'Evie, we could do it. We could host it at the villa itself, let people dine in the general's dining room. We could call it "A Night in a Roman Villa".'

'Something Latin would sound better,' Evie said without realising what she was walking into. '"La Nocturna, a Night at a Roman Villa." We could hang fabrics, damasks and silks.'

Dimitri exchanged a victorious look with Lady Milham. He framed the phrase with a gesture of his hand. '"La Nocturna, a Night at a Roman Villa." I like it. It will be the party of the decade, Evie.'

'Wait!' Evie saw too late what had happened. Dimitri nearly laughed at the incredulous expression on her face. 'I haven't agreed to anything.' But she was wavering. Her eyes were dancing, and Dimitri would bet his fortune her mind was starting to see the potential. He was too—the villa's courtyard, the dining room, a space that must have functioned as a grand salon of sorts at one time. It would be unique and magnificent.

Dimitri laughed. He hadn't had this much fun talking someone into something in ages and Evie was more than capable. 'Perhaps this will convince you. The four words every woman loves to hear: Money is no object. You won't be alone. You'll have your mother. Stefon will help you. You come up with the lists and Stefon will see it done. My crew will help you set up when the time comes and they'll clean up afterwards.'

He glanced at Andrew, who'd been minimised in the conversation. 'I think it's a fabulous idea, Andrew. A party will build commitment. People will support what they fund, what they feel part of. The project will become theirs. This could be the work of a lifetime for someone, someone like you, Sir Hollis.' Out of the corner of his eye, he saw Andrew blanch. Andrew had seen himself as the natural successor. But he didn't want the project in Andrew's hands alone. Andrew would sell it off piece by piece for personal gain. He saw that now. 'You can establish a museum with the artefacts, attract other scholars, attract tourists.' He could see the idea excited Sir Hollis and the man would be well placed to know who those scholars might be. They wouldn't be men like Lord Belvoir. They would be true scholars like Sir Hollis's son-in-law, the aspiring Oxford don.

Sir Hollis Milham rose. 'Why don't you and Evie take a stroll and talk through some ideas while they're fresh in your head and I'll see Andrew out.' It was all said congenially, but Dimitri understood the undertones. Andrew was being dismissed and he was being given a chance to be alone with Evie. He was starting to wonder who or what Sir Hollis Milham's remark about love was aimed at. At the time, it had seemed benign. Now, he wasn't so sure.

'The observatory would be nice tonight,' Sir Hollis suggested with a smile. 'There's still time to see the Perseids. There's nothing quite like wishing on shooting stars.' If only, Dimitri thought, one could take the risk. What happened if his wish came true?

Chapter Seventeen

Fresh air was good. Her head was reeling. Somehow she'd been manoeuvred into planning an enormous party, something she felt ill equipped to do. 'You tricked me, back there,' she said as she and Dimitri set out for the observatory, the lights of the house fading behind them, darkness and privacy before them.

'Oh, no, it was all fair and square.' Dimitri laughed. 'You walked right into it with your inspired idea. Besides, I couldn't tolerate the idea of turning it over to Miss Northam.'

That alone made her honour bound to accept. He'd stood up for her tonight. She hadn't missed that, nor had she been able to overlook how it had made her feel—cherished, important enough to fight for. Andrew had either been obtuse when it came to the undercurrents of her relationship with Cecilia Northam, or he simply didn't care enough to consider her feelings. But Dimitri, who had known her for a handful of weeks, had been her champion. Dimitri, who had been and would be her lover.

While they'd been arguing about parties, she had

been making decisions. It had not escaped her that planning this party would also be a countdown to losing Dimitri—pain with the pleasure. August was nearly done. There wasn't much time left. If she meant to act, it would have to be soon. And it would have to be her. She would have to let *him* know what the boundaries of their association would be.

At the observatory, Evie cast her eyes skyward, scanning the night. 'The Perseids will be visible tonight. It's one of my favourite things about August— the meteor showers. This is the last week of truly prime viewing. I suppose we can say, we'll catch the tail end of them.'

'No pun intended, I suppose?'

'*Every* pun intended. I've been waiting two weeks to use that.' She laughed and Dimitri laughed beside her, a warm sound in the dark. When she allowed herself to think about it, she was still amazed at their relationship. It was more than simply her initial awe that this handsome man found her interesting. Any girl who limited her appreciation of Dimitri to such shallows would be missing the real attraction. She loved how natural it was to be with him, to laugh, to joke, to share. They'd given meaningful, difficult pieces of their past to one another. He'd told her about his sister, his reasons for returning to Kuban, and she knew how much that decision weighed on him, what it would cost him in personal freedom. In return, she'd shared her most humiliating experience with him.

They climbed the tight spiral staircase to the top, where the large telescope stood ready. Dimitri blew out a whistle of appreciation. 'My father built it from different parts. He modelled it after the one in Greenwich.' She bent to the eyepiece to check the focus and stepped back. 'Come, see, the view is remarkable. Look to your right.'

Dimitri positioned himself at the eyepiece, his amazement instant. 'I can see all the way to heaven. Oh, Evie, you have to see this.' He backed away and moved her in front of him. 'Look to the left.' His hands were on her hips, directing her to catch the brilliant sight. 'To the left, Evie, I think it's the...'

'Ring Nebula.' They both murmured the answer in simultaneous awe.

'The colours are striking up close,' Dimitri whispered.

But even with the vibrant colours of the Ring Nebula in her vision, she was acutely aware of the warm press of his hands at her hips.

'The stars remind me how small I am, how finite my time on earth is,' Dimitri said close to her ear. 'It is perhaps a good lesson for a prince, to keep him humble.'

'But a hard one too?' Evie turned from the lens to face him. 'For a man who wants to be in control? Who wants to protect?' She was understanding him better each day. His sister, his family, herself. He was a born protector and protection required control. They were in close proximity now. She was within the circle of his arms and he made no move to take his hands from her waist. 'The universe is a good lesson for all of us. A life is but a moment.' Her voice was low and soft, her tongue ran across her lips as she gave words to the intoxicating thoughts in her head. 'We put so much into those small moments—what to wear, what to eat, who to dance with—so much concern over what others think. Sometimes control is an elusive thing, an illusion of smoke and mirrors only, something we fool ourselves into believing. Wherever we go, whatever we do, life will happen anyway. Regardless.' She'd never spoken such powerful words out loud before, afraid of being laughed at, and in truth, outside of Bea and May and Claire, who would she say such things to? But she wanted to say them to him, in the hope it would ease his sense of burden, perhaps bring him peace. He was trying to hide it, but he was troubled, it was there behind his dark eyes. He was wrestling with something.

She held him with her eyes. 'Did you know my mother has never left Little Westbury except to go to London? This is her universe, the entirety of her world.'

'Is that a bad thing?' Dimitri breathed.

'I don't know.' They were whispering to one another now because the truth was sacred. 'My father's lived here too, but he went away for school and a Grand Tour. He saw something of the world before he came home and married.'

'What of you, Evie? Are you comfortable with Little Westbury being your universe too?'

'I think I could be happy anywhere as long as I was loved the way my father loves my mother.' Two of her deepest, most hidden truths rolled out of her at once, without hesitation because he had to know. She needed him to know. Or perhaps because she needed herself to hear them in order to realise the other truth.

'I know now that Andrew would never give me

that. I don't know why it took me this long to see it. Andrew is a universe unto himself and there is no room in it for two.' She paused, letting them both take in her declaration. Her mind had let Andrew go before this, her subconscious had let him go long before to-night, but saying the words out loud was important. Sealing them with a kiss was even more important. Life could be built one kiss at a time.

She'd given up Andrew. She'd said it before but hearing it tonight carried a stronger sense of final-ity to it. It was a victory to know she'd freed herself from the rather limiting adulation of Andrew Adair. Not because he wanted to 'win'. It had never been a competition, he couldn't compete for Evie, for any-one. This victory meant Evie had found her personal value. He envied her the victory. She'd found a way to free herself while he was still chained by his duty, by his love, to Kuban.

What would he do if it was just him? If there was only himself to consider? Here in the observatory, with the stars above him, the heavens and Evie within his reach, the decision was clear. He would walk away from all of it for her, for this. This could be the sum of his world. His heart pounded with a clarity he'd never experienced as Evie pressed her lips to his and he gave himself a moment to be swept away by the kiss, by its promise.

Evie smoothed his hair and held his face in her hands, a soft smile on her face. 'Don't worry, Dimi-tri,' she said simply. 'Tell me what's on your mind.'

'I am glad you've given up Andrew. But I hope you haven't merely replaced him with me. I can give you nothing and...' He nearly choked over the last. 'And

I wish I could.' His hands tightened at her waist. 'I am a prince with worldly wealth and I can give you nothing. It is starting to kill me.' He shook his head. 'I was not prepared for this.' But that wasn't quite true. He had prepared for this moment all his life—the moment when love might find him and he would fight it. Only he wasn't prepared enough because he knew he was failing. He didn't want to resist. He wanted to give in to Evie Milham and all she offered even at an extraordinary price, a price that would not be paid by him alone, but by Evie, by his sister, by his family. 'I'd not thought of myself as a selfish man until now, Evie.' He felt rocked with emotions, but Evie was calm in the wake of his storm.

'The book my father finished is for her, you know. It's his version of a love song.' Her words were in earnest and their solemnity touched him, helped him. A love song. What a perfectly poignant way to think of the sacrifice he would make for Anna-Maria. It would be his love song to her. Just like that, Evie had restored his resolve. He was not sacrificing for Anna-Maria, he was performing an act of love. In letting him go, Evie was performing an act of love too. He would think of that in the years to come. He would think of this moment too. He would remember how Evie looked, how her voice had been sincere. How she'd felt in his arms, a warm autumn flame offering comfort without realising it. Perhaps that was the best kind of comfort—unsolicited, unedited, entirely honest.

In one accord, they moved down the stairs, silently into the night. They didn't dare stay too long without her parents worrying. But it had been enough to be alone with her, to hold her, to clarify his thoughts. In the dark, he reached for her hand, wanting to touch her as long as he could.

'Tell me about your sister.' Her voice was soft in response as if she'd known the direction of his thoughts and what he needed to say out loud. 'You love her very much.' Dimitri felt himself smile. 'She must be a wonderful person if her name makes you smile.'

'She is wonderful. She's been my life since I was twelve. My mother should never have tried to have another child. The doctors had warned her against a pregnancy at her age, especially since my older brother and I hadn't been easy. But in Kuban, it is an honour to give the country noble, handsome sons and she wanted to do her duty. My father loved her, he could deny her nothing. I was there when Anna-Maria was born. The birth had gone poorly from the start and everyone knew she wouldn't last. A nurse shoved the baby into my arms and I just stood there, staring at my poor mother fading away.' His throat tightened. He did not like this memory, but it was the last one he had and he would not give it up for the world. Evie's thumb moved in soothing circles around his hand. 'My mother looked at me one last time. There were no words but I knew what she wanted. I looked down into the face of my new little sister and I knew that it wasn't just what my mother wanted, but what Anna-Maria needed. A protector.'

'She had your father,' Evie put in, perhaps trying to imply he needn't have taken so much on himself.

Dimitri shook his head. 'Grief broke him. He was not the same father after that and in the years that followed, he wanted little to do with the baby girl who had stolen his wife. Anna-Maria was a double disappointment to him. His beloved wife had died for a daughter. Sons are everything in Kuban.' He drew a deep breath. 'Anna-Maria was mine, always. Even now, the relationship she has with my father is tenuous.' Beautiful, wild Anna-Maria was constantly testing their father's patience. It had been a difficult decision to leave her for this last journey but she'd assured him she'd be fine. She was nearly eighteen, hardly a child, and she'd known how much he needed this.

'I'm sorry,' Evie breathed, and in those words he heard more than bland empathy. She was sorry for a twelve-year-old boy who'd lost his mother and his father that day, for a boy who'd taken on more than what was fair to ask, who continued to take on unfair burdens in exchange for his own freedom. Evie understood him. 'Thank you for telling me.'

'Now you know,' Dimitri said, wanting to be sure she'd heard the warning in the tale, the reminder as to why he could offer her nothing that would last no matter how much he might want to.

They'd reached the edge of the gardens where the lights of the house took over. In a few more steps they'd be out of the darkness. Evie turned and wrapped her arms about his neck. 'Yes, now I know.' Her tongue flicked across her lips, her eyes dropping to his mouth. 'Dimitri, I would never ask for more than you could give. I would never do anything to diminish you, to make you less than you are. I understand what we can have.'

'And what is that?' He was almost afraid to ask, but more afraid to never have the answer.

'Everything. We can have everything. For a short time. And it will be better than having nothing for ever.'

He wasn't going to resist. This temptation was too much. The only question that remained was, when?

Chapter Eighteen

Her mother was waiting for her when Evie returned, in her room none the less, which never boded well. She sat on the edge of Evie's bed and rose when she entered, beginning to pace. Her mother was worked up about something. 'Evie dear, I thought we could talk before bed.' That went without saying. Evie hadn't missed the wringing of hands in her mother's lap. Ever since she was a little girl, her mother had always come to her room when there was a serious matter to discuss.

Tonight, though, Evie didn't want to talk. She wanted to think. Dinner seemed a lifetime ago—the observatory and all that had transpired in that short period embodied the present. In that short span everything had changed. Her choices, her direction had become clear. She had made her decisions. 'I'm a little tired.' Evie feigned a yawn. Perhaps her mother could be put off. 'We can discuss the party over breakfast tomorrow.' Hopefully, the party was all her mother had on her mind. Surely, she and Dimitri hadn't been gone long enough on their walk to raise any suspicions?

'I don't want to talk about the party.' Her mother gestured to the pink-striped bench at Evie's vanity. 'Sit down. I want to talk about the Prince. And you.' Hopes quashed. There was an edge of panic in her mother's voice and, this time, Evie couldn't quite discount her mother's worry as manufactured. Her mother was rather gifted at making mountains out of proverbial mole hills. Evie couldn't say that was the case tonight.

It was too bad her mother had chosen this evening to be intuitive. She should have remembered her mother's intuition was nearly infallible, even if it was couched in flighty worries that were often overblown. Evie sat. She had no choice really. She should have seen it coming. It had been like this when Diana and her earl had been courting.

Her mother pulled out the hair pins from Evie's *coiffure* to keep her nervous hands busy. Evie could never remember her mother sitting still for long. Her mother picked up the hairbrush, pulling it through her hair in long, gentle strokes. 'You have such beautiful hair, Evie. Maybe the prettiest hair of all my girls.' Evie let her prevaricate. It felt nice to have her mother brush her hair, it made her feel young, before the world had become complicated.

'The Prince has eyes for you, I think.' Her mother's eyes met hers in the mirror. 'He couldn't stop looking at you tonight. Of course, you looked very lovely. Your gown matched your hair perfectly. I thought, my daughter is Demeter.' She smiled and spread Evie's hair out along her shoulders. 'You looked like the goddess of the harvest. It was easy to see why the Prince was so taken with you.' She paused here to pick up the brush again. 'And you? Are you taken with the Prince? He's a very handsome, well-mannered man.' What to say to that? She was more than taken with him. 'Taken' seemed an inadequate word.

'I think he's a man who is easy to like wherever he goes.' Evie strove for a diplomatic answer.

'Wherever he goes. Quite right. We are lucky to know him for a short time. He's well travelled, a very worldly man. I can't imagine Little Westbury could hold his attention for long.' Despite her tendency to exaggerate situations, her mother had a shrewd underbelly when it came to husbands and wives. She'd known just how to help Diana with her earl and tonight Evie heard all of her mother's messages in the simple words: that she couldn't expect to hold the Prince's attention. Well, Evie had already beaten her to that conclusion. Moreover, she didn't want to hold that attention, not when it meant ruining him. She'd meant it tonight when she'd said she would never seek to diminish him. Trapping Dimitri into a life here in Little Westbury *would* diminish him. The honourable man she knew, the brave man she knew, would be destroyed if he couldn't return home and fulfil his duties.

'Andrew asked your father for permission to call on you formally tonight.' There was cheerful wariness in her mother's voice as if her mother didn't quite believe her dismissal of the Prince's interest as generic attention. 'Isn't that wonderful?' She smiled. 'Maybe Andrew is worried the Prince is stealing a march on him. I say it's about time Andrew realised what a catch you are.'

Evie carefully schooled her features. 'What did Father say?' This would have been wonderful news three months ago, perhaps even three weeks ago. Now, it was merely uncomfortable. Her infatuation with Andrew seemed a girlish flight of fancy against the backdrop of what she shared with Dimitri, of what she faced with Dimitri. That girl would have leapt at the merest attention from Andrew. And sold herself short in the process, she saw that now. She could not imagine having the discussions with him that she had with Dimitri, of doing the things with him she'd done with Dimitri.

'Your father says it is for you to decide.' Her mother watched her expectantly, waiting for her answer. 'Isn't it what you want?'

'I'm not so sure it *is* what I want,' Evie replied coolly, trying to give nothing alarming away. She didn't think she *looked* different. Perhaps there was no way to tell what she'd been up to with Dimitri.

Her mother's eyes sharpened. 'Is that because of the Prince? Is he what you think you want?' Evie braced herself. The conversation had circled back to what her mother had really wanted to discuss.

'I know you girls think I'm a worrier and maybe I am. But, I'm not stupid, Evie. I know when a man wants a woman. I noticed how long you were gone to look at the stars.' She fluttered a hand. 'I'm not even sure I want to think about why you were so late tonight. Perhaps it's best not to. That way I don't have to ask your father to take action.'

She placed her hands on Evie's shoulders. 'Evie, you might think you are infatuated with the Prince, maybe you might even fancy yourself in love with him. But think about what it means, if it means anything. If he loves you too, where does this lead?

Would you really want to marry the Prince? You wouldn't expect him to stay here. He can't possibly stay. It would mean leaving your home, your family, likely never seeing us again, your sisters, your nieces and nephews to come, living in a place where you don't even speak the language. It would mean giving up everything for him. Evie, I want you to understand that marriage is not all love and romance. It is the work of a lifetime and that work is more easily done when there are commonalities to build on. Hot kisses and passion don't last. Your father is occasionally annoyed with Andrew, but he's one of us, Andrew knows this place...'

Evie didn't listen to the rest of the argument. It wasn't unlike the arguments she'd once made with herself. But those arguments had already been beaten. She simply didn't want him, didn't think he'd suit her after all. Her mother would be rather shocked to know that Evie took hope from her warning about all that needed considering. In that warning was the answer. Dimitri couldn't stay. But she could go. If he took her to Kuban with him, he could return, fulfil his duty to his sister and not have to sacrifice his personal happiness.

Her mother hugged her one last time. 'All I'm saying, Evie, is that when the time comes for a decision, I want you to be sure what you feel is real.'

'Is it real?' The man turned the spearhead over in his hand, squinting in the dim light of the tavern's back room. Andrew didn't particularly care for the unsavoury meeting places that came with selling to the black market.

'Absolutely,' Andrew replied with confidence. Dimitri could at least be relied upon for that. 'It's a Roman spearhead, circa AD43.' He'd rather enjoyed carrying it around in his pocket last night. knowing that he would encounter Dimitri. Dimitri had been none the wiser. The Prince had sat there, ogling Evie and persuading her to plan the party, unaware that a few of his precious spearheads were on their way to new owners, men who had private collections of military hardware throughout the ages and who were willing to pay good money to add to those collections.

Maybe it was petty revenge, but Andrew was heartily sick of the Prince these days, especially since the Prince was stealing Evie. He did wonder how present tense the stealing was. Perhaps Dimitri had already stolen her. Evie was looking 'lush' these days. She seemed less mousy, her figure more bountiful, her hair vibrant instead of glaring. It wasn't that he wanted her, he still didn't feel she had any potential for him as a bride, but he absolutely despised the idea of losing Evie Milham, a nobody, to Dimitri. And, he needed her to keep drawing for him, to see things his way when it came to the future of the site.

He was getting impatient. His client was taking for ever to decide. Andrew reached for the spearheads. 'If you don't want them, I have other buyers.'

The man glared. 'I didn't say I didn't want them. All right. How much? They had better be for real or I'll come after you and cut you off at the knees.'

The thief was real. Dimitri blew out a breath and surveyed the case containing the spearheads. There was good news and bad news. Bad news: the thief had struck again. Five spearheads were gone. Good news: the spearheads were fake. But he would have preferred to have been wrong, would have preferred his trap remain unsprung. Now he had to consider who among them might be willing to steal from him and he didn't like the relatively short list of possibilities.

Dimitri strode towards his pavilion. A few of his crew called to him to join them for dinner, but he was not fit for company tonight. He'd be better off eating alone. This was not how he'd wanted to end his day. Taking assessment of the theft also meant he'd missed Evie. She was gone already and he hadn't been able to speak with her. He would write a few long-overdue letters and then return to work at the site if he was restless. There was always something to be done. He would stay busy and hopefully put this black mood behind him. No good could come of it. Dimitri pulled back the entrance flap and stepped inside, giving his eyes a moment to adjust to the darker interior.

He blinked. Once. Twice. The cares of his world started to slip away as he realized what lay before him. There was champagne, caviar and cold smoked salmon on the low table before his divan, but that was not what had him blinking. Evie was on the divan, dressed in his robe, her long chestnut hair falling over her shoulder in a thick silken skein, her body artfully arranged on the furniture, a sensual Botticelli.

'What is all this?' He could guess. He could hope. Something finally was going right today.

She rose and offered him a flute of champagne. 'Welcome to your seduction, Dimitri Petrovich.' Ah. Now he knew the answer to last night's burning question.

His mouth was dry with surprise, overwhelming want left him nearly speechless. The robe wasn't belted. His arid mouth was a desert now. Evie took a step forward, her eyes on him, her gaze confident. She licked her lips and gave a shrug, letting the robe slip down one shoulder, tantalising in its reveal of bare skin. 'When is now, Dimitri.'

Yes, he thought. When is now. He wanted her, wanted to bury himself in her until he was lost, until his cares were no more. The noble soul in him wanted to protest one last time, but the best he could do was 'Evie, are you sure?'

Her hands cupped his face, hushing him with the brush of her mouth over his lips. 'We settled this last night. I don't need promises, Dimitri, I don't need a commitment.' She kissed his throat. 'I don't need any of that. I just need you for however long that can be.'

He shouldn't allow it. She was offering him *carte blanche*. It was a decadent offer; an offer no sane man would turn down. 'Evie, a gentleman would never—'

Her interruption was swift, a hard, silencing kiss. Her hands steadied his face as she drew back, her voice a fierce, private whisper for him alone. 'Then don't be a gentleman. Don't be a prince. Just be a man. My man.' It was all he really wanted to be in those minutes—just hers—and he could feel logic slipping away, replaced by something headier, stronger and undeniable where doing what he wanted made sense.

'I am going to lose this argument, aren't I?' He could hear the desire in his voice, feel the beginnings of a smile on his lips.

'Yes, absolutely.' Evie gave his neckcloth a tug to

make it clear. 'If you're lucky, you'll lose more than that.' Yes, he could see that, starting with his clothes and quite possibly ending with his mind.

Chapter Nineteen

She was out of her mind and it felt wonderful! For her, for him. He was well aware she was undressing her first man. Her pupils were wide with desire, her jaw set to stubborn. She wanted this, she wasn't going to give herself an inch, not a single chance to back down from her choice. And he wasn't either. He was enjoying this, enjoying *her* far too much now that the seduction was underway. How long had it been since he'd been a woman's first anything? How long had it been since he'd let sex be making love? Had he ever allowed it to be that? Today it would be and the consequences be damned.

He held still, letting her fingers work the knot of his red workman's neckcloth; he let her tug the shirttails out of the waistband of his trousers. He felt her hands falter, unsure what came next, unsure how to execute it. Dimitri did not let her hesitate, did not give her an excuse to stop. They would both be disappointed if she did. 'Allow me.' He grabbed his shirt by the hem and pulled it over his head in one swift movement, gratified when Evie inhaled sharply.

'You've seen my chest before.' Dimitri gave a low laugh.

'I think I could see your chest a thousand times and still be amazed.' Evie's honesty made him rock hard. He knew she meant it. Discovering her beauty seemed an endless, infinite exploration for him. There was always more to see, more that caught his eye. 'I had no idea a man could be so beautifully made.'

'There's more to do than look, Evie.' He raised her hand and placed it on his chest, his eyes never leaving hers. She had touched him before, but never like this. There'd been pleasure given beneath his robe, but there'd been no time for exploration, for revelling, only pleasure. Today there would be time for both.

'Touch me, Evie.' That's when he knew: Evie was an instinctive master of the seduction game. In the short time it had taken to remove only some of his clothing, she'd managed to make him a partner in this seduction. He'd become complicit in the very thing he'd resisted for so long.

She took the invitation, almost reverently, tracing a circle around one flat nipple, a coy smile on her lips. 'You're like an atlas, all planes and ridges.' Her voice was quiet, her hand starting to move. His body was taut, savouring her touch, his mind already racing ahead to what else she might touch. 'I think you might be a map of Kuban itself. This is your famous river that gives the country its name.' Her finger drew a line down the centre of his chest, stopping at the ridges of his abdomen. 'Perhaps these are the Caucasus, the mountain ridges of your kingdom.' She splayed her hand over the flat of his stomach. 'The Steppes.'

'Travel south. There is more,' Dimitri murmured,

warming to her game. His hands lingered at the waist of his trousers. 'My "country", as you put it, is bigger than that.'

Evie cast him a dramatically sly look, eyes dancing. 'Bigger than this?' She might be untried, but she was *not* timid, not with him, and it pleased him inordinately when she took the initiative and flicked open the flies of his trousers, running a hand inside, tracing his length through his smalls. 'Very disappointing.' She sighed. 'I thought for sure you were a man who forwent smalls.' She shook her head in mock disapproval and issued the most provocative command he'd experienced to date. 'Take off everything.'

Dimitri cocked a brow. 'You're a greedy miss.' But he complied.

Boots, trousers *and* smalls fell to the ground, but Evie spared no glance for them. Her eyes were rooted on the sight before her—naked man in his most natural state. There was no robe, no rush, no hurried pleasure to get in the way of her enjoyment. It was as if his entire body was designed to draw her eye to the centre of him, the very core of his masculinity. The lean taper of his waist, the sculpted ridges of his muscles all led to his proudly jutting manhood, strong and large and…promising, as she knew it would be. It was perhaps one of the most primal sights she'd ever seen.

'Do you like what you see?' Dimitri's voice was a low, seductive prompt.

'I do.' Her own voice was little more than a reverent whisper. 'It's beautiful.' No wonder mamas cautioned their daughters to keep their eyes on a gentleman's face. If daughters knew what lay beneath a gentleman's clothes, London parties might indeed be quite different. They'd certainly be less boring.

'Evie?' The word was softer now, not a command but a question. She heard the unspoken question: Why him? Why now when there were limits on what they could be together?

'Signs of life,' Evie whispered. 'I feel more alive with you right now than I ever have before.' *And might ever feel again.* It was both a joy and a fear to feel this way.

Dimitri's forehead came down to rest against hers. 'That might be up for debate. I think you could very well be the death of me, Evie Milham.' They stood that way for long moments, foreheads touching, her hand about his shaft, simply together. Evie thought the moments were quite possibly the most peaceful moments of her life, their serenity transcending the usual calm. She would have been content to stand there for hours. But Dimitri had other ideas. His voice whispered low at her ear. 'Now, it's your turn. I want to see you. Take off everything.'

Evie stepped back from him, giving his gaze full access to her, her own gaze locked on him, both of them realising the solemnity of the occasion, the beauty of a woman disrobing for her man for the first time. She gave the robe a shrug, sending it down her body in a slide of silk. This had stopped being about discovering what men and women did together and had become discovering what Evie and Dimitri could do together, what they wanted together. She wanted to be naked with him. She did not worry if she was pretty enough, well made enough to match such a perfect man. She was. The look in Dimitri's eyes as the robe slipped down her body held her answer.

'I was not wrong when I thought you were a Botticelli goddess.' She felt his eyes sweep over her. His gaze lingered on her lips, her breasts, her belly, and lower still to the russet valley between her legs. Her own heat rose in response to his gaze, a tingling warmth spiralled outward from her core. 'It is such a difficult decision,' Dimitri murmured, 'to choose between stepping forward and touching you with my hands, or touching you with only my eyes.'

It was not a difficult decision for her. Evie knew precisely what she wanted. She stepped towards him, arms encircling his neck. 'Touch me with your hands, Dimitri, with your mouth.'

A small grin settled on his lips. 'As you wish.'

Dimitri Petrovich knew how to make a girl burn. It started slowly enough with a kiss at her collarbone, another at the notch of her neck, but the kisses didn't stop there. It might have been the hard kiss on the mouth that undid her, she did so love those, or it might have been the warmth of his hand sliding up her rib cage to cup her bare breasts, his thumbs running over her nipples in tantalising strokes. It wasn't important that she decide. She only knew she was grateful for the support of his body since her own bones were no longer interested in doing the job.

'We're going to need a bed.' His voice was gruff with his own desire. 'There are other ways I want to kiss you, other places.' She knew those other places. They were already weeping in memory and in anticipation of having that memory renewed.

She managed a coy whisper. 'I once wondered

what sort of man slept in the decadent bed beyond the curtains.'

'Come find out. Come to bed with me, Evie,' he murmured against her ear.

Part of her wished he'd carry her and part of her understood he couldn't. This walk to the bed made it her choice to be there, her choice to lie among the silken pillows. He came down beside her, stretching out the length of his body.

He moved over her, his mouth and hands making one of his slow trails down her body, kissing, licking, sucking until a moan escaped her and she arched up, her body recognising he had no intentions of stopping. What had once been the culmination of their pleasure would now merely be foreplay to something grander.

He moved to her navel, feathering it with a kiss before his mouth kissed the nest of her, the kiss a supplicant's offering to the altar of her feminine core. Evie shifted beneath him, giving him access, knowing what came next. Only today, it didn't come.

He came up over her instead, his eyes a glittering obsidian. 'I have it on good authority passion is to be shared. Today, we'll take our pleasure together.' He was entirely the Cossack warrior as he looked down at her, wild and untamed, granite hard, his arms braced at her head, muscles flexing as he lifted above her. It was not his mouth but his manhood at her entrance, pulsing and hard.

She arched up again, inviting, assuring him of entrance, of reception. This was what she wanted. From the feel of it, he wanted this too. He pushed forward, big and thick and strong, she remembered all too well how very large he'd been in her hand. But his progress was steady and her body was sure where her mind doubted. Her body shifted, adjusted, accommodated, granting entrance inch by inch until there was no more sting of pain, no more discomfort and he was well seated in her. A victorious smile took her face. She had all of him.

'That is just the beginning, Evie,' he whispered, his body starting to move; rocking slowly, his shaft retreating and returning only infinitesimally at first, each thrust took him out further from her core, only to come into her harder upon his return. Not unlike the tide, she thought somewhere in the recesses of her mind where cognition still lived, nearly extinct.

He was indeed a tide, a crashing, erotic tide that came to her hidden shores, withdrawing to only crash again and she welcomed each crash, each wave of his advance breaking against her shore, each wave larger than the last, pushing them towards some unseen destination with each sweep. There would be exquisite pleasure at the end, she knew this now, but this pleasure was far more intense, far more encompassing than the little pleasure of his mouth that had preceded it. Her hips drove into his, her body eager to claim that pleasure, unsure how much more she could withstand. They had reached pleasure's limits and then exceeded them.

Above her, Dimitri's muscles strained with the effort. He gave a guttural utterance, part-agony, part-ecstasy. She cried out, unable to hold back. They were pushing boundaries now, her legs wrapped about him, holding on to him, the only anchor she had. He thrust once more, hard and complete and deep, and they broke, together; her cries, his groans mingled with the half-choked sobs of disbelief and wonder that they'd been to these far shores and they had survived. What came next didn't matter.

Dimitri Petrovich was the most beautiful man alive, even when he was asleep. She didn't envy him his sleep. She was the lucky one. She got an unadulterated, unlimited look at him—*her lover.* Evie stared unabashedly, memorising every angle of his face from the straight plane of his regal nose to the sharp slant of his cheekbones. She wanted to hold these moments in her mind. Perhaps later, she would draw them, capture this man on paper. She wanted to capture the essence of him. He was more than the sum of his handsome features. Did others see that when they looked at him or did they see only the Prince? A man capable of carrying the burdens of many on those broad shoulders. Did anyone see just the man? There was a furrow between his eyes even when he slept that proved he was human after all.

Out of reflex, she reached a finger to smooth it away. Whatever had been bothering him when he'd entered the pavilion was bothering him still. She would erase those cares for him if she could, if she knew. What other burdens did he carry? She wanted to know. She wanted to know it all. In the wake of the physical intimacy between them another craving for another kind of intimacy had sprung up. She wanted to know *him:* the little things like his birthday, his favourite colour, his favourite drink, and the big things too. He'd shared about his baby sister, about how much his family meant to him. She wanted more of that. She would carry his burdens with him.

Dimitri stirred beside her, waking up slowly. He smiled at the sight of her. 'Have I slept for long?' He reached for her, tucking her close against him, and she went willingly into this new, easy physicality of being close to him.

'Not long.' She pushed his hair back away from his face.

'Are you all right, Evie? You look, ah, what is the word? Pensive?' He smiled sleepily and her stomach flipped with longing. If she wasn't careful, he would break her heart without meaning to. She had her precautions in place, she'd been through all the warnings to self before she'd decided to leap, but now that she'd leapt, those precautions were flimsy barricades against a look, a touch, the memory of his lips on her and the pleasure that followed.

'I am wondering what causes you to frown when you sleep.' She traced the line between his brows with the tip of her finger.

'Was I frowning? I'm sorry.' He sighed. She had the impression he was debating what to say next, what to tell her. 'I'm going to tell you something, but you can't tell anyone, not even your family.'

Evie lifted up on one arm, hair falling over one shoulder. Now she was worried. 'This sounds serious?'

'It might be. I think there's a thief at the site. A few more items have gone missing since the comb and the hair clips.'

This was horrible news. 'Who?' Evie sputtered.

Dimitri chuckled. 'If I knew, I wouldn't be worried. I have a plan, though, and I am certain the thief will be brought to justice before long. I just wanted you to know. You should be aware of any strange behaviour in cataloguing, of anyone who might approach you with a request to look at the collection, and perhaps you might encourage everyone to be extra-vigilant about locking things up at night.'

'You think it's someone here, then?'

Dimitri sighed. 'I suppose it's possible there are two different thieves. The spearheads went missing right after the lords' visit. Perhaps someone took them on a lark as a souvenir. But the hair clips and comb were missing long before then. If I had to guess, I would say it's someone here.'

Evie's heart sank. That meant it was an Englishman, a workman hired in good faith by Dimitri in an attempt to bring labour to the area. It was a cruel way to repay his kindness. 'I'm sorry.' She smoothed back his hair, wishing she could smooth away his cares just as easily.

'We'll catch him, but, Evie, you must say nothing or he might become alert to us and that would ruin the plan,' Dimitri cautioned.

Evie snuggled down next to him. 'Thank you for telling me. You can tell me anything. You don't have to be the Prince with me, you know.'

'What's that supposed to mean?' His arm tightened around her, holding her close. She loved the possessiveness of that gesture, of knowing that she was all his.

'That you take too much on yourself,' she murmured.

She let herself doze a while after that, savouring the warmth of Dimitri's body until she could no longer ignore that lateness. Shadows were falling outside, the summer dusk rapidly speeding towards true dark.

'I'll take you home.' Dimitri stirred, reading her thoughts. He sat up and rolled out of bed. He padded out of the room, giving her a glorious view of his backside in consolation, and came back with his clothes. He pulled on his trousers and flashed her a smile. 'It's getting late. Your parents will worry. We need to get you home.'

There was some irony in knowing that they had to be more careful than ever now that the act was done. She would not trap him into an impossible situation that would rob both of them of their happiness. And yet she couldn't help but feel she was already home, that home might always be wherever Dimitri was.

Chapter Twenty

He could tell her anything? The invitation was like a knife in the heart as he drove Evie home, her body close to his on the narrow bench of the gig as the sun slowly set. He couldn't possibly take her up on that generously made offer. When had anyone ever asked to share his burdens? Or seen that he had burdens to share? But Evie had. She'd always seen beyond the Prince to the man beneath, even that first day in the street when May had pressed the invitation on him.

Evie deserved so much more than he could give her. She deserved to be swept off her feet, deserved to be loved for who she was, deserved to live a happy life in the comfort of Little Westbury. She deserved the perfect happy-ever-after with a perfect man. What she'd got was him. How could he tell her that part of returning home to Kuban included marriage to a woman he'd never met? But how could he keep it from her now? Originally, that piece of his life hadn't mattered. He'd told her from the start he had to leave. He'd even told her about his sister. The other reasons were irrelevant. They didn't change anything, so why share them? But now he'd taken Evie to bed and that act had changed everything. It had changed *him*.

He had made *love* today for the first time and it had rendered him speechless. Not just sex, but love, earth-shattering, mind-blowing love that left him exhausted and sated, and with a clarity that had him upending the world as he knew it. In the clarity of post-coital release, he'd known without question what he wanted just as he had that night in the conservatory. He wanted Evie. Evie had been beautiful in her passion, her body arching, her hair falling, her little moans, her sobs of surprise as pleasure caught her. She'd given him all of herself, body and soul.

When he'd awakened and seen her beside him, a wave of contentment had rolled through him, fierce and primal. What would she say to these thoughts if he spoke them out loud? What would she say if he told her he'd give it all up, that he'd find another way to save his sister? For the first time in his life, he was a coward. He was afraid to find out.

So here they were, driving to Evie's house in absolute silence while he debated what to say and came up empty. The silence wasn't entirely uncomfortable, no silence with Evie ever would be. It was one of her many gifts. A person could be silent in her presence and not feel awkward. Maybe they would have driven in silence anyway. Her own thoughts had to be as far flung as his and there was much about the evening to appreciate without talking; the last of the summer light was fading, the sky was a lovely shade of purples and blues, stars piercing the twilight while crickets began to chirp.

He opened his mouth, looking for a way to begin,

but he'd waited too long. Now that he had something to say, it had to keep. They were nearly at Evie's house and someone was there. A carriage was parked outside.

He felt Evie's hand tighten on his arm as she whispered, 'It's Andrew.'

He felt as pale as Evie looked. 'It seems we're to have a welcoming committee.'

'I didn't plan this. He's not supposed to be here,' Evie said as he came around to help her down.

'Evie, I won't let anything happen to you.' Dimitri reminded himself Andrew knew nothing. What could he know? This drama was irrational. But should it become necessary, he would do whatever had to be done. Evie would not be shamed.

'No, stop, Dimitri.' She pressed a finger to his lips. 'Do not make promises. I understood exactly what I was doing and what the risks were when I stepped inside your pavilion today. You do not need to atone for any of my decisions.'

Did she not understand the seriousness of this? Her very answer was an affront to his honour. They might have agreed in the heat of the moment not to create expectations. But if *others* had expectations, those would have to be met, especially if those expectations cast aspersions on either of their characters.

Evie gave him a stubborn stare. 'I mean it, Dimitri. No gallantry is required. We'll start with "we were working late" and take it from there. Agreed?' Perhaps he hadn't been too far from the truth when he'd said she'd be the death of him.

They found her parents and Andrew on the veranda, enjoying tea and biscuits and a tray of fresh fruit. Apparently there'd been seed cakes from the looks of the crumbs. Sir Hollis must have relented. 'There might have been some left for you if you'd been earlier.' Andrew's tone was sharp, his eyes hard blue stones. He glared at Dimitri. 'Early bird gets the worm and all that, old chap.'

'We were working late.' Evie took a seat on a wicker sofa, smoothing her skirts under her, her own tone a little too bright. Would anyone notice? Was he being too critical? 'A particularly fine pair of artefacts has gone missing and I wanted to find them.'

'And did you?' Andrew asked, his gaze intent on Evie. Dimitri began to worry. Now that he looked at her, perhaps someone *could* tell what she'd been up to. Her lips were pink and slightly puffed, her face was soft, her eyes had a certain indefinable quality to them, the way a woman's face looks after she's been well loved. Perhaps in the dusk she could fool her parents. He doubted she'd fool Andrew. The only hope they had was if Andrew fooled himself. He'd been so adamant in the past that Evie Milham was of no interest, perhaps he'd find it hard to believe anyone else would feel differently.

'Where did you look?' Dimitri didn't care for the edge in Andrew's voice. He had to get Andrew out of here before things took a turn for the worse. 'Did you look in Dimitri's pavilion?'

'No, we did not.' Evie sighed. 'I am hoping they show up tomorrow.'

'Speaking of tomorrow,' Dimitri interrupted swiftly, 'it's late and there's a lot to do with the site and the gala. Andrew, you and I should take our leave.'

They managed a civil getaway, each of them in

their own carriages, and Dimitri drew a sigh of relief when Evie's house was behind them. But it wasn't over. Andrew signalled they should pull off to the side of the road and Dimitri steeled himself. Better to settle it between the two of them privately than in front of Evie and her parents.

Andrew jumped down and met him between the carriages, his temper evident even at a distance. 'You couldn't keep it in your trousers, could you?' Andrew shoved him hard, but Dimitri was braced for it. 'I knew something was going on when I saw the two of you at breakfast! I should have said something then.' Andrew shoved at him again. This time Dimitri grabbed his arm.

'You forget yourself,' he warned.

'Oh, right,' Andrew sneered. 'You're a prince of the royal house of Kuban and can't be touched.'

'No,' Dimitri countered, letting go of Andrew's arm with force. 'Because I'm better in a fight than you are. You remember Crete?'

'I remember Crete.' Andrew spat, beginning to circle, fists up, forcing Dimitri to do the same. 'I remember that I had your back that night.'

This was going to come to violence. Andrew was mad and Andrew was at his least logical when he was angry. 'I had your back,' he repeated, 'which is a sight more than I can say for you these days. "Working late"? I doubt it. "Looking for lost artefacts"? Where? In your trousers, in that damn bed of yours?'

'Be careful of your accusations,' Dimitri warned, his own temper straining at its leash. 'I will not tolerate Evie being slandered.' A fist in Andrew's face would feel good right now and the bastard had just about earned it.

'Not even when it's true? Do you think I can't tell when a woman's been bedded? What were you thinking? That we're stupid country folk because we don't have a kingdom waiting for us? That you can come here and do whatever you like?'

'Why do you care at all?' All this righteous anger was more than a bit suspicious, especially when it was aimed at a woman Andrew had sworn he had no interest in.

'Because you're *here*! Because this is *my* town.' Of course. He should have known. Jealousy. It was always about Andrew. Andrew was the centre of his own universe. '*I* invite you into my village and in the matter of a month, *you* manage to turn our most innocent spinster into a wanton whore.'

That earned it. The words had barely left Andrew's mouth before Dimitri's fist connected with his jaw. Andrew's head snapped back, he reeled back hard against the tailgate of the curricle, grasping at it for balance, his other hand clutching his face. 'What the hell was that for?'

'No one calls Evie Milham a whore. Our discussion is over.' Dimitri turned and sprang up into his carriage. If he stayed, he'd give Andrew worse than a sore jaw. Never mind that Andrew had spoken the truth, even if he disagreed with some of Andrew's adjectives. Evie was no more a spinster than she was a loose woman. But that didn't change the fact that he'd made a royal mess out of everything. He'd punched his so-called friend, had a thief on his hands just weeks before the important gala, he'd bedded a virgin and managed to do the one thing his father had warned him never to do: he'd fallen in love.

That disaster haunted him long after he had left Evie and returned to his pavilion, long after he lay on his empty bed staring up at the ceiling of that pavilion, trying not to think about Evie in this same bed that still smelled of her. His father had spent years warning him about the ills of love, how it could ruin a man. He'd seen the truth of it. His father was a good man, had raised him well, but his father had become a shadow of his former self. He was an ember, not a flame after his wife had passed. Love could indeed make a strong man weak. But his father had never told him love could also make a man powerful, brave enough to overcome impossible obstacles, or at least brave enough to try.

He ran through options in his mind. What if he took Evie back to Kuban? It would solve the returning issue. He'd be back before he turned thirty as required and perhaps some way could be found to spare his sister the marriage with the sultan's son. Even so, what would that do to Evie? To leave Little Westbury?

What a disaster that would be.

Wedding him would be like opening Pandora's box—there would be all nature of nastiness inside. Dimitri tucked his hands behind his head. Had Evie even thought of what marriage to a prince would require? But he had and it would be an unmitigated catastrophe. Perhaps this was why the Kubanian court had such strict laws about marriage requirements. Only other royalty could truly understand the burdens and duties that came with their position.

A commoner would be overwhelmed, and an outsider? 'Overwhelmed' didn't begin to cover it. If the culture shock and the language weren't enough to finish off a foreign wife, the court politics would be. The court would not be a friendly place for an unwelcome foreigner who had disrupted years of plans and he would not always be there to shield Evie from the worst of it.

There would be things she loved, though, things he would love showing her. The mountain trails full of wildflowers in the spring, the crystal rivers full of pure, cold glacier water, his house in the country where he'd grown up, where he'd played as child in the tall grasses of the fields. He could imagine too well his own sons running in those same fields. In that regard, he and Evie weren't all that dissimilar. Family was important to them both. Evie would be a good mother. She would make a good home, where children would be encouraged to be themselves. She would be kind and patient.

He had to stop his thoughts right there. Returning to Kuban would be a compromise of the worst sort , one that would leave both of them unhappy—Evie because she wouldn't fit in no matter how hard she tried. It would be like her debut in London, only worse. For him, he'd be tied to Kuban, tied to his royal position. The distaste that left him with was insightful and assuring. He wasn't considering giving up Kuban for Evie alone, but for himself, a reminder that this wasn't the first time he'd thought these things, toyed with these ideas. It was merely the first time thoughts of Evie had been tied to those mad schemes.

He got out of bed. Bed would only make it worse

tonight. She was there in the sheets with him. He wished there was someone to talk to. In Kuban, he'd have talked with his friends but they were a thousand miles away and he'd punched the one so-called friend he had here in the face. Andrew wouldn't be a willing conversationalist just now.

Dimitri reached for the decanter of vodka and poured a glass, sitting down hard on the divan. Did he dare think about it? He knew the path these thoughts led down—the path towards the most treacherous thought: what if he walked away from it all? What if there was a way to save his sister and decide for himself the course of his life? If all that were possible, would he do it? Would he give up being a prince? Would he give up Kuban?

Kuban was a 'thing', but to give up one's kingdom was never a small consideration. It was the kind of decision one could not step back from and re-do. There would only be going forward. It was a hypothetical game, only. For him, there was no way to do it without forcing his sister to take his place on the marriage altar. Even if he could find a way out, it was a difficult decision. What if he traded the life he knew for the life he thought he wanted, only to be disappointed?

It was a dangerous game to play. But tonight the words 'what if' kept whispering in his head, insistent and haunting. What the hell was he going to do? Normally, when faced with a problem, he would write out all of his options and discuss them with his friends over vodka until a solution presented itself. But his options in this case were so extreme as to be ludicrous. He couldn't imagine seriously contemplating any of them.

Perhaps if he pretended his friends were here? What would they say? He closed his eyes, trying to imagine it. Illarion, ever the dreamer, would commiserate with him as if the heartache were his own. He'd drink too much vodka and spout long lines from Russian literature about the fatal nature of love. There were no solutions there, but everyone needed a friend like Illarion to simply help one feel better.

Fierce, temperamental Nikolay would insist he marry for love, when what Nikolay really meant was that he should marry simply to spite the system. Nikolay despised the system developed in Kuban for keeping the peace. He rebelled against it at every turn and encouraged others to do so as well, even though he'd been warned several times that his actions bordered on treason.

Dimitri poured another glass. He played out in his mind how that scene would go. Nikolay would rise to his feet, pumping a fist in the air, probably voicing a few treasonous profanities before launching into a speech about how the court made whores of their royal sons by forcing these marriages, followed up by a personal plea that Dimitri break the contract and refuse Ayfer.

At which point, before Nikolay could get entirely worked up, Stepan would interject with a pointedly lazy drawl, 'And do what? Leave Kuban for ever? Turn his back on wealth and security? It is easy to speak of rebellion when it costs you nothing, Nikolay. But you are asking Dimitri to give up everything. You haven't the faintest clue what that even means.' The two would want to fight. Stepan and Nikolay had been fighting as long as Dimitri had known them and that was almost twenty years.

Ruslan would intervene, the inveterate peacemaker. He'd been the voice of reason between those two since he was ten. Dimitri could hear him taking Stepan's argument to its logical conclusion. 'It is unfortunate, but there is nothing for it. You must give up the English girl. You must honour the contract and marry Ayfer. The good of the many must always precede the good of the few. In time, you'll see it is for your own good too. Your whole life is in Kuban.'

Yulian would simply drink his vodka and glare his not-so-hidden resentment at his second cousin. Dimitri knew what Yulian would think—that he was a disgrace to the family. Yulian resented the fact that Dimitri had left for this Grand Tour of sorts throughout Europe. But Dimitri had wanted one more adventure, one more taste of freedom. Yulian believed he should have stayed and married Ayfer immediately, not waited. It was what Yulian would have done. Yulian was eager to prove himself to Kuban, eager to be a leader at court. There was some irony that the most eager among them was the one who didn't have vast plans already established for their future. Dimitri wished he was more eager to do his duty. It would make life simpler. Sometimes, Yulian's patriotic devotion shamed him.

Those were his options. Nothing new. Nothing he hadn't already thought of. Either he returned to Kuban and used his marriage to ensure peace on the border or throw it all away and stay for Evie, even knowing that he risked something larger than his family's pride, larger than his sister's future: the peace of a nation. Put that way, the choice seemed obvious. What honourable man risked all of that for a woman? Only the most self-serving scoundrel. He could not be that man. It was going to be a long, empty night.

Chapter Twenty-One

Evie couldn't stop smiling. It was making it difficult to focus on work and she needed to get these drawings done, but she'd spent more time covertly tracing her lips, tracing Dimitri's kisses on those lips, than she had drawing the latest artefact, a lovely bowl that had been found in two pieces and repaired. It would be a fabulous addition to the display she'd planned for the gala.

'You look like the cat who got the cream. What has you all smiles? Did we turn up a fabulous artefact today?' Andrew teased, startling her into nearly blotting the drawing. She hadn't even heard him approach. He took up his customary hitched-leg pose at the table.

'Is it that late already?' Surely the day wasn't over. She wasn't ready to leave, but she needed to place an order for the gala at the stationer's. Andrew could take her on the way home.

'Almost.' Andrew grinned, looking golden and well turned out in pale tan trousers and an expensively made tight-fitted blue coat of summer weight superfine. He was in a cheery mood. He cocked his head, taking in her paper. That's when she noticed it. Evie gasped.

'Andrew, what's wrong with your face? Your jaw is bruised.' He looked like he'd been in a fight. That seemed preposterous. Gentlemen didn't... Then she remembered how the evening had ended, with Dimitri driving her home and Andrew waiting there for her. Well, ostensibly he'd come to talk history with her father, but Evie suspected otherwise.

'Oh, this?' Andrew gingerly touched his jaw. 'This beauty is courtesy of the Prince, a royal shiner.' He laughed carefully as if the movement hurt. Evie winced. It probably did.

'I'll be ready to go in a minute.' Evie rose and put her things away. The drawing would have to wait. She didn't dare look for excuses to linger in the hope of seeing Dimitri, not if her suspicions were right. They'd fought over her and that couldn't mean anything good, except that Dimitri had got the better end of things. She'd seen him this morning. He'd looked tired, but he hadn't been sporting bruises. 'Perhaps you can drop me by the stationer's? I have invitations to order for the gala.'

Andrew managed another smile. 'I'll drop you anywhere you like, Evie. I am entirely at your disposal.'

Oh, what a difference a month made, Evie thought during the short drive into the village. Once upon a time not so long ago, she would have basked in the glow of Andrew's smile. Now, if it hadn't been for the chance to ride into Little Westbury and manage the invitations for Dimitri, she would have chosen to stay behind at the site.

In that other world, she would have been thrilled to drive into town with Andrew. Everyone would see them together. Women always noticed when Andrew was around. She used to notice when Andrew was around too. She could tell the exact moment he walked into a room, but she hadn't in a while. Everything had unfolded the way May had hinted it would if another man was involved. Apparently, men found a woman more appealing if another showed interest in her. But if that was what it took, she was doubly glad she'd let Andrew go. She didn't want to be a prize. Being with Dimitri, she'd learned she was so much more than that.

They pulled up outside the stationer's and Andrew helped her down. 'You look pretty today, Evie. Is that a new bonnet?'

'I re-trimmed it, so, yes, it's sort of new.' Evie touched the wide blue ribbons. She'd forgotten which bonnet it was. When she'd dressed this morning, she'd only thought about getting out to the site as quickly as possible.

'It brings out your eyes.' Andrew offered her his arm. It was a lovely compliment, one that showed he'd paid attention to the little details of her—the colour of her eyes, whether or not he'd seen the bonnet before. But it fell short when measured against other more intimate compliments. *You'd make a blancmange hard, Evie.*

The little bell over the stationer's jingled and she was glad to have something else to focus on beside hard blancmange. Evie smiled at Andrew, standing patiently beside her. 'Let's look at samples. You can help me decide between white and ecru.'

Was there a difference? White, onion, oyster, ivory, pearl, eggshell, alabaster—it was all the same to him. Andrew tried to hide his impatience. Evie was being nice, wanting to include him in the process, Evie was always being nice. Look where it had got her. Now, she was stuck planning Dimitri's party. When he'd suggested the party, he'd never intended that to happen. He'd hoped to use the party as a chance to lure Cecilia Northam to town. She'd be a fine prospective bride.

Evie didn't even want to plan the party, but she was being nice. He hated all that niceness, except when that niceness worked for him and it was working splendidly for him. That was why he had to be patient. He needed that niceness to keep her working for him. He needed those drawings and, shortly, he'd need more. That was why he'd driven into Little Westbury with her, why he drove her home every night, why he hadn't dared to spend an evening with the luscious and willing Lady Fairfield five miles from here in case anyone caught wind of his old affair heating up again. *Think about the money.* He had been paid well for the first instalment of her drawings. He'd be paid well too for the sale of some artefacts to another dealer if he could get his hands on them. That was where the real money was.

'Do you like the ivory or the alabaster?' Evie held up two samples.

'Ivory.' Andrew smiled. 'I think it offers a hint of elegance and a sense of the antique.' *Just order the damn invitations.* 'When did you say the gala was?'

'Two weeks from tomorrow.' Evie handed the sample to the stationer and gave the information.

Two weeks was perfect. Andrew began to feel a little more charitable. The gala would be the ideal evening for something to go missing. There would be too many people around to pin it on any one person. Andrew found one more smile to cover his boredom. 'Tell me, Evie, what other grand items has the Prince uncovered?' He was going to need more than pretty combs and spearheads if he was going to make money. It was always good to think optimistically. If he was going to pull off a heist, he wanted to make it a good one.

'There's a bowl. It was found nearly whole.' Evie signed the bill. 'Now you can take me home.'

'So soon?' Andrew cajoled. 'How about a short walk first, the leaves are beginning to turn.'

'I have a lot to do,' Evie prevaricated. This was new. Evie didn't want to spend time with him? Further proof his suspicions were more than that. He'd have to test that hypothesis.

'You've changed, Evie,' Andrew said, leading them out to the perimeter of the village where a stand of trees offered early autumn colour. 'Once, a walk with me anywhere would have made your day. Now, you barely have time for me,' he teased, trying to sound hurt.

'I haven't changed.' Evie smiled. Of course she'd smile. She couldn't imagine hurting anyone's feelings. She held up her ink-stained hand. 'I'm still Evie Milham, still drawing, still sewing.' *Still diddling the Prince behind your back*, Andrew thought uncharitably.

Andrew shook his head, playing the sincere friend-cum-suitor. 'It's more than that. This started when you met the Prince.' He dropped his voice and manoeuvred them into the trees. 'I hope he has not exerted undue influence over you, Evie. He's a very charismatic man. He's been all over the world, he's seen many things, *done* many things.' He imbued a sense of scandal into that word. He hoped the other implications were clear too: that she was a simple country girl who had taken a few turns in London which had been just short of disasters, whose head was easily turned, a girl too naïve for a man like Dimitri.

'You think I could never appeal to a man like him?' She sounded insulted, but Andrew didn't care. All of it was true. He was doing her a favour by warning her off.

'That's not what I said,' Andrew argued sternly, although it was in part exactly what he'd meant. 'Women are playthings to men like him. He is powerful. People exist to serve him.'

'I disagree. You have it backwards.' What? She dared to argue with him? Oh, he wanted to hear this. Dimitri must be phenomenal in bed if he had inspired such gumption in Evie Milham. 'He serves others. This whole excavation was his service to a community. If you think otherwise, you don't understand him at all.'

Andrew pasted on a look of exasperation. 'Evie, do you want to know how I got this bruise? I got it on the way home last night for defending your honour. I challenged his treatment of you and he swung at me.' Andrew covered her hand where it lay on his sleeve with his other one. 'He has not been careful of you and perhaps you've been too blinded by his looks, his manners, his attention, to notice. It's my job, as your friend, to notice on your behalf. He should not be alone with you and he has been on several occasions.' He could tell she didn't like him holding her hand. Her fingers were tense, looking for the first opportunity to pull away. He hated that she didn't like his touch. He would show her. He could touch a woman as well as any prince. In those jealous moments he wanted to ruin Dimitri and he had the power to do it. He wanted to ruin Evie too, wanted her to pay for loving a prince.

He dropped his voice. 'Evie, he will leave. He does not care what kind of reputation he leaves behind for you. But you have to live here. He has secrets, Evie. There are things he has not told you.'

'Such as? I believe you've indicated as much before, but not with any real evidence. We all have secrets.' Evie was a cool customer today. 'Why are you doing this? I thought you were his friend.'

Andrew rubbed a thumb over her knuckles, his eyes locking on hers. 'I am your friend and I'd like to be more. Do you really think I stopped by your house to talk history with your father? Have you asked yourself why I was there last night? Why I was willing to take a fist to the jaw for you?'

Now he had her on the run. There was a look of panic in her eyes. She was starting to notice how far removed they were from anyone else. How alone. 'I have to get back.' Evie tried to pull away, but Andrew held her hand tight.

'Not yet, Evie,' he pleaded. 'I want my answer. May I court you? Will you come to the gala with me? I would be proud to have you on my arm, to lead you out on the dance floor, to show everyone that the Prince has not corrupted you, that you are still respectable Evie Milham, who knows the value of one good Englishman.' He did not give her a chance to refuse. Andrew bent his head to capture her mouth, his kiss hard and brutal in its intensity.

She was shoving at him. He didn't care. He would have her remember her place. When he drew back, she wiped a hand across her mouth. Rage rocketed through him. 'It's true, then, that you've been with him,' he accused. 'How could you, Evie? You've given him everything and he will give you nothing. He won't marry you, Evie. He can't.'

That did not get the shock value he'd hoped for. Instead, Evie said calmly, 'I know all about his sister and the rules that say he has to return.' So Dimitri had told her, or rather he'd told her half of the truth.

Andrew smirked. 'There's more than a sister involved. Ask him what his duty is, Evie.' He pushed past her, leaving her alone. The bitch could walk home for all he cared. She'd thrown her lot in with the Prince and she was going to be disappointed. More than that, she was going to be ruined. He was sure Cecilia Northam would absolutely find the information that Evie Milham had bedded the Prince positively delicious. Even if it wasn't true. It didn't matter if she'd actually done the deed. It only mattered if people believed it.

Chapter Twenty-Two

Evie stomped down the long road home, fuelled by the adrenaline of their quarrel. It was hard to believe she'd ever liked Andrew or that she'd ever wanted his attention. Saying the words out loud to his face had felt good, empowering. It had been a chance to own the conclusions she'd reached in her mind, a final purging.

The infatuation of her girlhood was finished. From the distance of her adoration, Andrew had appeared perfect, but up close he had revealed his flaws. Everyone had flaws, but she could not live with *his*. Andrew did not wear jealousy well. She wasn't even convinced he was jealous over *her*, although he'd certainly tried to justify his behaviour along that line. He was merely jealous of Dimitri, of anything Dimitri had.

Knowing that made his kiss all the worse. He hadn't wanted to prove himself to her, he'd wanted to punish Dimitri. She wiped a hand across her mouth again as if this time she could erase those terrible moments, his mouth crashing down on her, hard and unforgiving, his tongue pushing its way into her mouth,

Andrew giving no heed to the shove of her hands on his chest. Her attempts to thwart him had been useless. That kiss had been nothing like Dimitri's. It had been forced upon her and there had been very little she could have done about it. *That* frightened her. The kiss had been unwanted, but she'd been helpless to prevent it.

Evie had to stop. She was starting to shake now that the moment and the adrenaline had passed, now that the full import of what Andrew had done sank in. What if he tried something like that again? What if he tried more than that? Evie drew deep breaths and pressed a steadying hand to her stomach. Surely she was exaggerating the situation now. Andrew had been angry. She had provoked him.

No. She would not make excuses for him any more. She'd not realised until now how often she'd done that in the past. She'd excused his behaviour at the lecture, she'd excused his tendency to overlook her presence on countless occasions. Now, she was excusing his entirely inappropriate behaviour. No more. What he'd done to her in the past, what he'd done to her today, was all of a same piece. She would not allow it any more. It didn't matter if a girl was plain or pretty, it simply wasn't appropriate to treat people with the disregard he'd shown her. Dimitri had shown her the utmost courtesy. Always.

Thinking about that gave her strength. She started walking again, her shaking under control. It did make her wonder what had brought on Andrew's rather sudden change of heart. Was it solely Dimitri's interest in her that had sparked Andrew's competitive nature or something else? Andrew paid attention to people

who could do things for him. What could she do for
him? She could draw and she had. She had made him
a copy of nearly every drawing she'd done for Dimitri's collection. A cold pit formed in her stomach. Why
did he really want her drawings?

Down the road, coming towards her on foot was a
tall figure walking rapidly. Evie stiffened, understanding more completely the danger Andrew's tirade had
put her in. He'd made her a woman alone on a road
in the gathering dark. The figure neared and she recognised him. Dimitri! He must have recognised her
too! He began to run.

She was in his arms, his embrace tight, his lips in
her hair as he muttered half-sentences. 'Evie, what are
you doing out here? I was so worried.'

'Andrew drove me into town to order the invitations.' She didn't want to leave his arms. She held
him close too. This was what she wanted to remember: how safe she felt.

'He left you there?' Incredulity marked Dimitri's
response. He stepped back, looking her in the eye.
'Evie, what *happened*?'

'He kissed me. He was angry...' She barely got the
words out before Dimitri swore.

'That bastard! He had no right to take his anger out
on you.' His dark eyes were a mixture of storm and
regret. 'I am sorry, Evie. This is all my fault.'

'I saw the bruise.' She tried for a smile. She didn't
want Dimitri going after Andrew for this. It would
only make things worse.

'He insulted you. I should have known he wouldn't
let this lie.' He pulled her close again and she breathed

in the vanilla of his soap. 'I don't think Andrew should drive you home any more.'

They started walking. She could enjoy the evening now that she was with him. 'What were you doing out looking for me?'

Dimitri smiled. 'I didn't get to say goodbye, today. I went over to your parents, but they told me you weren't home yet. I knew you should have been. They'd thought you were working late with me. That's when I knew something wasn't right.'

'I'm glad you came.' The lights of her house came into view, the long walk was suddenly too short. 'Will you come in?' They'd be with her parents. She wanted far more than that. She wanted to lie in the dark with him, wanted to find the pleasure again that could erase her earlier troubles. There would be no chance to be alone but it was the best she could do.

'For a short while only.' Dimitri paused. 'I have some thinking to do. But, Evie…?'

'Yes?' She was almost breathless, sensing he was about to say something important.

'Tomorrow. We'll be together tomorrow. I'll find a way.'

I'll find a way. The words became his motto throughout the sleepless night. He'd find a way tomorrow, and the next day, and the next. Somehow, he'd find a way. If tonight had shown him one thing, it was that he could not leave her here to be the victim of Andrew's anger, anger that wasn't entirely directed at her. But she would be the one who would pay. It had torn his guts out to see Evie on that road tonight, a perfect victim for whoever came along. It didn't mat-

ter this was Little Westbury. There was still crime. His
own temper rose to think Andrew had simply left her
to find her own way home when the blackguard knew
very well what could happen to her. More than that,
his determination wasn't only about protecting Evie.
He wasn't entirely that self-sacrificing. He wanted her
with him, wherever that was.

Dimitri didn't even bother going to bed. He sat
on the divan, feet up on the low table, vodka in one
hand. There had to be an answer and after what had
happened to Evie, he was more determined than ever
to find it.

He tried out the 'what ifs'. What if he didn't have
to give up the title? What if there was no peace to
risk, what if Anna-Maria didn't have to marry? There
was no help there. The peace was at stake and that
meant there had to be a marriage. But did it have to
be Anna-Maria's or his? Perhaps he'd been thinking
dichotomously for too long.

He tried it out: What if another marriage secured
the peace? What if someone married Ayfer in his
place? Then Anna-Maria would be safe. The nation
would be safe. He would be free to make his own
choices, to choose Evie. But who? This was the impossible part. There were no other males. His older
brother, Grigori, was already married. His father was
too old, too devoted to his mother's memory to marry
again and start a second family in his mid-sixties.
There was, however, Cousin Yulian—desperately de-
sirous to do his duty for the state.

Dimitri leaned forward, coming fully upright.
Yulian *was* family, even if only a distant second
cousin. Still, Ayfer would be marrying into the house

of Petrovich and that was the whole point of the exercise. Kuban would be honouring its agreement with the sultan. It hardly mattered who the groom was, as long as Ayfer's father was assured his daughter married equal to her station. Her honour would be intact with marriage to Yulian. Dimitri would ensure it. He would turn over his summer palace, his royal apartments at court to Yulian, who would positively drool on himself at such luxury. A wife, wealth, status at court now as a married man. Yulian would be beside himself. *If* his father could arrange it without harm to himself or Anna-Maria.

That was the only concern that remained. He didn't want there to be retribution. He didn't want his father and Anna-Maria or Grigori and his precious children to pay for his decision. The only way he could ensure that was if they were here, or if they renounced him along with the rest of the royal court.

Those were serious considerations indeed. Renouncing meant he would no longer be considered part of their family. It would be their only choice if they didn't renounce their own lives. It was one thing to ask oneself to give up one's life entirely. It was not something he could ask someone else to do for him or because of him.

All of this had to be handled with great care. His father would be initially disappointed in him. He'd gone and fallen in love and implicated the family in his romance. If he went forward with his idea, he'd need the help of each of his friends. He could not accomplish this alone. This would be a joint effort. He had to be sure.

A yawn surprised him and for the first time since

he'd taken Evie to bed, Dimitri thought he might sleep. There was peace to be had. Tonight, he had a possible solution. He'd sleep on it and see how it looked in the morning light. Just maybe, he'd found a way to claim the life he wanted, the woman he wanted. It was risky, but it was worth it. Evie was worth it.

Evie Milham wasn't worth it! Andrew downed another brandy and glared into the fire. It had been chilly enough tonight to light a fireplace after months of summer. But the homey comfort of the flames had done nothing to soothe his temper. She'd scorned him! He didn't want her, but it did gall that she didn't want him. Who was she to resist such a handsome man as himself? A man who had his pick of girls. He was done with her. He had enough drawings now to complete his contract with a London publisher who had signed on to put out a book regarding the site. With luck, the book would be ready to unveil at the gala. Wouldn't she be surprised to see her drawings in a book with his name on the cover? Hopefully, the surprise would render her speechless because there wouldn't be anything she could do about it.

He'd submitted all the catalogue entries too as captions to explain the drawings. All he'd written was the introduction that gave a brief history of the site and some background on Lucius Artorious, most of which he'd borrowed from the two-page entry Dimitri had. Andrew preferred to take the most amount of credit for the least amount of work possible. Debuting the book at the gala would make it impossible for Dimitri or Evie to contest its legitimacy. Meanwhile, he would have a tidy sum of money stashed away in his accounts for very little effort. His interest in Evie remained purely financial. She'd been good for business. Now, she'd become a liability, a problem to manage and managed she would be. When this was over, Evie Milham would wonder why she'd ever risked stepping into the light. Wallflowers weren't meant to blossom. The best part was, it was the Prince who'd dealt her the death blow. Whatever he or Cecilia did would merely be the aftermath.

Chapter Twenty-Three

Finding a way to be together turned out to be easier than finding a way to tell Evie about his plans. At first, it didn't matter. It only mattered that they spent their precious time together. After all, there was plenty of time to discuss the details of his plan. They'd taken to picnics during the lunch break, going off beyond the rim of trees to find privacy in the crisp, early autumn afternoons. There were afternoon teas that provided a chance to go over artefacts and gala plans in private. He'd become infinitely creative at getting Evie alone, at loving her furtively in the out of doors on blankets beneath blue autumn skies or covertly in the silken depths of his pavilion.

But secrecy did not become him. He didn't want to hide Evie. He wanted to shout to the world that he loved her, that he wanted her. But how could he shout it to the world when he couldn't find the words to tell her? Soon, he told himself. Soon, he would tell her his plan. Soon, he would put that plan into motion with her approval and yet he put it off. Each day brought a certain joy, a certain pleasure that he didn't want to destroy with talk of the uncertain future and he put that difficult discussion off until 'soon' was 'now'. The gala was tomorrow. He had run out of time.

Perhaps Evie sensed it too. He was scheduled to leave the week after the gala. Only he wouldn't be leaving, not if he had his way. But Evie didn't know that. Her desperation seeped out in her lovemaking as the gala inched closer. There was a frantic quality to her kisses, a recklessness to her release. Today, she sat him astride, her skirts rucked up, her hair down, sated from their latest bout of outdoor lovemaking, while her blue eyes burned with a pensive breed of satisfaction.

'A penny for your thoughts.' He reached a hand out to touch her hair. He knew what was on her mind. It was on his mind as well. Perhaps it had been right to wait this long and let her be the one who brought up the subject.

'Save your money. You don't want to hear these thoughts, not on a beautiful day like this.'

He levered up on his elbows, careful not to dislodge her from her erotic position. 'We have to talk about it, Evie.'

Her eyes sparkled, starting to water. 'I knew you were going to leave. I knew this wouldn't last. I knew I was going to fall for you, that I couldn't stop myself and it was going to hurt when I landed.' She gave a sad smile that broke his heart. 'If I knew, why does it still hurt? Why can't I just accept that all is true and move on? Every time I'm with you I have to learn to lose you all over again.' She made a fist and pounded it on his chest.

She loved him. He knew she did, of course. Evie

would never give herself lightly. In spite of all he couldn't offer her, she'd fallen anyway. He was so unworthy of her affections and yet he'd so readily craved them, needed them. Dimitri captured her hand. He did not want her to cry over him, over anything. His Evie deserved only happiness. It was time to give that to her. The thought gave him courage. 'Evie, will you walk with me?' He'd brought her here for a reason. There was a little valley he wanted to show her.

'It's pretty out here.' Evie made small talk to fill the silence, but she was nervous too, no doubt wondering what they were doing and how it fit into the discussion they were both so desperate to have and yet had avoided.

'I'm glad you think so.' Dimitri drew a breath. Very soon there would be no going back. His heart was starting to pound with excitement—he'd had enough time to think about it, he didn't want to go back, only forward into this new life he was building—but also with trepidation. What would Evie think? 'Close your eyes, Evie.' He covered her eyes with his hands and led her to the edge of the hill. 'Now, look!'

He waited, seeing the valley below them through her eyes: the tall green grass, the sturdy, brick manse with its outbuildings and barn, the paddocks for the horses, the road leading to the drive. To his eye, it looked like a place that could be home, a place that would do a country gentleman of some means proud, not unlike Evie's home. 'The property is for sale. The couple who live there are elderly and looking to move in with their daughter.' He'd found time to make enquiries, to make an offer.

'It's a nice property, too big for a couple. It's made

for children. That tree needs a swing.' Evie smiled, but it was a questioning smile. She was unsure what to make of this.

'I am hoping it's made for us and our children, Evie.' The words were out before he could take them back. This wasn't the order of conversation he'd imagined in his mind. He'd thought to work up to that slowly, telling her first about his plan and then asking her to marry him.

Evie stared. Apparently, she hadn't thought the conversation was supposed to head this direction either. 'You're leaving.' They were both feeling their way off script now.

'I've decided not to go.' He wanted her to look at him, but she refused, keeping her gaze staunchly on the smoke curling out of the chimney in the distance.

'You cannot decide that. Your sister needs you. Your family needs you.' Her voice was flat, her face stoic. She said the phrases as if they'd been a silent litany she'd carried with her and repeated as needed over the past weeks.

'I have a plan for that. I meant to start with it, but I got a little ahead of myself.' He gave a chuckle but she didn't smile. Oh, God, how he wanted Evie to smile. He'd give his kingdom for that smile if he hadn't already decided to give it up for something far more worthy. 'I'm going to renounce my title.' She did look at him then, but not with a smile. The look on her face was one of abject horror.

Good God, he thought to renounce his title for her! Disbelief coursed through her as the world reeled. Now she knew why Cinderella had bolted; the poor girl had seen something in the Prince's eyes that scared her—something that resembled for ever and the determination to make it happen at all costs. That was exactly what Evie had seen in Dimitri's eyes.

Everything became surreal in those moments. She'd been wrong. Dimitri leaving wasn't the real nightmare. *This* was the real nightmare, the part where romance turned into hatred. He was doing this for love, but he would come to hate her for it. Some day he'd realise how foolish he'd been. He had everything to go back for and no reason to stay except her. She did not want to be that reason. Her own mother had counselled her against such rashness, that love didn't last. There had to be something more to base a life on together. When that love died, he would despise her and then the nightmare would begin—knowing the man she loved hated her. That would be even worse than Andrew's rude neglect.

She found a few, simple words. 'No. I can't allow that.' Her mind was racing. It was almost too much to take in and yet she had to reason with him, help him to see the error of his choice. 'Your sister, your family, they need you to return.' But she'd already said that. She needed something new. 'Don't renounce. I will go to Kuban with you. Then you can have the best of both worlds—we can be together and you don't have to give up your country and your sister will be safe.'

It was his turn to stare. Is that what her face had looked like a few moments earlier? 'I can't go back, Evie. It's more complicated than that,' he said quietly, taking her hand and clutching it tight. 'I should have told you earlier. I just didn't think it would matter. If I go back, there's a woman I am expected to marry.'

The hillside might as well have collapsed beneath her. She could hardly breathe from the shock of it. Dimitri engaged! Promised to another and he'd known the whole time, when he'd kissed her, when they'd made love. Should she be devastated or angry?

'I know what you're thinking.'

That made her angry. 'How could you possibly know? *I* don't even know!' She walked away from him. Maybe distance would help her think. She should have listened to Andrew. Hadn't he tried to warn her? Hadn't he said there was another reason Dimitri wouldn't marry her? In her naïvety she'd not thought it would be another woman.

Dimitri was behind her, his voice tenacious and low, and her own perverse curiosity didn't want to miss a word. 'Please let me explain about Ayfer.' Oh, heavens, that made it worse. The woman had a name. He didn't wait for an answer, perhaps he was smart enough to know she wasn't going to give him one.

'She's a sultan's daughter. The marriage is meant to keep the peace on the border. If I don't marry her, Anna-Maria will have to marry the sultan's son. I told you most of this before.' Except for the one thing that mattered. He didn't just have to return to save his sister, he had to marry.

Dimitri was still talking, still explaining. 'I've never met her. This was negotiated as part of a treaty put together by the sultan's representatives and my King. I understand there's some sort of backwards irony, that to save my sister from an arranged marriage to a stranger who will take her away from her country and her faith, I am condemning another woman to the same fate by marrying me, but the ends justify the means.'

Of course he would and that was why she couldn't stay mad at him. She could only be hurt by the insurmountable impossibility of being with him. She had offered him all she could offer, to go with him, and it wasn't enough. *Couldn't* be enough. All that would go to Kuban with Dimitri when he left was the small tapestry she'd finished last night.

'I told you I have a plan,' Dimitri said with quiet fierceness. He was going to be listened to. 'I have a cousin, Yulian, who I believe will marry the sultan's daughter in my place. I will renounce all claims to any wealth I possess that is tied to the state and turn it over to him.'

Against her will, Evie asked, 'And your family? What happens to them?' She couldn't imagine the kingdom accepting Dimitri's resignation blithely and going on its happy way.

'They can renounce me and affirm their loyalty to the crown and all will be well.'

'And you will never see them again,' Evie supplied, the last of her anger seeping away, replaced by great sadness for him, that this brave man should have to face such a decision. Even more it saddened her that he'd had to puzzle out such a decision alone, so far from home.

'I am willing to accept it if that is what happens.' She couldn't imagine never seeing her mother, her father, her sisters, her baby nephew. 'That might have been your fate had you come to Kuban,' Dimitri argued softly. 'It's not fair that you should be willing to give that up, but not allow me to do the same.'

She turned then to look at him finally and whispered the great fear that had burst open in her when he'd laid out his plan. 'You will come to hate me.' She pressed two fingers to his lips, those beautiful lips she'd kissed countless times in the last weeks. 'I know you don't think so now. But in time, you will. I can't live with that.' Then came the great truth that accompanied her great fear. 'I am not worth it.'

'Will it make you feel better to know this isn't only about you? It's about me in the same way that I hope your decision to give up Andrew wasn't about me, but about you deciding he wasn't the one regardless of who or what waited for you. Long before I loved you, Evie, I'd been looking for a way out, wondering if it was possible to escape my fate and live my own life. This is what I want.' Dimitri tipped her chin up to meet his gaze. 'As for the question, are you worth it? Yes, you are. You've always been worth it. London doesn't know what they've been missing. But I do. I see the real you, Evie, and I love her. I love *you*.'

He was not making it better and he certainly wasn't making any of this easier. 'You weren't supposed to.'

Dimitri smiled. 'I know. You like people at a distance, people who are unattainable. That way you aren't disappointed, you don't have to risk anything. But I made you risk everything and that has had you reeling since day one.'

A smile stole across her face in spite of her best efforts. Perhaps she did do that. Distance made it easier to see the best in them. 'I'm not sure I like having myself explained to me.' She was seriously weakening. She was starting to believe happiness was within her reach if she would just close her fingers over it.

Dimitri held her hands against his chest, his eyes locking with hers. 'I've made my choice for our future. Now, you have to make yours. I am asking you to marry me, to live with me in that house down there and raise a family with me, study history with me and make love with me every night until we're too old, and can only make love on Sundays.'

Evie laughed. 'Only Sundays?' And then, because she could deny him nothing, and because it was nice to believe for a moment that it all could come true, Evie said, 'Yes.' But in her heart, she knew what she had to do even as he kissed her. *She* had to be the one to leave. Already a plan was unfolding. She'd go after the gala. She'd visit Bea and May up north. Then, Dimitri would have no reason to stay. He could return home and make good on his promises. She had two days left and then she had to let him go because he loved her and she loved him. Too much, it seemed. She kissed him hard. She'd always believed people in love belonged together, but now she saw she was wrong. Sometimes you had to love someone enough to give them up.

She loved Dimitri enough.

Chapter Twenty-Four

She said yes!

Dimitri walked to his desk in the corner of the pavilion and lit a lamp. He'd left Evie at her parents' and headed home, prepared for a night of writing. Everything could be set in motion now. He was going to do it. He was going to renounce his title and become Mr Petrovich, the man he'd always wanted to be. He was going to need help. Titles were not renounced easily. He needed someone to watch over his father and Anna-Maria, someone to negotiate these arrangements. Quite possibly, he was going to need a great many someones. That's what friends were for.

He pulled out several sheets of paper, his confidence building as he began to write. He wrote to his father first, the one man in the entire world he trusted to see it done, and the one man who would understand how agonising the decision was because he too had loved deeply. He wrote to Yulian next, carefully outlining the benefits and great patriotic honour of taking on this duty for Kuban.

Then came the letters to Stepan and Ruslan. He

would entrust them to help his father with the negotiations. To Nikolay he entrusted the duty of protecting the family quite literally. Nikolay's firebrand temper didn't make him an ideal political ally, but his sword arm was never in doubt. Nikolay would defend the house, would defend Anna-Maria to his last breath.

To Illarion fell the job of keeping up the spirits, a shoulder to cry on. Anna-Maria would be devastated when it came to renouncing him. Her letter had been the hardest of all to write. He'd begged her to understand that she had to do this for her own future and safety, that he wanted a secure future for her above all else where she had choices.

When the sun came up, his hand was cramped and a stack of letters sealed with the great bear, the mark of the house of Petrovich, lay piled on his desk. He counted the days in his head. One day to the embassy in London. The diplomatic pouch would take three days to reach Ostend across the Channel and then a week of hard riding to make Kuban. Ten days at best until his father opened that letter. One of the benefits of being a prince: one's mail went fast. Dimitri twisted the ring on his finger. He'd enjoy the privilege while it lasted. He didn't fool himself that this transition would be easy. Doubtless there would be some adjusting to going from a prince to ordinary man, but there would be benefits too. For one, he could go to the privy without being tracked down by voracious females.

It would take ten days for a response to arrive plus whatever time lay in between to settle negotiations. He hoped they would be quick. But he knew better than to hope for too much. There would be protocol and ceremony to follow and if the sultan's representative wasn't lounging around court, he'd have to be summoned. Dimitri pushed a hand through his hair. All of this would take time. He was taking an enormous leap of faith that his friends and his family wouldn't fail him. He could not wait for permission to move forward. He had to assume it would all happen according to his plan. He had one more letter to write, to the couple in the valley. It was time to enquire about the house. *Mr* Petrovich and his wife were going to need somewhere to live.

Dimitri stretched and smiled. A great weight had been lifted from his shoulders. Almost. There were still a few things that needed wrapping up. There was still a thief on the loose who had managed to steal a few more items. Whoever the thief was, he wasn't a very good one. He had no idea the items he'd taken were merely replicas.

There was also the gala to get through, one more night of people staring in awe at the Prince of Kuban and treating him like some precious artefact himself that might break if they didn't fawn over him enough. If they weren't busy kowtowing, they were busy speculating how they could best use their association with him. That would soon be over. People wouldn't care so much when he was regular Mr Petrovich, the foreign chap who'd married Evie Milham.

But *after* the gala, real life could begin with Evie beside him. He would dance with Evie, keep Evie by his side all night because he wanted to and because he wanted no one in Little Westbury to be surprised when he called on Sir Hollis Milham the next day and asked for his daughter's hand in marriage. Instead, they would say, 'It all makes sense. Didn't you see them together at the gala? A perfect pair.' It could all begin tomorrow. He just had to get through the gala. He could hardly wait for it to begin *and* he could hardly wait for it to be over.

'Careful with that!'

'It has to be carried flat or it will crack.'

'You would crack too if you were a thousand years old.'

'Yes, over here with that crate. No, put the other box over there.' Evie ran a hand through her hair, trying hard not to bark orders, trying hard not to be overwhelmed as she managed three tasks at once. The whole morning had been like this, everyone relying on her for instruction and for direction. Evie looked down at the tablet in her hand, covered in lists and ticks, the ticks a testament to the progress she was making and to the amount of work that still remained to be done. Thank goodness for all the work. It was supposed to keep her mind off what was to come.

It would all be over tonight. The gala was a culminating event in more ways than one, a thought that Evie was struggling to push away no matter how hard she worked. She and her mother had been up early, at the site overseeing preparations for the evening's party. Everything had to happen in a specific order.

First, the 'set designers', as her mother liked to call them, had to assemble the curtains that would cordon off unfinished areas of the site and guide guests through the rooms Dimitri wanted to display tonight towards the *pièce de résistance*, the dining room with its terracotta-rose design carved into the floor. Setting up the curtains would take most of the morning. After that, the flowers could be arranged in tall urns replicating Roman style, the long table brought in for dining could be laid and Evie could work on getting the displays of artefacts ready for public viewing. There would be a separate pavilion set up for dancing that would have to be supervised as well. Then and only then could she think about dressing and getting herself ready. Her gown for the evening was already at Dimitri's pavilion. There would be no time to go home and change.

But that was hours away, nearly an entire day. The gown was beautiful, one she'd made herself and just finished last night out of the silk from London, and yet she didn't want to think about putting it on and what that would symbolise, taking her one step closer to leaving Dimitri. No, she couldn't think of it like that. She was one step closer to setting him free, not giving him up.

Out of the corner of her eye she caught a glimpse of Dimitri working hard to help assemble the curtains. He flashed her a smile, looking entirely too handsome in rolled-up shirtsleeves, looking entirely too much in his element. He looked like he belonged here with these people. No. She could not second-guess her decision. She had to be firm. He would thank her for it later when he realised a man didn't simply give up a kingdom for a girl like her. She was making the right decision in leaving. She knew it was the right decision because it was hard. Every time she thought about it she wanted to cry. Right decisions were hard decisions, the ones it cost you something to make. This was costing her plenty.

* * *

She could not turn back time. She couldn't even manage to hold it back. The long day which had seemed endless in the cool of the morning, and the tasks that had seemed impossible to accomplish in the warmth of the day, had given way to the long purple shadows of evening.

'It looks spectacular.' She turned at the sound of Dimitri's voice. He had been everywhere today, raising curtains, moving tables, carrying heavy urns full of flowers, patiently moving them from niche to niche at her mother's behest. Now, that labouring man was gone, replaced by a resplendent prince in dark evening clothes, immaculately groomed.

'*You* look spectacular.' Evie reached up and adjusted his cravat, a useless gesture since it was perfectly tied, but it gave her an excuse to touch him.

'This exceeds my wildest expectations.' Dimitri motioned to the site, taking in the transformation with a sweep of his hand.

How she'd miss those wide gestures. Together, they looked at the lush setting with its silk hangings and displays. Guests would be able to wander through the corridor and view artefacts displayed in cases while reading carefully scripted programmes that detailed everything in the cases. She had worked hours on those. That reminded her of something. 'Did you have any luck catching the thief?' She still regretted the loss of the pretty comb and hair clips.

'No, but no further harm has been done.' Dimitri winked. 'I would like to catch him. But if I don't, I feel assured he will be punished. People who discover they've been duped into buying false antiques aren't friendly about it. His crime will catch up with him.' He wrapped his arms about her and planted a secret kiss on the back of her neck.

'People will see!' she scolded, caught off balance by his boldness. They'd spent the last weeks being careful, being private.

'Let them see.' Dimitri nuzzled her ear. 'Very soon you'll be mine and I can kiss you in public all I want.'

'It would be a scandal.'

'I hardly think anyone would care what an ordinary fellow does with his wife. They'll just say it's "common".' Dimitri laughed and she wished she could laugh too. But she knew better. Dimitri's little fantasy would never come to pass.

'You'll never be common. With or without a title, you will always be the Prince to these people. People won't stop staring at you.' Didn't this man ever look in the mirror? Women would stare at him if he were dressed in sackcloth.

His arms around her tightened, she could feel him growing hard where her buttocks nestled against him. 'I only care if you stare.' For a moment she wondered if she'd been too hasty. Maybe he was right, maybe he knew what he was doing. Maybe she was the one who was throwing away happiness while he was the one bravely reaching for it with all he was worth. She had to put a stop to all of this second-guessing.

'I have to get ready or the guests will be here and I'll be in my apron.'

Dimitri turned serious as he let her go. 'I did want to tell you something. Andrew will be here tonight. He's coming with Lord Belvoir and Miss Northam.

But he won't cause you any trouble. I give you my word, I won't let him near you.'

She squeezed his hand and looked down at their hands. 'I know. I always feel safe when I'm with you.'

'Then you'll be safe for the rest of your life.'

Not really, she thought as she headed to the pavilion to change. She'd be safe for the next sixteen hours. Then she'd be on a coach to Scotland and Dimitri could go back to Kuban without guilt. She would just go on. Somehow.

'Are you changing your mind about leaving?' Her mother stepped behind the curtain leading into Dimitri's private chambers. He'd given the area over to the two women to get ready for the gala. Evie was nearly ready now. Her mother had finished earlier and looked exceptionally lovely in a dark blue silk.

Evie looked up from the vanity. 'Why do you ask?'

'Because you've spent the last five minutes staring in the mirror, doing nothing.' Her mother walked the room, trailing a hand over the covers on the bed. 'This is an impressive space. I don't think I've ever seen a bed quite like this. It stirs the imagination a bit, doesn't it?' She gave a nervous little titter, a warning she was leading up to something.

It stirs more than the imagination, Evie thought. 'What do you mean, Mother?' she asked warily. This conversation was going somewhere, she just wasn't sure where that was.

Her mother sat on the edge of the bed. 'Evie, something has happened between you and the Prince, even since the last time we talked.' She pursed her lips and looked down at her hands, perhaps unsure how to broach the subject. 'I know about Beatrice. Her mother told me.' Her mother smiled. 'The perks of being long-time friends, I suppose.'

What did Beatrice have to do with this? Evie was having a hard time keeping up. 'I thought we were talking about the Prince.'

'We are.' Her mother sighed. She sounded concerned, her usual flightiness absent, a sign of just how worried she was, worried to the point of weariness—too weary for flight even. 'I was young once, Evie. I was in love, I had emotions that ran hot and cold. I did a few things that might surprise you. I know young girls aren't all that innocent and I don't hold that against them. I think the Penroses have dealt poorly with Beatrice's situation and my heart breaks for that girl.' She paused. 'What I am saying, Evie, is that you can tell me whatever it is that has happened with the Prince and we will sort it out.' There was that wisdom again, coming when Evie least expected it.

The kind words broke her. Evie felt the tears come and they wouldn't stop. It had all been so very much to bear alone. She choked out the words. 'Dimitri has proposed.'

Her usually highly strung mother did not faint, did not lapse into excited hysterics. Instead, she met this news with an unflappable reserve that reminded Evie of when Diana's earl had proposed. 'Tell me everything.' Her mother knelt beside her at the vanity, taking her hands.

The story came out between sobs and tears. She had to repeat herself to make sense, had to take deep breaths to remain coherent. The enormity of what

Dimitri had done was overwhelming. 'He has renounced everything.'

'What did you say to that, my darling girl?' her mother asked quietly when she'd finished.

'I said yes because he'd tolerate nothing less. But I knew I couldn't let him do it. I can't let him renounce his title, his country, turn his back on his family. I knew then I had to be strong for both of us. He'll come to hate me once he realises what he's done.'

'That's not what I asked,' her mother said softly. 'What do you *want* to say? Do you love him?'

'I wasn't supposed to love him. I never meant to love him. I thought I loved Andrew for years. But Dimitri came along when I least expected it. When I am with him, everything seems possible. When he looks at me, I feel beautiful, like I am more than I ever thought I could be.' Evie drew a breath. 'It's too fast, isn't it? How could I love Andrew for years and then love Dimitri instantly? Love at first sight doesn't really exist. Does it?' How could it when her mother said marriage was the work of a lifetime?

Her mother laughed and smoothed back her hair. 'Evie, love doesn't work that way. Some people do fall in love over the course of several years, so gradually they don't realise it. Others fall right away. There is no timetable and perhaps you were merely infatuated with Andrew. It would be easy enough. He's handsome and charming in his own way if one doesn't look too closely, like costume jewellery, no? He's all you've known in this small corner of the world.'

She smiled. 'I've long thought it a great disservice to our women that we don't send them abroad the way we do our young men. We should let our women see the world, see what it has to offer before they settle down.'

It was the most liberal thought Evie had ever heard her mother voice—her mother, who was traditional to her core, a woman who'd raised her daughters by the book, who did not challenge society by reaching too high above her. She knew her station.

'I see I have surprised you.' She squeezed Evie's hand. 'It might also surprise you to know that your father and I weren't always this old married couple you see before you.' There was a soft look in her eyes, a faraway look. 'Once, we were young and hotly in love like you and your prince.' Her voice trailed off. 'I never told you this, but I had another suitor, in London, while your father was on his Grand Tour right before the wars broke out. Henry Northam.'

Lord Belvoir? Evie almost fell off the vanity bench. The most feared man in Parliament? The man whose daughter was the toast of the *ton*? The man who'd tried to block Claire's husband's appointment to Vienna. 'Cecilia's father?' she said in disbelief. 'I can't imagine you with him.'

'Apparently neither could I.' Her mother gave a little laugh. 'I tried to, though. He was handsome, a superb dancer and he could have anyone he wanted. He was like Andrew in that regard. It was flattering that he was taken with me. I had nothing to offer him that a hundred other girls couldn't also offer him. He was the catch of the Season that year, but I never felt quite right with him. I felt as if I were always thinking about what to say next, what to do next, hoping it would be the right thing. I wasn't myself around him. Then your father came home from his Grand Tour early because the revolution in France had become too dangerous. I remember watching him walk into Lady Chatsworth's ballroom in the middle of July and I knew I was going to marry him. He looked at me and it was over.' A satisfied smile played on her lips. 'I did marry him, three months later, a very fast wedding considering the circumstances.

'Your father made me laugh, he still does. When I was with him, I didn't question who I was and neither did he. Had I married Henry Northam, I would have spent the rest of my life doubting my place. Some people say I gave up everything, but I have never felt that way. I've gained everything. I loved the man, not the title, not all the trappings that went with him.'

'But you told me marriage is work, that passion doesn't last,' Evie argued.

'It is that too. You will quarrel and you will disagree, and the passion changes into something far better than what you start out with. So you see, you can fall in love at first sight.'

'He is giving up too much. I don't need him to be a prince. But I fear he does.' She did not want him to become less than he was. 'I don't want him to humble himself for me, to give up his family. I'm not worth it and some day he'll figure that out.'

Her mother's response was sharp. 'Stop right there, young lady. Perhaps he should not humble himself for you, but you are worth loving. You hold yourself too cheaply and I fear people take advantage of you for it.' Her mother made a sad smile. 'Even your own family, sometimes. Your father and I love having you here. It would be hard to lose you. Maybe we haven't handled it the right way, giving you too much freedom. But we didn't want you to feel pressured to leave or too suffocated if you stayed. Perhaps in being *laissez-faire*, we've create the impression we didn't care. But we do care, Evie, about your happiness very much and you can't be happy *with* anyone unless you're happy with yourself. Can you live with yourself if you let the Prince go? Don't answer, just think on it.'

Her mother rose. 'Let me help you with your dress or we'll be late for our own party.'

The russet silk slid over her and Evie felt peace, confidence descend with it. This gown was her armour. In it, she felt beautiful. Beautiful enough even to stand beside Dimitri Petrovich. Evie wasn't arrogant enough to think she would be the centre of attention at the gala, but she would be *in* the centre of attention. Any woman standing beside Dimitri would always be in the centre of attention. Old Evie would have played the hostess behind the scenes. But the Evie who stared back at her from the mirror as she smoothed the gown over her hips, the New Evie who had taken a lover, would be Cinderella at the ball, a ball she'd planned. She would stand beside Dimitri as his hostess for the first and only time with a smile on her face and act as if her world wasn't about to fall apart. She was glad she was wearing quite possibly the best dress she'd ever made. She was going to need it. It was becoming more difficult with each hour to maintain her belief that she had made the right choice.

Chapter Twenty-Five

Dimitri came to an abrupt halt, his heart pounding in pure male appreciation as Evie stepped out from the pavilion. He vaguely registered that her parents were with her or that other carriages had begun to arrive at the site like a little parade. All of that could wait for just a moment while he looked at her.

The gown was daring, a design all its own that was at once modern with its rich russet hue and yet a throwback to earlier days of fuller skirts and tighter bodices—a fashion he was developing an immediate appreciation for. The bodice was cut low, with the merest nod to sleeves in the slim off-the-shoulder bands that called more attention to what was *not* there than what was. A black choker at her neck drew the eye upward to the delicate bones of her shoulders and the cream of her skin, the upsweep of her hair a perfect match for the richness of her gown. But when she walked, the gown and the woman took on a life of their own. A man couldn't help but notice the tight waist, the gorgeous, sweeping bell of her skirts as she moved. The woman in the gown moved with grace that bordered on regal. He'd never seen Evie like this, yet it was still her, still his sweet, beautiful Evie. It was there in the smile she bestowed on him.

He moved towards her, offering her his hand, taking hers in its long, white, elbow-length gloves, raising it to his lips. He let his eyes brave her face as he kissed those gloved knuckles, not caring if he gave away too much. Let the world see how much he loved her. By tomorrow, it would be over. She would be his. He beamed at her, but her lovely smile faltered. Nerves, perhaps? He tucked her arm through his. 'I want nothing more than to be alone with you.' His voice was low. 'As lovely as that gown is, I can think only of taking it off you.'

She shook her head. 'Not now.' She was right, of course. He had a party to host. There was no time. Guests were arriving and the future of this wonderfully begun excavation depended on his success tonight.

'Certainly not now, guests might find that a little awkward. Later, then.' He gave a chuckle just for her and led her towards their guests. 'Their'. He liked the sound of that. There would be a lot more 'theirs' and 'ours'. 'Come and see your party, Evie. It has turned out magnificently.'

He wanted her to see it as a guest, not as a worker who had laboured all day to make the magic happen. It had overwhelmed him in its elegance when he'd stepped out of the pavilion. He'd helped the curtained walls go up, seen the swathes of fabric give shape to the party space all day long, but it was wondrous to see the transformation after stepping back from it. It was even more wondrous to see it through Evie's eyes, to see her face brighten with a genuine smile of joy when she saw the rich fabrics, the lit candles, the flowers all in their places.

They took up their place at the entrance to the site, his Kubanian crew turned out in the livery of footmen, standing behind them ready with trays of chilled champagne in the phalanx that discreetly ushered the guests through the site without letting them veer off to unfinished areas. In the distance, the dancing tent gleamed white in the falling light.

'Mrs Jeffers, Mr Jeffers, how good of you to come. Your necklace is lovely, is that a topaz?' Dimitri greeted the first guests with a smile. The party had begun. It was a start. He was happier than he had been all day. Evie was beside him and it gave him confidence that they would sort out whatever lay between them. He devoted himself to charming the guests, but most of all, he devoted himself to selflessly charming Evie. *Let her see that I can do this, that I can fit in in her little part of the world, that I can be her man.* He knew the guests by name, knew small, personal details about each of them, encouraged them to enjoy the party.

Beside him, Evie was a revelation. Her natural tendency to help others made her the consummate hostess to his host. She discreetly saw to everyone's comfort, making sure people were paired with others they could talk to with ease as he moved around the gathering space with her. At each group, he stopped and talked briefly about the project, the progress and the future. More than ever now, he needed funds for the project. He would no longer have vast unlimited wealth to throw at it.

He watched Evie with Mrs Stone, listening politely to a story about the lady's grandchildren. Tonight was a glimpse of what life would be like; hosting parties with Evie. Perhaps nothing as grand as this, but other events at their home in the valley. His offer had been accepted. If he had a private moment with Evie tonight, he'd tell her. He wanted to show her the deed. Signs of life. Proof of life. Their life. Not even Andrew with Cecilia Northam on his arm laughing and tossing her head could diminish the evening.

If there was one blight on the evening, it was a small one indeed. Evie was everything a hostess should be and yet he felt she wasn't quite herself. Every so often, he'd sneak a glance and catch a sadness in her eyes and then she would look at him and it would disappear as if he'd imagined it.

After a dinner of Russian foods, all of his favourites—he could see Evie's thoughtful hand in the menu—he led her out for the first dance, a Russian waltz beneath the enormous canopy with its dazzling chandelier that had stolen everyone's breath. He had waited all night for an excuse to hold her close, to put his hand at her waist and claim her in front of all these people, all of her neighbours, and announce through his possession that he meant to make her his. After tonight, there could be no doubt that this was what he wanted and this was the woman he wanted it with.

He swept her into the early steps of the dance, his mouth close at her ear, letting it wash over him. 'I love you, Evie.' He closed his eyes, inhaling deeply the clean lavender fragrance of her.

She looked up at him with fierce blue eyes. 'I love you too, don't ever forget it.'

'I want to tell you a secret, Evie,' he murmured. 'This is the best night of my life.' It was. The chains were gone, chains he hadn't even known he carried. His father's bittersweet view of love, while understandable, had coloured his own views far more than he'd realised. He'd had to throw off those chains and the limits they shackled him to in order to find his own understanding: love was powerful. Love could free a man.

A movement at the dais where the orchestra played caught his eye. A man mounted the steps. On closer scrutiny, he could see who it was. What was Andrew doing up there? Worry began to hatch. The music came to a stop as the waltz ended. Andrew had something in his hand. With his other hand, he gestured for attention. What was the man doing? Dimitri feared 'the grand gesture' Andrew was so fond of making. He felt Evie's hand tighten on his arm and protectiveness surged. The man had tried to hurt Evie and here he was pretending to be the golden boy in front of his neighbours—neighbours who didn't guess what a bastard the man was at heart, that he'd left a woman to walk home alone at dark after forcing attentions on her.

The crowd silenced and Andrew's voice filled the room. 'Good evening, everyone. Welcome to our celebration, and I mean "our" in the most encompassing sense. This is Little Westbury's night. Tonight we celebrate the excavation, a project that has lain dormant in our community for too long, but has now come to life.' There was applause and Andrew waited for it to die down before continuing. 'I can think of no better way to crown that celebration than with the unveiling of this book that chronicles the early work on our site.' He held up the item he carried in his hand, reading off the title in gilt letters on a green leather background, *'The Life of General Lucius Artorious: A Sussex Excavation, complete with illustrations by a local artist.'* He held the book open to reveal a very fine drawing of a goblet. Dimitri did not miss the self-satisfied glance of smugness he tossed their way.

What the hell? Next to him, Evie stifled a horrified gasp. There was so much wrong with this presentation, Dimitri's mind raced to take in the implications. Andrew had stolen his work and claimed it. 'How did he get his hands on your drawings?' It was obvious to him who the 'local artist' was.

Evie was trembling. 'I gave them to him. I had no idea. He said he wanted a keepsake.'

Around them, more applause broke out, no one aware of the little drama playing out in front of them. To the people gathered here, this was indeed a perfect capstone to an evening designed to honour the excavation. They saw nothing wrong with had happened. It never occurred to them Andrew had stolen work that did not rightfully belong to him.

'Why would he do this?' Evie's eyes were wide with betrayal, her face mirroring the shock he felt in his gut.

'Revenge,' Dimitri growled. Evie's pain was worse to bear than his own. Andrew hadn't just done this to him, he'd done it to Evie, Evie, who had given so selflessly of her time and skill to help with all of this. This was not Andrew Adair's excavation, it was his. He alone had the privilege to write about it. He alone had the obligation to defend it, to defend Evie. 'I will make this right.'

Dimitri moved through the crowd. He would put a stop to this with all the royal finesse he possessed. Being in public wouldn't protect Andrew tonight. It was time to expose a traitor. He was starting to suspect a man who would steal another man's work wouldn't stop there. He had found his thief. He stepped up on the dais to join Andrew, throwing the guests a charismatic smile. He was enjoying the fact already that Andrew was off balance.

Andrew had not expected this. He'd expected anger, he'd been planning to offset an outburst as if he thought Dimitri would rush the stage and do violence. Andrew should have thought like a prince. A prince would never engage in a public brawl.

Dimitri quieted the crowd. 'What an evening! Andrew is too modest. I think under these circumstances we can expose the real name of our illustrator. We are all friends here; we don't need to hide. Our illustrator is none other than our own Miss Evaine Milham. She has given generously of her time and talents and deserves to be acknowledged for it. Her beautiful drawings have brought our shards and pieces to life, some of which you've had a chance to view tonight.' He was gratified at the oohs and ahs that went up, the applause that met his announcement.

'Secondly, to cap off the evening, we encourage you to continue enjoy dancing, and to wander over to our special display cases containing some of the best items in our collection. There, you can see the fruits of your labour because this project has taken all of us.' He shot a glance at Andrew. 'Let me tell you what you'll find in the case. First, we have a hair brush and mirror most likely used by the general's wife. Secondly, we have a bowl, which was found in two pieces. We have glued it back together and if you look carefully, you can see the seam where it shattered. Finally, we have a pottery goblet, which bears the general's personal insignia on the bottom, which, of course, as any good collector knows, is one way to tell a piece is authentic.' He turned to the orchestra and gave the signal for music. It was time to return his guests to the dancing. Beside him, Andrew looked pale.

'You look ill—too many seed cakes?' Dimitri joked, trying to keep his tone light, trying not to give away his anger. He wanted Andrew flummoxed. He wanted Andrew thinking he actually approved of his actions. There was nothing better for foiling revenge than to simply not be angry over it. It was hard, especially when he really wanted to haul Andrew outside and thrash him in a most unprincely fashion. This man was no longer his friend and he disliked pretending otherwise. 'Walk with me.' He had Andrew by the arm, giving him no choice. They strolled over to the display tables, Evie coming to link her arm with his. He rather wished she hadn't. He worried Andrew in his desperation might become violent. But she had a right to see a thief brought to justice. Andrew had stolen from her as surely as he'd stolen from him.

'These are beautiful. Signs of life, Evie and I call them,' Dimitri said casually, watching Andrew's face go chalky. It was time. He clapped a hand on Andrew's shoulder. 'Did you think I wouldn't notice?' His voice was low for Andrew alone. 'You stole from me. However, beyond the first item you took, everything else were reproductions only. I sincerely hope you didn't sell them to discerning buyers. They will not be pleased if they discover you've been passing off replicas. People who buy on the black market aren't known for their scruples.' Dimitri didn't think it was possible for Andrew to get any whiter, but he managed it, his jaw tightening, his eyes fierce in their desperation. 'I might have tolerated the crime against me, but not Evie. She liked you once upon a time and you used her quite sorely.

'Well, enough said.' He offered Andrew a smile and forced a final note of bonhomie into his tone. 'You might need a head start. I hope you take it. Out of remembrance of the good times we once had, I don't want to see your throat slit in an alley.' He made a small nod with his head as if he were merely finished with a conversation instead of having offered Andrew an ultimatum. 'Now, if you'll excuse us, we have guests to see to.'

He turned away from Andrew, his hand at Evie's back, a most dismissive gesture and a most dangerous one. It nearly proved fatal.

'No, I don't think I will excuse you.' Andrew's voice was menacing. 'Turn around, Prince Dimitri Petrovich, and face me like a man.' Dimitri turned. Andrew's eyes flickered downward towards his hand. Dimitri's heart pounded. This was what he had feared. In Andrew's hand was a small, palm-sized gun, perfect for roués and gamblers who found themselves in sticky situations. The gun was aimed at Evie's stomach. 'A gut shot is a terrible way to die. One lingers long enough to really hurt, to know their life is slipping away and no one can do anything about it.

There's a little relief at the end. You go numb right before the world goes dark. That's how you know it's nearly over.'

Andrew grinned. 'How does it feel to have your life stripped out from under? That's what you have done to me. You've signed my death warrant and you know it. Now, give me the artefacts and we'll all live.'

'You should shoot me instead if that's how you feel.' It seemed surreal they could have this discussion and no one was any wiser, but the room was loud, the gun was small and they were supposed to be friends. No one saw what they didn't expect to see.

Andrew sneered. 'Your kingdom for a whore? Is she really worth it? Must be incredible in bed.' His eyes flicked over Evie. 'I never would have guessed it, my dear. But back to business, Prince. You have until the count of three. One—'

Dimitri didn't wait. Decisiveness was the best offensive weapon at anyone's disposal. Strike fast, strike hard. Always fight like you mean it. Men like Andrew bargained on fear working in their favour. He stepped forward rapidly, his body between Andrew and Evie, his foot coming down hard on Andrew's instep, his hand closing around Andrew's wrist, knocking the gun away. With his other leg, he brought his knee up into Andrew's groin. Andrew groaned and doubled over. Dimitri motioned to two footmen. 'Mr Adair isn't quite himself. Please show him out.'

Evie was reeling. Dimitri had her, though. She could feel his arm around her, could hear his words at her ear. 'Don't faint now, Evie. It's over. You're safe.'

He had saved her. Andrew had pulled a gun on her. She could barely grasp the events of the last two minutes, could barely sort them out. Then Dimitri had stepped in front of the gun. He could have been killed, although he'd not acted like it for a moment. She had been horrified, frozen, in fact. But he had been swift, decisive, and the next moment Andrew had been doubled over. She started to sway and Dimitri picked her up, his voice warm. 'Well, that's certainly one way to get you into my bed.'

She felt better outside, better still when they were safely inside the pavilion, away from the ballroom and its noise. The pavilion was dark and softly lit. Dimitri pressed a glass of vodka into her hand with a command. 'Drink.'

'Andrew pulled a gun on me.' Disbelief was the only way she could handle the shock. Andrew, her neighbour, her girlish infatuation, had threatened to *kill* her. '*You* could have been killed, Dimitri.' That part too was surreal. She didn't think there was enough vodka in the world to soften that reality. 'I meant to thank you for what you did; getting on that stage and standing up for me tonight, but now I have so much more to thank you for and "thank you" seems entirely inadequate.' But it did reassure her she was doing the right thing in letting him go. He'd already given his life twice for her—tonight in a more physical sense. But one didn't have to die to give up one's life and he'd been ready to give up the life he knew for her and live a new one. It was too much. 'There are no words, Dimitri.'

'There don't have to be.' He leaned towards her, his own hands shaking as he reached for her. For the first time, she was aware of the toll the evening had taken on him. He'd been so sure, so confident when he'd strode on stage, when he'd confronted Andrew and disarmed him, when he'd swept her up into his arms and carried her away to peace and safety. One could easily forget he was only a man, a very mortal man. It was her turn to comfort him, her turn to be strong for him. He needed to know she was all right.

She covered his shaking hands. 'I am safe,' she murmured. 'We are safe.' Then she kissed him, slow and hard, to show him they were alive, to show him how much she loved him. There was so much love she wanted to show him.

Evie gave his lips a last kiss and slid to her knees in front of him, her hands working the fall of his evening trousers until he was free and hard in her hand. She let a wicked smile take her lips as she looked up at him. 'I am going to put my mouth on you, do you think you'd like that?' she whispered, her own breath catching in anticipation, then her lips were there, at the base of his shaft, kissing it gently where it rose from his dark tangle. She licked up his length, trailing her tongue along its ridge, delighting in the moaned plea that escaped him; mercy and pleasure and celebration mixed together.

His pleasure drove her to greater lengths. She closed her mouth over the tender head of him, her tongue probing the tiny weeping slit at its summit with wicked strokes. She felt him rise beneath her, felt his hands grasp for purchase in her hair, his hips press forward as he arched. She felt his body gather, rushing to its conclusion. She pulled back at the last and took him in hand. She loved this—watching him pulse, watching his body wrack in pleasure and knowing she'd had a part in it. This was life at its finest.

Except when he was kissing her.

Or caressing her breasts.

Or undressing her.

His hands were at the laces of her gown, the russet creation falling to the floor, forgotten in passion's wake. His recovery time, impressively immediate. Her mouth work had served to encourage rampant passion, perhaps fuelled by the realisation that Andrew's threat had passed and they were both indeed alive and well.

'I'll be ready by the time I get you out of all these clothes,' he growled, nipping at her ear. 'I've never understood why women wear so many clothes.' So many clothes or not, they were all vanquished in relatively short order. Her underskirts and chemise joining her gown in an ever more frantic undressing. Desire rose, her own hands pushing at his dark evening jacket, tugging at white shirttails and patterned waistcoat. She wanted him naked as soon as possible. He kissed her hard as he ripped his arms from his shirtsleeves, throwing the shirt aside, her own hands busy with his trousers.

It had become a foregone conclusion that they weren't going to make it to the bed.

Chapter Twenty-Six

The divan was as far as they could go for now, the limits of their perseverance. She knew this in her bones, in the heated core of herself. They were both rough in their need, craving each other with a new intensity. She bit his lip and he gave a fierce growl, dancing her backwards to the divan. This coming together would be fast, furious, a celebration and a secret farewell. She opened her thighs to him, dragging him down, her body urging him onward. She was already wet with wanting. He was pulsing and hard at her entrance and he did not wait for further invitation.

She welcomed the roughness, the wildness of him. Her nails raked his back and she arched up into him, fierce in her own passion. He thrust hard and she moaned, feeling climax approaching fast and sure. This would be over in moments. He thrust again, his mouth close to her ear, his voice harsh with his own desire. 'Say it, Evie.'

His next thrust didn't come. She shoved her hips upwards to coax him. She tugged at him. 'What are you waiting for?' Her body was frantic as it hovered on the edge of pleasure satisfied, the treat of shattering denied.

'I'm waiting for you.' His muscles were taut as he braced above her. 'Say it, Evie. Say we'll build a life together, one day at a time.'

Or she'd never climax with him again. 'You don't fight fair.' Her body was already hating her hesitation.

He gave a hoarse laugh. 'Not true. All is fair in love and war, and, Evie, I mean to win.'

Her resistance crumbled at that and she gave him the words he wanted, the words she wanted and in the moment they might have been true. 'Then, yes. Now, would you please claim your victory?' He grinned and her legs went about him, holding him close as he took them the rest of the way to pleasure not for the last time that night.

She gave herself over to the pleasure. Dawn seemed a long way off and what she had to do seemed a long way off too. There were times in the long night when she thought perhaps sex would indeed hold the morning at bay. They moved to his decadent bed, and she took him astride, her breasts brushing his chest as she moved on him, wanting to remember the feel of him, the look of him as joy swamped him.

But they were mere mortals. There was indeed a point of exhaustion and they reached it there in the dark in each other's arms.

Then there was light. And reality. She allowed herself the luxury of watching him sleep, this beautiful man who had saved her, not just from Andrew, but from a life of oblivion, of being a shell of a human. Now it was her turn to save him. Everyone needed a champion, maybe the strongest needed them the most. Today, she would be his hero.

She rose quietly and dressed, leaving a soft wrapped package on the vanity, a note folded on top. He would understand. He was a prince, he was used to putting others first, she assured herself. He would come to appreciate her choice and he would understand the necessity for it. 'All's fair in love and war,' she whispered, blowing him a goodbye kiss and disappearing through the curtain before she could think better of it, before her courage gave out.

At the inn, the coach was waiting. She checked to see that her trunk had arrived and was already strapped on. Fussing over details, checking the schedule, were distractors. They kept her mind in the present, kept it from wandering back to images of a sleeping man.

'Miss, you need to board if you're coming. It's time,' the coachman said, roughly, irritated at the delay. He and the horses were eager to be off. She took one last look down the road. It wasn't as if she wasn't coming back. She was merely going for a visit to see May and Beatrice. Little Westbury would still be here. But he wouldn't be. When she came back everything would be different.

She climbed in and settled herself on a seat, grateful the coach held only one other passenger. She'd have her privacy. The other man would too. His hat was low and his head was buried in a book. A reader. Good. Perhaps they would have something to talk about if she felt like talking later. She pulled out her own book and tried to busy her mind and forget her heart was breaking. Dimitri would be hurt when he woke. But he would understand, she took comfort in that. The carriage lurched into action. There was no going back now.

Five miles down the road, after a lengthy silence that bordered on odd—what sort of stranger offered nothing, not even a greeting—the stranger in the corner lifted his head and fixed her with blue eyes. 'Hello, Evie. Seems we have a coach to Scotland to share. Four days on the road ought to be time to get reacquainted.'

Andrew. Her heart began to race. She didn't want to be alone with him. Not after last night.

'I hear Scotland's great for exiles.' He smiled coldly. 'That gives us something in common. The Prince has ruined us both. That's something else in common. Peas in pod, we are.'

'I'm nothing like you.'

'Oh, you are, you just don't want to admit it. The Prince has shafted us, one of us more literally than the other, I am guessing. But he's forced us both to flee our homes.'

She would not dignify that with a response. She was not going to tell Andrew all Dimitri had offered to give up for her just to prove him wrong. Evie turned her attention to her book, trying to treat Andrew as she would any prying stranger. How had she ever thought him attractive? Costume jewellery indeed. But it was hard to ignore Andrew. He was no longer just annoying, he was potentially dangerous. On two occasions he had threatened her with physical harm. This man was not her friend, perhaps not even her ex-friend. The realisation made the coach that much smaller. She glanced out the window, considering her options.

'Do you think he'll come after you? He doesn't know I'm on this coach too.' He made a general gesture with his hand. 'This is all very serendipitous, you and I together. He has no reason to believe you're in any danger or in need of rescue. Can you imagine how this might look to him? You and I running away to Scotland, land of the quick marriage, together right after you've left his bed. Perhaps I can explain to him how you gave me the drawings and then how I used the drawings to market the artefacts to buyers. He'll think we were in it together all along.' Andrew made a pouting face. 'I don't think that will go over well at all, considering he was most willing to take a bullet for you last night. Of course, how much this betrayal hurts, depends on whether or not he loved you.' He paused. 'Oh, I see. You think he *does* love you.

'How quaint. The mighty prince in love with the country girl.' He sighed. 'He doesn't love you, Evie. He is going to marry Ayfer Hanimsultan, a princess of sorts in his part of the world. It's all been planned for years. I tried to warn you. He's the real villain here. He misled you entirely.' She was not going to cry. Of course he was going to marry Ayfer Hanimsultan. She'd given him permission when she'd left. It was what had to be done. She just wished it didn't hurt so much.

To her horror, Andrew pulled out a small knife and began to do his nails. 'I have to go armed now, Evie. The Prince has the made the world more dangerous for me.'

'You shouldn't have stolen his artefacts.'

He gave her a leer of a look. 'I might steal more than his artefacts before this trip is over. It seems you never did give my kisses a fair try and I never did give you a fair try. Apparently, you have charms I've been unaware of.' Andrew licked his lips. 'Let's play a game. It's called obedience. My last mistress liked it quite a bit.'

Evie's skin began to crawl, her pulse accelerated with fear. She could not let herself be afraid. She had to be more like Dimitri. Last night, he'd been decisive. Andrew was counting on fear to work in his favour. 'Here's the rules. I tell you to do something. You can choose to do it, or you can choose to be punished for refusing. My mistress liked spanking. Maybe there's a foreign trick or two you can show me, something Dimitri liked.'

Andrew's hatred of Dimitri was fully unmasked now. He'd never been Dimitri's friend, just one of many who tried to use him for their own gain. It was the key she needed to unlock her own strength. This game would not conquer her. Evie sat up a little straighter and looked Andrew in the eye. 'I will never like anything associated with you. I was wrong to have ascribed certain values to you for as long as I did.' She made a point of returning to her book.

Bravado had been a mistake. In a lightning move, Andrew slid onto the seat next to her, knife at her throat, his hand in her hair, yanking her head up so that she cried out. 'That is *not* how the game works, Evie,' he growled.

He released her and she rubbed at her neck, panic becoming real. 'Now, let's try again, Evie. I'll show you some mercy. We'll start easy. Take down your hair.'

She had no choice. She was trapped in a moving box with a mad man. She was going to have to play. But she didn't have to lose. It occurred to her that losing wasn't defined by merely doing what Andrew asked, but rather by giving in to fear. Andrew wanted her in tears, wanted her to beg, as revenge on Dimitri and perhaps revenge on her. She would not give him either. She could do this. Taking down her hair was nothing. It was only embarrassing if she let it be. She would wait for her moment and when it came, she would seize it with both hands. With a fierce stare, she took her hair down, pin by pin.

Dimitri stared, dumbfounded at the note. He didn't think Evie was the type to go back on her word. He'd read it and re-read it. She'd left? Because she loved him? That made no sense. He rubbed his hands over his stubbly jaw. He'd woken and found her gone. The bed was cold. It had been a while. She'd left and he'd missed it.

With fumbling fingers, he unwrapped the package, more out of reflex than curiosity. His mind was going through ordinary routines while it tried to assimilate what had just happened. Inside lay an exquisite piece of needlework depicting Kuban the way he'd described it to her: the river, the mountains, the shining palaces with their domes. He ran a finger over the threads. He understood the note better now. She was telling him to go to Kuban and fulfil his destiny because she loved him, because she would not take his life away from him.

That was unacceptable. She didn't want to leave him. She only felt she had to. Everything last night made sense, the hint of sadness in her eyes, the desperation with which she'd made love. She'd known she was saying farewell. He had saved her life and now she thought she was saving his.

Dimitri dressed hurriedly. He would go to her parents' house and convince her, convince them, he didn't need saving. Somehow. He'd given her all his best arguments. He'd make them all again if need be. He'd show her the deed. He'd kiss her. He would think of something. He saddled one of the horses he travelled with, a shiny, fast black stallion, and ran through the options all the way to her house, only to learn she wasn't there. She'd left for Scotland to visit her girlfriends.

The stallion was hot beneath him, wanting to run in the fine morning. Dimitri gauged the time. The coach couldn't be more than an hour or two ahead of him, on a fast horse, even less. He wheeled the horse around and gave him his head. There was only one road north. He would find her and he would bring her back.

Chapter Twenty-Seven

'Someone's coming.' Andrew dropped the curtain back in place with a scowl. The coach was slowing. Whoever was out there had ordered the coach to pull over. Evie could hear loud voices outside over the rumble of hooves. She tried to right herself as best she could. Her gown was undone, her chemise ripped, but she'd survived the game. She could not say the same for Andrew. He had a nail scratch down his cheek and he looked less immaculate. She'd made him pay for everything he'd demanded of her. The goal was to survive intact and that meant modesty had to be sacrificed. In some cases, even pride. Her motto had become there was worse he could do and he hadn't done it. Not yet.

Andrew pointed the tip of his knife at her. 'Don't think for a moment about making yourself decent. If it's highwaymen they'll not thank you for it. If it's your Prince, I want him to see what he's done. This is all his fault. He took from me and now I take from him.'

Andrew lifted the curtain again now that the coach was at a full stop. 'Maybe he does love you.' He shot her an appraising look. 'I can understand that attraction better now after our little game.' He motioned to the door. 'We are getting out together, you first, my knife at your throat, so go cautiously and don't think about blurting anything out. They could very well be your last words. Keep your hands down.'

Her moment was nearly here, Evie reminded herself as he dragged her against him, the blade at her neck, the edge pricking. It was frightening indeed to have one's skin that close to death, but there was hope just the other side of that door. 'I'm going to kill him, you know that, don't you? Unless the sight of you kills him first,' Andrew growled.

It was the very thing she feared. She'd not wanted to tidy her clothes for herself as much she'd wanted to tidy herself for Dimitri. She didn't want Dimitri to see her like this, her hair mussed, her clothes torn, her body exposed. He would think the worst. She wanted to protect him from that, from the anger that would come. That anger would be his enemy. It would drive him to foolishness and Andrew would not hesitate. Andrew wanted him dead, but not before he had suffered.

She wanted to spit at him, wanted to fight, but Andrew was not above letting his blade draw blood. It was one of the lessons she'd learned early in the game. She had the cut to prove it. Only a coward would kill in the isolation of the country. Sunlight hit her eyes and she squinted, trying hard to keep her eyes open, not wanting to be blind for a moment. Even so, she heard him before she saw him.

'Evie!' Oh, God, that was the voice of her salvation. She wanted to give in to weakness and weep with relief even though Andrew held her a mortal prisoner against him. Dimitri had come for her, to save her from her own foolishness, she saw that now. She never should have left his bed. And now this good man who loved her, who was willing to give up everything for her, might very well end up giving his life. He'd not come expecting danger, only a stubborn woman. But Andrew was armed. To the teeth, it turned out. There was the little gun, the knife, and a larger knife and a larger pistol under the seat. She would go for those weapons the first chance she had. She would not let Dimitri fight alone.

'Andrew, let her go.' The command came, regal and loud atop the black stallion.

'What? Is that all you have to say? Don't you want to know why we're together, or what we've been doing? Maybe she doesn't want to come with you now that she's had a taste of a real Englishman.' Andrew's other arm came up, the long pistol a deadly extension of his hand. 'Shall I shoot him, my dear? Shall he join our little game? It's more fun with three. Imagine what we could do.

'Get off that beast of yours, Prince, and face me man to man and I'll let her go. I was about done with her anyway.'

'No, Dimitri, don't get down. He'll kill you!' The blade bit and she felt a trickle of blood rise on her neck. The words were worth it. All that mattered was that Dimitri ride away from this, alive and well. He deserved that.

Dear God, Andrew was going to kill her. The man had gone mad. It became obvious this was going to be over in a matter of seconds. There was no chance to negotiate. Heaven only knew what she'd endured in that coach, and now this. He was trying hard not to imagine what these hours had been like for her, not while she was depending on his cool head and cooler hand. She'd made it this far, she deserved to have him help her the rest of the way. He would have only one shot. His hand closed around his first pistol, lying low against his saddle. There would be no chance to draw it. He would have to shoot from the holster, through the holster. He angled the horse, letting the horse prance. He could make this shot, but his margin for error was slim. If he missed, he risked hitting Evie. The shot would cripple her.

'Evie, stand still.' His words were cold and crisp and loud. He'd never been more terrified in his life. The woman he loved was at risk. He could not miss this shot. He squeezed the trigger. There was a breeze past Evie's skirts. Fabric rippled. Andrew went down in a howl of pain as the bullet took him in the knee. Relief swamped Dimitri. He came off the horse in a fluid motion, drawing another pistol, tossing away the empty one as he advanced. "Evie, get behind me!" He barked when she glanced towards the coach. There were probably weapons inside and his brave girl would want to fight but he needed her safe.

Out of the corner of his eye, he saw Evie scramble towards the horse, towards safety behind him. Now he could give all of his concentration to Andrew. The coachman on the box began to protest. 'I don't take with violence on my stage.'

'A little too late for that,' Dimitri growled, his eyes

never leaving Andrew. 'You've allowed a woman to be molested in your coach.' He trained his pistol on Andrew. 'I should shoot you.' This next bullet would take him between the eyes. Andrew began to whine, to beg. Dimitri cut him off with harsh words. He was beyond mercy. 'Stop your snivelling, you coward. I won't shoot you. I will, however, throw you in this coach with enough money for a doctor and your promise that you'll never leave Scotland. If I catch you on English soil or near my wife ever again, I will shoot you on sight.'

He didn't see Andrew's hand move. A blade flashed on his periphery. Behind him, Evie screamed a single word. 'Knife!' Without her warning it would have been too late. All else happened in slow motion. The blade came up. There was no time to think, only to time to act. Dimitri fired his second pistol without hesitation on Evie's warning. When the roar of the bullet ebbed, Andrew lay dead. But his other thought was: Evie is safe. Andrew could never hurt her again.

She half-ran, half-stumbled to him and he wrapped her in his arms, pulling her away from the scene. He was never letting her go again. He shrugged out of his coat, draping it about her. His brave girl was shaking. 'Are you all right, Evie? Did he hurt you?' They were inadequate words. Of course Andrew had hurt her. Her clothes were torn, her hair was tangled. The thin red line of a cut was visible on her neck, another high above her right breast. But he couldn't bring himself to mouth the words he feared the most: Had Andrew *forced* himself on her?

'I'm all right.' She clutched at his shirt, her eyes

searching his. She knew what he meant to ask. 'He didn't hurt me, not like that. But he would have. He made me play this game…' She held nothing back, perhaps understanding his need to know. When she finished, he knew one truth. If Andrew were not already dead, he would have been now.

'After all that, you still had the presence of mind to save me, Evie.' He wanted to get her away from here more than ever as if putting miles between this place and Evie would help her forget. He boosted her up into the saddle and settled behind her, taking her deep into the vee of his thighs, letting her feel the press of his muscles around her, strong and alive, a reminder too that she was strong and she was alive. They were alive together. 'You know, in Kuban, we have a tradition. When you save a life, that life belongs to you. You become responsible for it.'

He kneed the horse forward, back towards Little Westbury, back towards the life that was about to start. 'Do you have any idea how I felt when I woke up and saw you were gone? That my life was over, Evie. You're my life now. The life I've chosen and I don't want you to ever run from that again.'

'I left because I chose you.' Evie half-turned, to stroke his face with her hand, her eyes shining with tears. 'I didn't think giving up a kingdom for me was a good trade.'

'You're right. It's not a good trade. It's not nearly enough. Not even two kingdoms, three kingdoms, would be enough for you, Evie.' Sapphire tears glistened, threatening to spill. He wanted to lick them away with his tongue. His Evie should never cry. 'I just need you to believe it.'

'I do. You came for me. Not because I told you to, but because you wanted to.'

'Because I *needed* to, Evie. You are my freedom.' She smiled at him then—the smile he'd fallen for from the first. He knew he was home. It no longer mattered what the news from Kuban was. He would manage it, whenever it came, with whatever verdict it held. If he had to go back to Kuban and spirit Anna-Maria away, so be it. 'Did you know, the first thing I noticed about you was your smile? I knew then I was in trouble. Just not how much.'

Evie laughed, facing forward. She snuggled her buttocks deeper against his groin. 'What's so funny?' He would swear she was doing that wiggling bit on purpose.

'The first thing I noticed about you was your trousers,' she said coyly.

'My trousers?'

'Yes. We all did. Every woman in the assembly room wanted to get into your trousers that night, me most of all.'

'Well, it looks like your wish came true, soon-to-be-Mrs Petrovich. How long does it take you to make a dress, Evie?'

'What?' The question caught her off guard. 'Three weeks, I think. Maybe less if I don't have any distractions.'

'Three weeks? Good. Then you can wear it to your wedding.'

'Hmm.' She arched her neck and looked up at him

with a considering stare, ready to tease him in return. 'I like how this story is developing. Who would have thought I'd marry the Prince of Pleats?'

Dimitri laughed and held her tight. Who would have thought indeed? He'd not come to Little Westbury expecting any of this, but it was fast becoming his experience that the unexpected made for the best endings.

The three weeks leading up to the wedding had been filled with activity and unfortunately a large amount of tradition, which from Evie's point of view, seemed ironic coming from a man who apparently liked unexpected endings. Dimitri had insisted on having the banns read, just as he'd insisted on a traditional wedding in the Little Westbury church where she and all her family had been christened. She could tolerate those foibles, as she called them. The third foible was less tolerable. He'd also insisted on celibacy before the wedding night, something Evie didn't understand the reason for, especially now when they were to marry and it could not be considered compromising even if they were caught. But he had insisted and they had stuck to it. Mostly.

It hardly mattered. In less than an hour, she'd be Mrs Petrovich and they could have all the sex they wanted for the rest of their lives. There was a knock on her bedroom door and May poked her head in. 'Are you ready? The carriage is coming.' May had made the trip south for her, one reason why she'd even considered tolerating the three-week wait. Even then, May had barely arrived in time.

Evie nodded and smoothed her skirts with a final look in the mirror. The dress was another reason she'd consented to the wait. She wanted a wedding dress of her own design and this one was hers down to the final stitch, with its full skirts that rustled delightfully when she walked. The ecru silk had been specially ordered from London, the deep off-white shade perfect for a harvest wedding. A border of autumn-coloured flowers was embroidered around the hem and the bodice had been a work of art with its matching profusion of flowers. May had helped sew the remaining bit of trim last night.

'I'm going to be bride. At last.' Evie sighed.

'And a very beautiful one, Evie. You're radiant.' May reached for the veil lying on the bed, a long sheer confection crowned with a wreath of autumn leaves that matched the dress. She set it on Evie's head. 'I wish Claire and Bea could be here. You know they're happy for you.' Claire was too far away in Vienna and there was no question of Beatrice travelling at this late stage of pregnancy even if she could be seen in public.

'It's enough you're here. More than enough,' Evie assured her. May would stand up with her today as her witness. Stefon would stand up with Dimitri. She grabbed her bouquet from the vanity and gave her room one last look, her throat squeezing. Evie Milham would never come back here again. She wondered how Dimitri was handling the morning. It was emotional enough for her and she was surrounded by friends and family for support. Suddenly, she wanted to get to the church, wanted to be next to him so he wouldn't be alone.

The church was filled to capacity, not being all that large to begin with. Everyone from town must be stuffed inside. She knew her family would be in the front pews; her mother, her sisters and their husbands and Diana's little baby. She knew too that the aisle would be festooned in a rich ivory ribbon with nosegays of flowers attached at each pew. She'd helped with the decorating yesterday. It was a good thing, or else she wouldn't have noticed any of that today. As soon as the heavy oak doors of the church were opened and her father took her arm, she had eyes for nothing except the man waiting at the end of the aisle for her.

Dimitri was dressed in an English morning coat of blue superfine with perfectly pressed buff trousers, *with* pleats, she noted. His shirt was starched, white perfection, his cravat a simple, elegant navy blue, his waistcoat a tiny blue-and-white stripe. But no one would mistake him for an Englishman. No one ever would. His dark hair was sleek and immaculate, pulled back in his usual style, and his eyes were on her. She might have walked down the aisle a little too quickly, she might have smiled too broadly. She would not be a solemn bride. A girl had only one wedding day.

If her decorum wasn't all it should have been she had a good excuse. The most handsome man in the world was waiting for her. Dimitri took her hand, kissed her knuckles and lifted her veil. She remembered that much. There would be other highlights too. She would recall, emotionally, Dimitri slipping his mother's wedding ring on her finger and she would recall, vividly, Dimitri kissing her at the end.

The wedding breakfast awaited at her parents' home, they would honeymoon at home in their new house in the valley but before any of that happened, there was the carriage ride, her chance to be alone with him. She could hardly wait.

She pulled off her veil the moment the door was closed behind them and Dimitri kissed her hard on the mouth. 'There, now I can kiss you properly the way I want to.'

She smiled at him and sank back against the leather squabs. She let out a little groan. 'Do we have to go?' She'd rather skip straight to the wedding night, or the wedding afternoon, as the case may be.

'Yes, we do.' His eyes danced mischievously. 'But not just yet. How much are you wearing under that skirt?' He eyed the voluminous dress.

'Hmm.' Her eyes flicked to his pleats. 'Maybe the better question is how much are you wearing under those trousers?' She slid her hand over him, cupping him through the fabric, running her tongue over her teeth in contemplation as she undid the fall of his trousers.

'Why, Mrs Petrovich, you are full of good ideas.' Dimitri grinned and spread his legs as she closed her hand over him.

'Do you want to know another good idea?' She leaned close with a wicked whisper. 'I know a long cut.'

He furrowed his brow at the unfamiliar term and she laughed. 'We can take the back route to the house. It will take longer.'

He waggled his eyebrows. 'Then by all means.'

It might have taken them a little longer than usual

to make the ten-minute drive from the church to the wedding breakfast and the groom might have looked just slightly less immaculate than when he'd left, but no less satisfied.

* * * * *

*If you enjoyed this story,
make sure you don't miss the
first book in Bronwyn Scott's*
WALLFLOWERS TO WIVES *miniseries,
UNBUTTONING THE INNOCENT MISS.*

*And watch out for two more books
in this series, coming soon!*

She would become the best songstress in all of London.
She knew it. The future was hers. Now she just had to
find it. She was lost beyond hope in the biggest city of
the world.

Isabel tried to scrape the street refuse from her shoe
without anyone noticing what she was doing. She didn't
know how she was going to get the muck off her dress.
A stranger who wore a drooping cravat was eyeing her
bosom quite openly. Only the fact that she was certain
she could outrun him, even in her soiled slippers, kept her
from screaming.

He tipped his hat to her and ambled into a doorway
across the street.

Her dress, the only one with the entire bodice made
from silk, would have to be altered now. The rip in
the skirt—thank you, dog who didn't appreciate her

trespassing in his gardens—was not something she could mend.

How? How had she gotten herself into this?

She opened the satchel, pulled out the plume and examined it. She straightened the unfortunate new crimp in it as best she could and put the splash of blue into the little slot she'd added to her bonnet. She picked up her satchel, realizing she had got a bit of the street muck on it—and began again her new life.

Begin my new life, she repeated to herself, unmoving. She looked at the paint peeling from the exterior and watched as another man came from the doorway, waistcoat buttoned at an angle. Gripping the satchel with both hands, she locked her eyes on the wayward man.

Her stomach began a song of its own, and very off-key. She couldn't turn back. She had no funds to hire a carriage. She knew no one in London but Mr. Wren. And he had been so complimentary and kind to everyone at Madame Dubois's School for Young Ladies. Not just her. She could manage. She would have to. His compliments had not been idle, surely.

She held her head the way she planned to look over the audience when she first walked onstage and put one foot in front of the other, ignoring everything but the entrance in front of her.

Don't miss
THE RUNAWAY GOVERNESS by Liz Tyner,
available November 2016 wherever
Harlequin® Historical books and ebooks are sold.

www.Harlequin.com

HARLEQUIN®
A Romance FOR EVERY MOOD™

Love the Harlequin book you just read?

Your opinion matters.

Review this book on your favorite book site, review site, blog or your own social media properties and share your opinion with other readers!